THE LOST
GALLOWS

D1424934

531 070 01 8

THE LOST GALLOWS

JOHN DICKSON CARR

with an introduction by
MARTIN EDWARDS

This edition published 2020 by
The British Library
96 Euston Road
London
NW1 2DB

The Lost Gallows was originally published in 1931 by
Harper & Brothers, New York and London

'The Ends of Justice' was originally published
in *The Haverfordian*, May 1927

Introduction © 2020 Martin Edwards
The Lost Gallows © 1931 The Estate of Clarice M. Carr
'The Ends of Justice' © 1927 The Estate of Clarice M. Carr

Cataloguing in Publication Data
A catalogue record for this book is available from the British Library

ISBN 978 0 7123 5363 2
eISBN 978 0 7123 6767 7

Front cover image © NRM/Pictorial Collection/
Science & Society Picture Library

Typeset by Tetragon, London
Printed in England by TJ Books Limited, Padstow, Cornwall

CONTENTS

INTRODUCTION

The Lost Gallows, John Dickson Carr's second novel, saw the return of the Parisian detective Henri Bencolin, who had solved the mystery in Carr's first book, *It Walks by Night*. This time, however, Carr set his story in England, in foggy London.

One need only glance at the chapter titles to get a flavour of the story. The first chapter is called "The Shadow of the Noose" and others include "How We Played Hare and Hounds with a Corpse", "The Street of Strangled Men", and "The Trap Falls At Last". This was a young man's book (Carr was a stripling of twenty-four when the novel first appeared in 1931) and it's full of youthful swagger and zest.

The opening scene is set at the Brimstone Club—a wonderful name, typical of Carr—where Bencolin and his friend, the American Jeff Marle, are staying. They are in conversation with Sir John Landervorne, who lives at the Brimstone. Sir John is "one of Bencolin's oldest friends, with a genius for organization" and a former assistant police commissioner at Scotland Yard. Sir John had previously appeared in a handful of Carr's early short stories, one of which, "The Ends of Justice", is included in this volume. It may be that Carr originally conceived Bencolin and Landervorne as a cosmopolitan updating of the Holmes–Watson type of detective partnership popularized by Arthur Conan Doyle, but by this time, he had created Jeff Marle to act as a narrator as well as loyal sidekick, much more in the Watson vein than Sir John. And indeed this book marked Sir John's last appearance in Carr's work.

Sir John tells his colleagues a strange story about a young man called Dallings; they talk about the discovery in Paris of the murdered corpse of a man dressed in the sandals and gold robes of a nobleman from ancient Egypt and the subsequent suicide of an Englishman in a prison cell; and they chance upon a model, a toy gibbet, which someone has left in the lounge of the Brimstone.

Carr describes the club with his customary brio. The Brimstone is said to be the most disreputable in the West End and its membership subscriptions are the highest of any in London: it "collects the wealthy and drifting scum of the world. For the past thirty years it has been the club of the wanderer... Through it float English, French, German, Russian, Spanish, Italian faces; the soldier, the pawned title, the castaway, the game-hunter, the seeker of far places; the bored, the aimless, the foot-loose, the damned... One is hushed by the massive dreariness of its luxury, its sombre lamps, its thick, muffled carpets, its hint of suicide."

Lashings of atmosphere of this kind help to create the ideal environment for the mysterious "impossibilities" that were Carr's stock-in-trade. Here there are three intriguing riddles. The first concerns a limousine, which seems to have been driven through the London streets by a murdered chauffeur. The second concerns the mysterious appearance and disappearance of a number of items within a locked room. The third is: how was a man hanged on a lost gallows in a lost street—Ruination Street?

The main puzzle concerns the identity of the culprit who hides behind the name of "Jack Ketch", the legendary hangman. After the discovery of a body, Bencolin accepts a wager from Sir John, to identify the killer within forty-eight hours. Bencolin, a man who is as diabolic as his secret adversary, is one of those Great Detectives who likes to play God. He keeps his cards close to his chest and asks Jeff to obey his orders "even if they involve as deadly danger as you are ever likely to encounter." This is a big ask, and not surprisingly Jeff is put out: "I should at least like to know what this is all about. You make all these mysterious remarks..."

Predictably, his plea for enlightenment falls on deaf ears. Bencolin refuses to show his hand, despite piling the pressure on himself as he ruminates: "if I have misread the signs, if I have made the slightest error in all my calculations, then there are unutterable horrors in store for all of us. A theory, nothing more!"

The original American first edition of this book was a "Harper Sealed Mystery", and the publishers Harper interrupt at an appropriate cliffhanging moment (the end of chapter fifteen) to demand of the reader: "Do you know Jack Ketch?... If you can resist the desire to read what lies within this seal, to discover how this ghastly vigil terminates and end the fearful uncertainty and harrowing suspense of this tale, return this book to your bookseller with the seal unbroken and your money will be refunded".

All is finally revealed in what Carr's biographer, Douglas G. Greene, has described as "a powerful conclusion, and one that fits this inhuman, mad world Carr has created." The American bibliophile, editor, and publisher Otto Penzler is among those who have named *The Lost Gallows* as one of their favourite Carr novels.

John Dickson Carr (1906–77) proceeded to become one of the most popular and influential authors of Golden Age detective fiction. Bencolin appeared in five novels in the 1930s, having previously appeared in four short stories printed in *The Haverfordian*, a college magazine. "The Ends of Justice", a baroque tale with a distinct anticlerical flavour, was published in the May 1927 issue. Carr established a reputation as a master of the locked room mystery and in her essay "Detective Writers in England", Agatha Christie described him as a "master magician... He is a male Scheherazade." His work continues to be admired around the world; on a recent trip to a festival in Shanghai, I discovered that his ingenious stories are warmly regarded by a large number of young Chinese fans and in recent years more than twenty of his books have been published in Chinese translation.

To write fiction of such enduring and widespread appeal is no mean feat. *The Lost Gallows* is an enjoyable mystery in itself as well as a milestone in the literary apprenticeship of one of the genre's great entertainers.

MARTIN EDWARDS

www.martinedwardsbooks.com

THE LOST GALLOWS

JACK KETCH: A familiar hobgoblin of nursery tales, appearing also in the showbox history of Punch and Judy. A hangman, an executioner, applied in general to all hangmen. The first Jack Ketch officiated at Tyburn in the latter part of the seventeenth century...

—LORE FOR THE CURIOUS

I

The Shadow of the Noose

I T STOOD ON THE TABLE BEFORE US, AMONG THE TEACUPS, A small and perfectly constructed model of a gibbet. Standing no more than eight inches high, it was made of cedar wood painted black. Thirteen steps led up to the platform, to a trap held in place by tiny hinges and a rod. From the crossbeam dangled a small noose of twine.

I can see it yet, brought into grisly relief by the white cloth, the cups, and the plate of sandwiches, in the yellow lamplight of late afternoon. Beyond the bay window where we sat, dingy fog was strangling out the street lamps along Pall Mall. It curled and billowed past in thick yellow-brown, smearing every light. A muffled rumble of traffic shook against the windows, pierced by the siren-hoot of a bus. The faces of Bencolin and Sir John Landervorne were reflected in the glass as they studied this ugly toy.

The two man-hunters were a contrast.

Sir John's face was sallow and austere. He had a high, narrow forehead, with shining grey hair. But the eyebrows were very thin and black, pinched over a sombre gaze from behind gold-rimmed eyeglasses on his thin nose. His eyelids moved slowly up and down as he fondled his grey moustache and close-clipped grey beard. He stared intently at the little gallows. On the other side of the table, Bencolin watched him behind cigarette smoke. Sir John Landervorne had been formerly assistant commissioner of the metropolitan police.

The Frenchman opposite him was a tall and lazy Mephisto—Mephisto with a lifted eyebrow. His black hair was parted in the middle and twirled up like horns. Thin lines ran from his nostrils down past a small moustache and black pointed beard, past a mouth which showed now the glittering edge of a smile. His cheek-bones were high, and his eyes unfathomable. The face was brilliant, moody, capricious, and cruel. There were rings on the drooping fingers which held his cigarette. He was M. Henri Bencolin, *juge d'instruction* of the Seine, the head of the Paris police and the most dangerous man in Europe.

The time was five-thirty in the afternoon of November 16th; the place was the lounge of the Brimstone Club in London. With the finding of that model we were introduced into the celebrated murder case of the Lost Gallows on the Lost Street, and it had come about in this fashion:

Bencolin and I had come over from Paris to witness the opening performance, at the Haymarket Theatre, of "The Silver Mask." This, it may be remembered, was the play which Edouard Vautrelle had written, and which furnished so terrible a clue in the Saligny case the previous April. We had arranged for rooms at the Brimstone, where Sir John lived, and he was to meet us on our arrival. Sir John was one of Bencolin's oldest friends, with a genius for organiza- tion which had done much at Scotland Yard. Before the war he had been assistant police commissioner under the Honourable Ronald Devisham. I had met him in Paris, where he came occasionally to visit Bencolin. He was a tall stooped man, courteous but austere, with little humour, and with the air of one brooding perpetually over a puzzling position on a chessboard—the sort of person whom the old romances would have described as a man with a secret. Bencolin said that he had never quite recovered from the loss of his son during the war. Since his retirement in 1919 he had become a recluse, living in Hampshire until he had taken up lodgings in London the previous year.

He met us that afternoon at Victoria; he was the first person we saw standing on the sooty, foggy platform when the train coughed into the dimness of the shed. He greeted us with a sort of embarrassed jollity, but nobody felt in a particularly gay mood. The chill of the weather, the iron gloom and the hollow roar of the Channel in a gale, had depressed us no less than our mission. When our talk did begin, after we had been installed at the Brimstone, it turned inevitably to crime.

We ordered tea in the lounge, a brown-panelled room of bay windows and those grotesque carvings which are associated with the club's history. A wood fire lighted the immense stone fireplace, that monstrosity of gargoyles, above which hangs the portrait of the founder, by De Suérif. I think he would have relished our conversation. Rake, duellist, horseman, drunkard was Sir George Falconer, in that galaxy of Georges round the Prince Regent. He stands there rich-coloured in his bottle-green coat, his Brummel cravat, and his skin-tight tan trousers. His hair is curled, and his insolent eye stares down in the low light of the amber lamps. From high up in the tall room he looked now at the back of Sir John Landervorne, who was sitting in a deep chair facing Bencolin across the tea table.

Sir John spoke with a hesitant air, as though he frowned at each word before he uttered it.

"You know, Bencolin," he said, "what has always amazed me is the picturesque quality of crime on the Continent. I've been dipping into your records. Amazing, some of them! Gruesome imagination—it's devilish."

He adjusted his eyeglasses more firmly on his nose and blinked through them at his cup. He continued:

"It may be the Gallic mind; yes, I fancy it is. People killed with scorpions, and cords made of women's hair, and spiked cradles like the Iron Maiden—"

Bencolin turned from the window, where he had been studying the fog-swirls with his chin in his hand.

"What do you mean by the Gallic mind?" he asked.

"Well… emotionalism. Flighty lot, as a rule."

Staring past him into the fire, Bencolin smiled obscurely.

"'Emotionalism,'" he repeated. "When you say that you think of some wild-eyed Frenchman flying into a rage, seizing a dagger and stabbing his sweetheart. That, Sir John, is a product of sentimentalism, pure and simple. Such things are done by the sentimental Anglo-Saxon, who insanely stabs his sweetheart and then weeps over a crushed flower she left in a book. Your Anglo-Saxon is simple and direct. A blind passion, a desire to kill; *ergo*, somebody *is* killed, without further fuss. He goes straight to the point—a process at which the Gallic soul revolts, in anything from committing a crime to bargaining with the grocer."

Sir John said, "H'm," noncommittally. He cast a dubious eye across the table.

"The Gallic type," said Bencolin, "loves devious ways. He would never enter your house through the street door when he could enter by a secret passage. But he is cold, hard, and cunning. If he kills, he kills with logical care. Where he expresses himself is in the theatrical gesture, the flourish, the purple-cloak drama—which is the surest evidence of coldness at heart. True and spontaneous emotion is always incoherent. A man really in love can only gurgle foolishly to his lady; it is your unmoved Don Juan who writes her the fine, elaborate, theatrical love-verses."

He paused.

"I am not trying to distinguish between English and French, of course. I merely point out two types of mind, of whatever nationality. But of all things I delight in, this latter sort—"

"I have observed that tendency in you," Sir John said, dryly.

"—because it makes for the super-criminal." Bencolin's eyes were half shut, and they glittered. "The blind, mad little brain which buzzes forever round in its own conceit. That is why it *is* mad, in its own way, because it thinks about itself all the time. One of the strangest crimes I ever knew..."

After a long silence he went on:

"Once, some years ago, the Paris police found in the woods at dawn the body of a man dressed in the sandals and gold robes of an Egyptian noble of four thousand years ago. He had been shot through the head. Yes, it was an odd murder. Its sequel was that an Englishman hanged himself in his cell at the Santé prison. He had made a rope of bed-sheets—"

A flush had risen under Sir John's sallow cheek-bones. He sat curiously rigid.

"May I ask," he said, "what put that into your head?"

"It seems to startle you. Do you know the case?"

"Why, as a matter of fact, I was thinking along the same lines. Different business, but it concerned hanging..."

The rigidity left him. He tapped with his fingers on the chair arm, and the eyes behind his glasses seemed to be watching something weighed in a scales.

Bencolin asked, "What was it?"

"Cock-and-bull tale," replied the other, idly. "Dallings had got a drink too many in him, I fancy. It was a young friend of mine. He seems to have been involved recently in some queer business, in the course of which he got lost in the fog, and swears he saw on the side of a house the shadow of a gallows and a rope. Says a shadow of Jack Ketch was walking up the steps to adjust the rope. He made quite a ghost story of... Good God! what's the matter?"

Bencolin had been looking sideways at the darkened window. He whirled round suddenly.

"You know," said the detective, "pardon my interruption, old man, but a moment ago I imagined I saw a ghost myself, in that window there."

Sir John looked at the glass.

"Your poetic way of saying what?" he asked, annoyed.

"That I saw a reflection of somebody passing the door of this room—in the hallway out there."

He nodded across the dim room, at the end of which the door to the passage made a rectangle of bright light. It was empty now. In stillness we could hear the fire crackling and the distant hoot of a cab. Bencolin had risen. He stood tall and rather tense, his shoulders poised as though he were listening.

"I think he was starting into the room here, but he changed his mind when he saw us... It was a man I once knew. An Egyptian named Nezam El Moulk. Do you happen to know him?"

"No-o, I don't believe so. Wait a bit, though... Oh yes! I thought I'd heard the name," Sir John muttered. "He has rooms here, I believe. We're not very—choosy, are we? Why do you ask?"

Bencolin sat down and shrugged.

"A whim," he said. He contemplated the fire. In shadow, the cruel and powerful angles of his face had hardened, with bright unwinking eyes on the blaze. Sir John looked at him curiously, but said nothing. He was addressing some commonplace to me when Bencolin spoke again.

"Do you know, old man, that random ghost story you mentioned interests me very much. The shadow of a gallows! Who is this friend of yours who saw it?"

"Oh—that? His name is Dallings; friend of my son during the war. We shall probably meet him at the theatre tonight, by the way."

"And what was the nature of his adventure?"

Sir John's glance said, "What the devil ails you?" But he answered:

"Why, I can't tell you the whole affair—something about a mysterious woman he met and took home in the fog. I didn't pay particular attention; fellow'd been drinking. The upshot of it was that he found himself without a cab—"

"Where?"

"That's the point—he doesn't know. When they drove there, the woman gave the address to the driver herself, and Dallings didn't hear it. Apparently she must have paid the driver, too, and told him to leave directly. Dallings let her out to say good night, and then there wasn't any cab and the woman had gone.

"The fog was so thick that he couldn't see a foot in front of him. Dallings says he kept groping round and round, down over kerbs and across streets, without the slightest idea where he was going. It was past one in the morning; not a soul abroad, or a light he could locate. In the course of his wanderings he blundered into a brick wall of some sort. Then he lost the last shred of reason. While he was standing there, he says an immense rectangle of yellowish light appeared ahead of him. It was blurred by the fog, but up against it stood a gigantic gallows with a noose hanging from the crossbeam. So Dallings says, mind! Then he says that somebody was mounting the steps to it, and that the figure appeared to be waving its arms in the air…"

The Englishman paused. His lips wore a wintry smile.

"What then?" inquired Bencolin.

"Nothing. It disappeared. Dallings thought he must have been fooled by some trick of light. He was in a beastly mood and didn't investigate further. Then he resumed his wanderings. Eventually he found a lamp-post, and stopped there until he heard a cab pass. He was in Ryder Street then, not far from Piccadilly. Heaven knows where he'd *been*."

Sir John poured himself more tea, dismissing the matter. But he added:

"If you're curious, ask Dallings about it. He's full of the story, and he isn't ordinarily—loquacious. Seems to have been particularly impressed by the lady; she was French, by the way."

Bencolin stopped suddenly with a match halfway to his cigarette, staring at Sir John. Then he laughed, lit the cigarette, and sat back, amusedly contemplating its tip.

"French!" he repeated. "Ah well, your infernal fog is doing things to my nerves, I fear. Let's speak of something else. The fog itself, for instance." He turned to the window again. "Don't you find it fascinating?"

"No," said Sir John.

Mephisto winced. "My friend," he said, "you are a tonic. You are a shower-bath. You are gifted with all the lyric charm of a load of bricks falling through a skylight. In brief, you are good for me…

"But there *is* a fascination about it. A troll cavern, a masquerade, a city under the sea! Common things are made alluring by being blurred—an active principle of theology, Sir John. Or made terrifying because we see them out of their proper places. That was what so startled your friend Dallings the other night. To see a gibbet at Pentonville would be quite ordinary. But to see a gibbet under one's own window, on waking in the middle of the night…"

Sir John interrupted, "I can see one in this room."

There was an abrupt silence. Sir John's eyes were fixed on a chair near us. He rose slowly, and his stooped shoulders loomed up on the light as he moved towards that chair. That was how the model of the gibbet was found, lying on its side there. He placed it on our table, among the scattered tea-things, and still nobody spoke. The thing was uncannily real. It cried aloud for a doll victim to mount its steps.

Bencolin clucked his tongue, nodded, and examined it with an air of refreshed interest, as though he said, "I had not hitherto suspected the English of this quaint custom of putting toy gibbets in the lounges of their clubs. Undoubtedly it has its points of merit."

Sir John snapped, "What sort of stupid humorist—!" He paused and looked at Bencolin. The detective sat silent, and was absorbedly walking his fingers up and down the steps. He pulled a tiny wire at the side, so that the trap fell.

Pressing the bell for the lounge steward, Sir John sat down and glowered.

"Victor," he said, when the steward came in, "may I ask who is responsible for this?"

"Is anything wrong, sir?"

"No, nothing's wrong. But who left that damned thing in the chair there?"

Victor was rather funereal-looking. Had he shrunk before our eyes to the size of a tin soldier, he might have made a very suitable figure to mount the little steps.

"I'm very sorry, sir! I—"

"Never mind. Take it out."

"Er—just a moment, please," said Bencolin, looking up with wrinkled forehead. "I'll be responsible, Victor, if Sir John doesn't mind."

He turned his attention again to the model. Victor started. An idea seemed to strike him, rather as though he had been jabbed in the rear with a pin. "Oh!" he said, and as Bencolin looked up he continued:

"Oh… yes, sir. Thank you. I fancy I know to whom it belongs."

"Well?"

"I think so, sir. I believe it belongs to the Egyptian gentleman, sir—Mr. El Moulk."

"To Mr. El Moulk," the detective repeated, thoughtfully. "You mean he collects them, or makes them himself, or what?"

"I really can't say, sir. I remember, however, that Mr. El Moulk received a box by the post this afternoon…"

He paused, and Sir John, who was regarding him curiously, said: "Go on, man."

"He was in this room when I was emptying the ash-trays, sir. I saw him opening the box—it was about of a size to contain *that*—and when I heard him rustling the paper while he opened it, I noticed that he was looking very strange, sir; frightened, as it were. When he had got it open, he stood very still for a moment... I hope I am violating no confidence, sir?"

Victor looked about, and seemed to take strength from the sight of Sir John. His wavering black outline became solid.

"He said, 'Victor, take the model that's in this box and burn it.' He looked very queer, sir. I thought he was ill. Then he seemed to remember something. He took the model—I suppose it was the model, though I didn't see it—out of the box and dropped it in the chair over there. After that he threw the box and the wrapping-paper into the fire, and then walked out very quickly. That's all I know, sir."

"And why didn't you burn it?" asked Bencolin.

"I intended to, sir. But I was carrying out ash-trays at the time, and I fear I overlooked—"

"Ah yes. Do you happen to know whether he returned to the room afterwards?"

"Why, I am positive he didn't, sir. I saw him go out afterwards, and he didn't return until a short time ago. The porter can tell you..."

"That's all, Victor, thank you."

When he had gone, Sir John asked: "What was the purpose of all those questions? After all—none of our affair, you know."

Bencolin did not reply. He sat motionless, his elbow on the table and his chin in his hand, staring at the evil toy. A burning log exploded sharply in the fireplace. Over the rumble of London we heard the slow, sonorous gong notes of Big Ben striking six.

II

How We Played Hare and
Hounds with a Corpse

NOW THE BRIMSTONE CLUB IS ONE OF THE MOST CURIOUS, AND certainly the most disreputable, institution of the West End. It used to stand at the eastern corner of Pall Mall and St. James's Street; four floors of dun-coloured granite, grimy, bay-windowed, and sedate. Considering its earlier reputation, it now wears the rather forlorn air of a young lady trying to look wicked in an 1890 bathing suit. But it is still spoken of (in the deafer and more polite circles) with a clearing of the throat and a deprecating "Hum!" The smell of top-hats and hell fire lingers strong in its vicinity.

It was founded in 1798 by Sir George Falconer, so it is yet a parvenu among those ancient clubs whose first quiet chop has long since petrified. In the time of the Regency it housed some high gaming and full-blooded devilment. Its subsequent luridness, from the eighteen thirties on, was of a lace-valentine nature very pretty to contemplate. When you walk upon the thick rugs of its galleries, and look at the tall portraits there, it is difficult to realize that those starchy and slab-faced gentlemen in the elaborate whiskers were bucks in their day. Their plaid trousers illumined the oyster bars of Leicester Square; they could star a knee-cap in a little affair of honour with pistols, at not too discreet a distance; and at the card tables, under gimcrack canopies of lights, they could toss away their wives' fortunes with the utmost nonchalance. Their red-plush rooms were full of gilt mirrors, billowing skirts, and a vague scent of horsiness. Pleasantly frail ladies had a convenient habit of fainting when you locked the door (which made everything much simpler), and of not reviving until it was too late to make a convincing protest against your intentions.

All this culminated, in the late 'eighties, when pretty Kitty Darkins jumped to her death from a top-floor window, and young Lord Rayle blew out his brains in the same room—for no apparent reason, except that everybody appeared to think it a very romantic idea. Rayle's friends (men like Compston and Mirch, for instance) had much more reasonable views in these matters. When a lady had such bad taste as to mess up your doorstep by killing herself on it, you simply took a few more drinks and went out to find another woman. But Kitty Darkins's conduct, in a club, was profanation. The Brimstone has not, therefore, ever been an institution for gentlemen. They said all manner of foolish things; among them, that there was a lost suite of rooms where Rayle housed his lights of love, with a hidden door whose secret died with him. It was all very alluring, and quite untrue.

But, though now the club has fallen upon peace, it is a peace more evil and morbid than that of any hauntings from the past. The paper-lantern chivalries have crumbled. One does not hear in the passages (as they used to swear) the click of the hammer on Falconer's ghostly pistol. But, at the restless doom which is on it now, I fancy that I can hear Falconer laughing in the good Anglican hell to which dice and adultery gave him the passport. For the Brimstone Club is haunted by its own members.

Membership is allowed to men of any nationality and of any type. They are not passed on by any committee; they need no qualifications except a willingness to pay the most fantastically high dues of any club in London. The Brimstone collects the wealthy and drifting scum of the world. For the past thirty years it has been the club of the wanderer.

It is run precisely like a hotel, and is generally empty. Through it float English, French, German, Russian, Spanish, Italian faces; the soldier, the pawned title, the castaway, the game-hunter, the seeker of far places; the bored, the aimless, the foot-loose, the damned. They have sullen mouths and a restless eye. The same face rarely appears for more than a few days at a time. For one night they will be seen sitting in the bar, staring into a glass, speaking to nobody; and the next morning they will have gone. They disappear, nobody knows where, on their secret paths through a world rich in twining colours like an Eastern rug. A jauntiness is on them, and the lure of other suns. But they will always look baffled when they reappear at the Brimstone after months or years. And then Martin, who presides over the bar, will mix each man's favourite cocktail without a word, and put it before him as though he had been doing it each night since the club began.

This, I think, is the reason for the atmosphere of melancholy and doom which seeps into every room. One is hushed by the massive dreariness of its luxury, its sombre lamps, its thick, muffled carpets, its hint of suicide. Its lighted windows on the fog of a raw night do not suggest comfort inside. They suggest, instead, the lights of steamers in all the foggy harbours of the earth, slow-moving to the hoot of steamers' sirens—that hoarse and mournful cry. They suggest strange smells, strange ghosts, and the weird roofs of Xanadu. If the model of a gallows were to be found at any club in London, it came most appropriately here…

Or so I thought when we had left off looking at the toy that afternoon. Bencolin was moody and distraught. He prowled about the lounge, shaking his head, and I know that everybody felt relieved when Sir John suggested we adjourn to dress for dinner. Bencolin put away the model in a cabinet at one side of the fireplace. He clicked shut the door of the cabinet slowly, as though he were shutting up his own thoughts.

We did not refer to the matter again, and at shortly after six we all left the lounge. Sir John's rooms were on the ground floor, at the rear;

Bencolin had quarters on the second floor, and I on the fourth. The passage from the lounge gave on a lobby, like a hotel again, with a lift at the back. Its gloomy rotunda, swathed in tapestries and lighted by pale wall-lamps, was deserted. Our footfalls echoed, and small wreaths of fog were floating across it.

Bencolin got out of the lift at the second floor, and I ascended to the fourth alone. I was in such a state of depression that I was not aware of my surroundings until I heard the whir of the descending lift. This top floor had not been wired for electricity. The hallway was huge and bleak, lighted by gas-globes on its tarnished gilding, and mounting to a peak in the manner of a Gothic arch. It was even more quiet than the lower regions; so cold, too, that I could see the smoke of my breath. Now the number of my door was twenty-one. It communicated with the only set of rooms on the floor, except an immense suite at the rear. I had remarked, vaguely, the dark archway at the end of the hall which led to these other chambers. And so preoccupied was I with the whole dismal affair that, without thinking, I walked straight past my own door, into the archway beyond.

At that moment I collided with somebody. In the dark, I had struck a human shoulder.

There was a gasp, a choking and unearthly gasp, from the other person. I cried, "Who's there?" For a queer instant we stood there, trying to see each other, so that I heard his heavy, laboured breathing. Then he shoved past me, and we both emerged into the lights of the hallway.

He was a small, thin man in a dressing-gown of flowered silk. His skin had a brown tinge, his nose was beaked, and the thick black hair fell in disorder on his forehead. But what struck me was the strange expression of his eyes. They were of a staring, bestial shade of yellow, opened so wide that a ring of white showed entirely round the iris. They remained transfixed, motionless, like the eyes of a wax figure, although the man was panting thickly. They were hypnotic, and seemed to grow larger in that dead cold stare.

When he spoke, it startled me anew; I had not fancied that his lips moved at all.

"Did you put this damned thing on my desk?" he asked.

Abruptly he thrust out his hand, opening the palm. In it lay a tiny wooden figure, not an inch long. It seemed to be the figure of a man. The head had over it some sort of cap, and the neck was twisted sideways.

I looked at it in silence, and still I could hear his thick breathing. In the brown palm that little black figure had assumed a monstrous significance. Nor was his accent necessary to tell me that I had run into Nezam El Moulk. I said something like,

"No. Sorry... Rooms on this floor. Got in here by mistake..."

The brown palm shut. When I looked up he was studying me with those wide-open eyes. He began, "Somebody came into my room—"

Without any further words he stuffed the little figure into the pocket of his dressing-gown, whirled about, and disappeared into the archway. I walked rather quickly back to my door.

A bright fire was burning in the bedroom of my suite. In the next room I could hear Thomas, the most comfortable of servants, moving about, laying out my clothes. These fancies were all nonsense. But they persisted while I bathed and dressed. It was seven o'clock when I started downstairs...

In the hallway I met Nezam El Moulk. We almost collided again as he passed my door on his way to the lift. The change in the man was marked; he no longer wore that dreadful face which, I thought, must be quite as bad as the thing he dreaded. About him now was a gloss and jauntiness—coat and top-hat wore a rakish air of defiance. With his stick he poked the button to summon the lift, as though he tossed at it a casual thrust with a sword. I noticed then that he was wearing the most immaculate white gloves. Now the brown face was placid. His eyes had an absent, almost stupid look. He smiled, stared at the shaft, and hummed something from a musical show.

Suddenly he turned and addressed me, in slurred soft English:

"I *say*… I hope you will pardon the outburst"—he gestured— "back there. Eh? It was"—casting up his eyes and smiling—"a joke. You understand?"

"Of course. It was my fault."

"No, no, *no!*" he protested, lifting his hand. "I will not have you say that. And please do not mention—eh?"

As he opened his eyes wide again, a glimpse of their earlier expression came back. In the lift going down, he examined himself in the mirror, straightened the wings of his white tie, looked very pleased, and fell to humming his tune. He paused in the lobby to light a cigarette, and I wandered into the lounge. There was no sign of Bencolin or Sir John; I sat down by the window to wait.

The fog had lifted somewhat, and the lights from the club shone out through a thinner brown dinginess across the pavement. A long Minerva limousine, of a peculiarly violent shade of green, loomed up duskily at the kerb. I saw El Moulk saunter down the steps, slapping at the balustrade with his stick. A gigantic chauffeur opened the door for him, saluting. The door slammed, and presently the Minerva's tail-light moved away into the stream of traffic.

It was nearly half an hour before Bencolin and Sir John appeared. No further reference was made to the events of the afternoon, and so I did not mention the episode upstairs. We had a cocktail in the bar, that snug place of red curtains and lights in inverted bowls, where the great porcelain monkey leers down from the mantelpiece. Sir John, with his hatred of crowded places, was for dining at the club; and I suggested a short theatre dinner in the Pall Mall restaurant, adjoining the Haymarket Theatre. But Bencolin would have it at Frascati's in Oxford Street.

Frascati's was gold and silver. There were crowds. There was clatter. There was a sniping fire of pulled corks, and the music of an orchestra astir under lights. There were the steam and blue flame of chafing-dishes, the clink of their lids, the vanishing goblin-waiter, and the yellow, luminous hue of wine. Sir John blinked at all of it like a man who has just come out of a dark room. Slowly the wine flushed up into his sallow cheek, and a guilty twinkle appeared in his eye. Over the coffee and *fine*, when we were all warmed, he began to chuckle. Leaning forward confidentially, he told a number of absolutely pointless jokes, after each of which he would chuckle again, draw himself up with a roguish eye cocked, and beam, *"Eh?"*

When we took a cab to the theatre, I had almost begun to look forward to this play. London that night was a wet chaos of fog, screeching with taxis and smeared on the sky with a blur of electric signs round Piccadilly. But as we turned down the Haymarket, there was a sense of intimacy crowded into these dun-coloured walls. The heavy-footed traffic rumbling past, the shine of light on wet pavements—clank, babble, shrill policeman's whistle, and loom of big arm in water-proof—all carried a suggestion of companionship through mere virtue of the fog. It was not until we entered the theatre, until the house darkened and the curtain rose on that pale mimic world of terror which was Vautrelle's play, that the afternoon's devils returned...

At the end of the first act it was a relief to go out for a cigarette. None of us had seats together, for the house had been sold out. In the foyer I found Sir John introducing Bencolin to somebody who had just come up. He turned to me.

"—and this is Mr. Marle. Mr. Dallings, Mr. Marle."

I found myself shaking hands with a youngish, languid man whose hand was hung in the air, and whose grip was so very loose that you felt you were taking hold of a dead man's. His eyes were fixed glassily on a point somewhere past your shoulder. He murmured something that sounded like, "Chrugulph!" and gave us a pale spectral smile before he began to inspect his finger nails. He was just becoming stout, and was good-looking in a fashion at once pallid and robust. Oxford, and not quite out of it after some years. Conversation was going to be difficult.

There was a pause. Somebody said, "I trust you're enjoying the play, Mr. Dallings?"

"Aoh?" queried Dallings, coming out of his reverie with a vague start. "Aoh!" he repeated, in a tone of comprehension, and the spectral smile dawned again. "Don't know, really. Just got here. Fearfully late, I'm afraid. D'you like it?"

Now I was convinced about the difficulty of conversation. There was another pause, so somebody suggested a drink. By degrees Dallings thawed; at length a faint spark appeared, and before the beginning of the second act he was almost friendly. Careful attention was necessary, however, to extricate his syllables from their conversational clothes-wringer. I felt as I once had in Heidelberg when an earnest Teuton, firmly convinced that I spoke German, had buttonholed me and lectured fervently for three-quarters of an hour about God knows what, pausing now and then for corroboration. So I had just nodded, saying, *"Ja, ja,"* and looking wise, and at intervals had deprecatingly murmured, *"Bahnhof."*—Finally Sir John asked:

"Oh, by the way, George, you remember that wild story you were telling me? About seeing the shadow of a gallows, or something?"

"Seinglows?" inquired Dallings, wrinkling his forehead. "Aoh, that? Quite!"

Sir John had apparently been primed by Bencolin. He was vague; he mentioned some excitement at the Brimstone in connection with it; at length he invited Dallings to the club for a drink after the performance. The other looked startled, for no apparent reason, when Sir John said he would like to hear the tale again. But he agreed, and said he would be delighted.

"Incidentally, Mr. Dallings," Bencolin put in, lazily, "you don't happen to know a man called El Moulk, do you? Nezam El Moulk, I think the name is."

Now Dallings was really startled. He passed a hand over his thick dark hair, he blinked, and stammered, "Why, as a matter of fact, I've *heard* of him—" Then he broke off to regard Bencolin with some suspicion.

The second act began at that moment, and I returned to the theatre more than a little puzzled. Bencolin was smiling.

We exchanged no more words until the end of the play. Its eerie effect had laid hold of all our spirits, and the whole crowd thronging out of the theatre had a sombre look. When Dallings joined us, we walked out to the street in silence. It was intensely cold, and a fog as transparent as tobacco smoke hung round the bright lamps. A honking mass of cabs cluttered the street, but they were being snapped up as quickly as lifted stick could hail them, and we could find none vacant. We walked up almost to Piccadilly Circus in the hope of finding one.

"Oh, let's walk," Sir John said, petulantly. "The fog's thinning out now. Turn round; it isn't far."

At that moment we were at the corner of Jermyn Street, on the side towards Piccadilly. There were not many pedestrians—which was just as well, because I was not looking where I was going. A policeman's arm had halted traffic, and I saw my companions turn and cross the street. I had just stepped down to follow them, when, vaguely, in the blurred glow of an electric sign high over our heads, I saw Sir John turn about. He whirled up his stick and cried:

"Look out, man!"

The shout jabbed into my mind. I whirled about, jumped backwards, and almost fell. Traffic was halted—but one of the cars had paid no attention to the policeman's signal. It loomed up out of Jermyn Street soundlessly. Distorted by the muddy fog, it had a devilish life of its own, and its staring lamps bounded towards me as I turned. I heard the officer's cry and the shrilling of his whistle. Then the great green limousine swept past me into the Haymarket.

But what made me stand there, shaken with a sickness of horror, was not this. As the car roared past, I had caught a glimpse of the chauffeur's face.

The chauffeur of that car was dead.

The picture was swift, but hideously vivid. Through the dingy mist, the face had been almost thrust into mine. He was a gigantic man in livery, and his face had now turned grey. It hung over his right shoulder, with white eyeballs staring out and jaw fallen wide, and his throat was cut from ear to ear... And yet the limousine careened on, turning down the Haymarket. It was El Moulk's car. I became aware that my hat had tumbled off and lay in the mud; I was standing in the middle of Jermyn Street and cursing in a voice I did not recognize.

Bencolin was at my elbow. He had seen it, too, and he wasted no time. Behind us, held in the traffic, was a cab with its flag up. As the policeman came hurrying towards us, Bencolin was bundling us all into the taxi.

"Get in, all of you!" he yelled. "I'm going to use *you*, Sir John. Scotland Yard," he said to the driver. "Follow that green limousine ahead—the one up there. See it?"

I was falling over Sir John's knees as the four of us tumbled inside. Dallings, breathless and astonished, had got jammed into the corner.

His muffler was blown about his face and his strangled voice was protesting:

"I say! Look here!—"

The big top-heavy cab snorted and trembled. In a screech of gears it knocked past the infuriated policeman, who was shaking his fist at the window. From the cavern darkness of the interior I saw a segment of buildings reel round in a blur of lights as we turned into the Haymarket.

"—can't *go* faster!" the driver was shouting to Bencolin. The roar deepened. We dodged round a tiny Austin in a way that jolted us into a swearing wedge, but we could see the green Minerva moving just ahead. It was not until then that the ultimate madness of the thing took hold of me: this comedy of lunacy in which we pursued a dead man on his joy ride through London. We were flying in pursuit of a corpse. Dallings and Sir John started to talk at once, but Bencolin, who was leaning out of the window, silenced them with a fierce gesture.

The driver was still shouting to Bencolin. "Fog's too thick, guv'nor!" he cried in despair. "*There!* 'E's turnin' into Pall Mall..."

A thick billowing of fog was bearing down on us. Ahead, as we swung to the right, was the long field of lamps which was Pall Mall. It was level and almost deserted, so that through the blotching of mist the Minerva's red tail-light shone clearly.

We flashed past Waterloo Place and straight on. The corpse on its grisly ride was breaking all speed laws. I could fancy it shaking its arms and threshing about with the joy of the race. Over the low growl of London lifted the boom of Big Ben striking twelve. Past the Carlton Club, only gathering speed! The lamps of a car jumped in our eyes; swerving with a sickening plunge, we skidded, crashed a mudguard, and tore ahead with a burst of profanity in our wake. A policeman's whistle shrilled thin blasts across the street...

Now the limousine was slowing down, and Bencolin's fingers clenched. We were almost to St. James's Street when it suddenly swerved across to the right. Sir John said in a queer voice:

"He—he's going to the Brimstone."

As we turned to the right after it, the Minerva came to a slow stop. I could distinguish its outline dimly, and on the right the light from the door of the club made a haze along its green side. We swept in and ground to a stop only a few feet behind it. The dead man had placidly come home.

We thumped out on the sidewalk. With a stately tread the doorman was coming down the steps of the Brimstone; we could see his vague ghost silhouetted against the lights from behind. My heart was pounding, and I suppose the others felt as insane as I, for none of us moved. The attendant opened the rear door of the limousine and stood waiting. Nobody came out.

There was a terrible minute of silence, while the rumble of London beat away behind us. In that swimming dimness, the doorman craned his neck to peer into the back of the car. He seemed to be puzzled. Still nobody appeared. Shaking his head, he walked up to speak to the chauffeur.

At that moment Bencolin moved out of our group. His tall figure loomed in and out of fog-swirls as he went with steady steps towards the front of the car... Then the doorman uttered a horrible screech and jumped away as though he had been burnt. I could see Bencolin's sharp profile under his silk hat, bent forward in the glow of the dash lights. Out went his long arm, and he yanked the door open. A huge bulk seemed to rise up past him, and then it dropped with a sodden flat *thud* on the pavement at his feet. Now in the light of the dash lamps I could see Bencolin's face set in a devilish mask as he stared down at it, unmoving.

III

Ruination Street

I LOOKED ROUND AT MY COMPANIONS. SIR JOHN STOOD EXPRESsionless, a dumb wonder in his eyes, his motionless hand holding out a bank note to the taxi-driver—who was leaning out of the cab, too startled to take it. Dallings's pallid, dark-shadowed face looked from side to side with a sort of bewildered petulance. In the next moment we had all crowded up.

The big chauffeur lay spread-eagled on his face, and the cap had fallen off his kinky head. But his spine was raised and his legs doubled under at the knees; *rigor mortis* had set in while he was in a sitting position, and it was as though he were salaaming before the detective. His dark-green livery stood out in the fog like the back of an enormous beetle. Inside the car and down the running-board was such a welter of blood that all of it had not yet dried, and still dripped into the gutter. Dallings, who had absently put his hand on that door, jumped and drew back; then he began to rub his hands together as though he were trying to shake off a piece of clinging fly-paper.

We heard Bencolin's harsh, level voice.

"Sir John," he said, "where is the nearest police station—Vine Street?... Good. Doorman, hop inside and phone there. If possible, get the divisional inspector himself. We want somebody up here at once."

"He's dead, of course," said Sir John, quietly.

"He has been dead for some time," answered Bencolin, touching the body with his stick. Then he drew a deep breath and knelt beside it.

Dallings came to life with a jerk. He cried, "But, look here!—he was *driving!*—"

Bencolin rose. He peered into the back and front of the car, and nodded.

"So it seems, my friend. All very neat; he has turned off the ignition and"—he bent further—"put on the emergency brake, I think—I don't want to touch it. There's nobody in the back seat."

"Wait," Sir John said to the doorman; "wait a bit. I'll ring up Vine Street myself. Talbot's the D.D. inspector there. I know him very well; he worked under me. He'll come at once.—Whose car is it?"

"A very famous limousine. Better known on the Continent, I think, than here. It belongs to Nezam El Moulk. Lend a hand, now, and let's get the poor devil inside. We can't leave him out here to draw a crowd. Take his shoulders, there, doorman, and"—he beckoned to the taxi-driver—"you take his feet. Don't be afraid! He won't hurt you. Steady... he's heavy."

The weird procession moved and staggered up the steps. Just before Sir John went in to telephone, a wrathful policeman came pounding out of the fog to arrest everybody for the violation of all traffic rules; but his mood changed as Sir John drew him inside to explain. Fortunately, we drew no crowd. Bencolin and I were left alone in the drifting mist when Dallings went in, too. We stood for a time silent beside that evil car whose doors were both open to the night.

"Bencolin," I said, "where is El Moulk?"

He shrugged. "Not in his car, anyhow. Why do you ask?"

I told him of my two encounters with the Egyptian, and of his leaving shortly after seven in the car. He heard me out, but made no comment. Leaning into the tonneau, he felt round and found the switch for the interior light. By its yellow glow from the roof we saw that the back of the car was upholstered in dark velours. On the seat lay an ebony stick and a pair of white gloves. Beside them was a square cardboard box which bore the lettering, "Wills, Florist, 8 Cockspur Street, London W. 1." There were no signs of disorder; not even of dust.

"Look at these back doors," said Bencolin. "You see?"

"The glass looks uncommonly thick."

"It is bullet-proof," he said, knocking lightly against it with his knuckles... "And judging by the thickness of that cane there, I'm inclined to think it's a sword-stick. The man seems to be taking every human precaution against attack."

Extinguishing the light, he remarked, softly:

"But they got him, Jeff. They got him."

"Who got him?"

He was peering into the front again. "What an excessively small space up here! It must have cramped our big chauffeur... H'm! Well, the police deserve first turn at it. Let's go inside."

"Bencolin," I said, "when that car went by I could see straight through past the driver. There was nobody else in that front seat! I swear there was nobody else in that front seat! Do you mean to say that a dead man—"

"Nonsense, Jeff! Somebody was driving it, of course. He could have slipped out under cover of the fog and gotten away as soon as the car stopped; it's a right-hand drive, you see, and he must have left by the other side."

"But I tell you—!"

"Very well, then; have it your way. Let's go inside."

The awed taxi-driver was coming down the steps, muttering incredulous blasphemies. Bencolin gave him some money and told him to watch the car. We left him staring grimly at it as though he expected it to start up and drive away of its own volition. When we went inside, we were met by the portly doorman, who was mopping his brow with a handkerchief.

He led us across the lobby, down a passage past the lift.

"We took him to the billiard-room, sir," he explained, "the old billiard-room, I mean. We don't use it, now that we have the new tables off the lounge. And, begging your pardon, sir, I didn't want anybody to see…"

Opening a door, he led us into a large cold room where much dust had accumulated. An old billiard-table, with its green cover scarred and ripped, stood under two bright drop-lamps in the centre. They had placed the body on this, and thrown over it a dusty couch-cover from under which the huge boots projected grotesquely. Behind the table stood Dallings, his hat on the back of his head, looking at the lump in horrified fascination. He started as we opened the door, pointed at the body, and said, unnecessarily:

"His throat's cut. D'you see? His throat's cut!"

As we came in, I had seen Victor with pail and mop hurriedly at work on the marble floor. I shuddered again when Dallings's finger indicated the stain that was crawling across the green table towards one of the billiard pockets. Watching that blood, it was horribly as though you were waiting for a ball to drop there in a game, and wondering whether it would. Dallings pointed again. He said, hysterically, "Made it, by Jove!" and started to laugh. The doorman bolted out of the room. He almost collided with Sir John, who was coming in, looking perplexed and distrait.

"Did you get Vine Street?" asked Bencolin. "Be still, Mr. Dallings, please!—"

"Yes; I got Talbot too, fortunately. But there's something queer…"

"What do you mean?"

Sir John was biting at his upper lip. His thin dark brows were drawn together, and he squinted at the body without seeing it.

"Why," he said, "why, about Talbot. Never heard him so excited. Said he'd come over immediately, and asked me the oddest question. He said, 'Where is Ruination Street?'"

Bencolin turned round with his hand on the cover over the chauffeur.

"Well?" he demanded. "What about it?"

"That's the question," Sir John replied, nodding his head—"where *is* Ruination Street? Why should he ask me that? I—I hope I'm not getting fanciful." He made this remark as though he said, "I hope I'm not going insane," hesitated, and went on: "When I was in the service, I thought I knew every street and alley in London. But I never heard of that one."

Then he raised his eyes and stared at Bencolin through the gold-rimmed glasses.

The detective murmured, "Nonsense!" He turned again to the body. When he drew back the couch-cover, Dallings retreated. The young man tried to take a cigarette from his case, but the case jumped out of his hand and spilled on the floor. The white eyeballs of the dead man were turned sideways over his shoulder, and glistened beneath the bright lights. A heavy gash on the left side of his neck, thinning out under the right ear, had almost stopped bleeding now. It looked like the slash of a razor. His left hand, pulled up on his breast, bore an imitation diamond ring. The fingers of this hand had been nearly severed, as though the assassin had tried to hack them off to get at the ring. The green coat was soaked and sodden with blood, but just over the heart you could see a tear in the cloth where some instrument had been driven into his chest. Pulling the cover farther down, Bencolin uttered an exclamation.

"What is it?" demanded Sir John.

"All the buttons have been cut off his coat," said Bencolin. "And see here." He picked up the ends of a couple of tawdry gilt cords hanging from the chauffeur's shoulders. "*Diable!* What a taste in livery El Moulk has! These cords had gilt tassels hanging from them. The tassels have been cut off."

He stepped back and stood with his hands on his hips, glancing up and down the body.

"I should like to go through his pockets," he added, "but we shall have to wait until your inspector arrives."

When Victor told us that Divisional Detective-Inspector Talbot had arrived, he strolled into the shadow beyond the lamps. I could see his dim figure leaning against the mantelpiece, and the moving glow of his cigar.

Inspector Talbot was not particularly impressive. He was a little man with a stolid, square-cut face which looked dusty, a broken nose, and an unpleasant habit of clicking his teeth together audibly. But the eyes in that somnolent countenance had a singular quality of seeming to absorb all details before him as the sun draws up water. His dark hair was growing grey round the temples. When he removed his water-proof, we saw that he was well dressed to the point of dandyism. He showed no surprise whatever, greeted Sir John with profound respect, and glanced casually at the rest of us. A notebook appeared. Even when Sir John had finished telling about the chase down the Haymarket he only nodded.

"Very well, sir," he said at length. He meditated. He clicked his teeth. "Now this whole business," he continued, making a gesture about him, "it's very queer indeed."

He pondered this a moment, as though wondering whether he had made an overstatement, and then confirmed himself:

"Yes, *very* queer. Now we'll have a look at his things."

"Wait a bit, Talbot," said Sir John. "What's all this you were telling me about Ruination Street?"

"Ah!" Talbot muttered dubiously. He frowned. "Now *that*—that's the queerest part of all, Sir John. As I understand you, the car belongs to an Egyptian named Mr. El Moulk. I had a look at it as I came in. Mr. El Moulk apparently *was* in it. Stick and gloves, all neat and orderly, on the back seat."

"I saw him leave the club in it tonight," I volunteered.

Talbot made another note, and turned his dusty face slowly. "Ah," he repeated. "And what time was that?"

"After seven. Five minutes, possibly."

"'After seven. Five minutes, possibly.' Now—"

"Well?" interrupted Sir John.

"Tonight we got a telephone message at Vine Street. Person insisted on speaking to me. The voice was indistinct. What it said was, '*Nezam El Moulk has been hanged on the gallows in Ruination Street.*'"

There was a pause. From the dense shadow where Bencolin stood, the red glow of his cigar jerked in midair and then stayed motionless.

"It rang off then," continued Talbot. "I didn't trace the call. I thought, of course, it was a crank or else somebody playing a joke. They do it, you know," he explained, smiling vaguely. "We get all sorts of reports. They say the Prince has been kidnapped, or somebody has run off with the Marble Arch, or something...

"But I got to thinking about the queer names, and it bothered me. I kept thinking, 'Where *is* Ruination Street?' Finally I asked several people at the station, but nobody had ever heard of it. Then, when you rang up to say Mr. El Moulk's car had driven up here with the chauffeur dead—why, it put the wind up me for a second."

He uttered a sound which was strangely like a sigh, gave several rapid little clicks of his teeth, and shot out:

"I don't suppose any of you gentlemen know where Ruination Street is?"

The opaque eyes were rather disconcerting as they turned towards me. I shook my head, and so did everybody else.

"H'm!" said Talbot. "Just so." Without any more words he approached the body and bent stiffly over it. The pencil jabbed rapid little words into his notebook.

"A few coppers; no other money—"

"Robbery?" queried Sir John.

"Can't say, sir... Billfold, empty; no name. Cigarette case..."

"Good Lord!" said Sir John. He was pulling at his clipped beard, and he pointed suddenly. "That cigarette case is platinum! A chauffeur with a platinum cigarette case!"

Bencolin's cigar had begun to pulse and dim again, but still the detective did not move. In a matter-of-fact way Talbot noted:

"Platinum. Didn't know it myself, Sir John. Thank you. Full of cigarettes. Bunch of keys. Stub of a cinema ticket. 'Pocket Guide to London.' Package of peppermint drops. That's all."

Talbot shut up his notebook.

"Now, gentlemen," he went on with a show of energy, "I don't know that the superintendent will like your disturbing the body. Should have been left at the wheel, you know. It destroys any indications when you—"

Sir John interposed, stiffly:

"I think we knew what we were about, Talbot. Did you catch the name of that man over there?"

The teeth clicked again. Talbot's eyes narrowed. For the first time he showed a flash of surprise and looked inquiringly at Sir John, who nodded. To my own astonishment, all of Talbot's briskness went out of him. He grinned as Bencolin advanced out of the shadows—a homely, slow, suburban grin—and put out his hand.

"Nearly put my foot in it, sir. You don't remember me, but I'm very certain I remember *you*. I was a sergeant at Vine Street when you helped us on that Grovane case. All the same"—he caught himself up and scowled—"all the *same*, you shouldn't have disturbed that body."

"I feel most guilty, Inspector," said Bencolin. "However, I don't think it matters a great deal... Your fingerprint men are here, I take it?"

"Yes. I'll clear out now and let the doctor have a look at him. I'm interviewing all the servants here, and I'm afraid I shall have to ask you gentlemen to wait for me in the lounge... Fine mess it 'u'd be," he added with sudden fierceness, "if Mr. El Moulk should walk in that door, no more dead than I am!... See you later in the lounge, gentlemen, if you please."

Bencolin looked after him whimsically as he went out.

"Inspector Talbot sees our difficulties much more clearly than we think he does... *He* believes in Ruination Street. This afternoon, Sir John, you interrupted my little lecture on the possibilities of fog. Talbot knows, or suspects—"

Sir John was polishing his eyeglasses moodily. He jerked up his head.

"—that a street has got lost in London."

"What the devil are you talking about?" asked the Englishman.

"Well, where is Ruination Street? The thing intrigues me. There might be nothing strange about the disappearance of a man. Some crack-brained soul might even telephone to say that the man who disappeared had been hanged. But suppose a whole street disappeared, a whole thoroughfare blotted from London. What could be more fantastic?"

He paused.

"Who lives in Ruination Street? How would you send letters there? Man, this vision of El Moulk swallowed up in a lost street is the prettiest fancy in the whole realm of nightmare!—How could a murderer better dispose of his victim than by hanging him on a high gallows, up before the sight of all heaven, but on a street the police couldn't find?"

Sir John made a gesture of exasperation. He said:

"See here, Bencolin—seriously—this romancing has got to stop. You'll damned well have everything so muddled that we shan't know what we're about. You'll never know it from Talbot, but he looks on you as a kind of god. I know him. He'll take your suggestions like a shot. And then—"

His clipped beard was thrust forward and his sallow face pinched with earnestness. Without knowing it, he had touched a spring in Bencolin. The Frenchman's charlatanism shot up like a jack-in-the-box. He threw back his head and laughed in that way of his, opening his mouth hardly at all. He spoke coolly, but I knew he was furious.

"So, my friend, you think my methods of work will only muddle things?"

"If you call those 'methods of work'—yes."

"Ah yes," said Bencolin, still coolly. He ran a thoughtful finger along the edge of the billiard-table. His voice trembled. I had seen him in that mood a few times before, and on the last occasion he had broken a man's back in a frowsy café on the rue Brisemiche.

"We have often argued, you and I, about this matter." The poison crept into his voice. He looked up. "I know little about this case. I do not yet even know what has happened. But I will make you a small wager. I will bet you dinners for the three of us that I can name this man's murderer within forty-eight hours."

His voice broke. He crashed his fist down on the edge of the billiard-table. "God damn your slow methods! I have no use for the plodder. We will see whether I 'romance' or not. Do you accept?"

Sir John stood very straight and rigid. Colour was in his cheek, and his cold eye said, 'Swank!' What he replied was:

"Please be serious."

"I was never more serious in my life."

"I may remind you that our law requires evidence. We can have none of your spectacular methods here. You love induction. You assume one or more things are true, to show the criminal must have done this or that, and then you go to work to prove it. It is flashy, I dare say, and suited to your law. But it would land the English detective in trouble. The qualities of a detective are practice, patience, and perseverance."

"In short," said Bencolin, "the qualities one finds most highly developed in the trainer of a flea-circus."

Sir John answered, stiffly:

"Why quarrel about it? I will accept your wager... You will guarantee to produce evidence also, I expect?"

"Yes." Bencolin was leaning against the table. His face looked tired and ugly.

"Well," said Sir John, smiling dimly, "*that's* settled, then. Come, old man! We've gone too far along the road to row about a ridiculous point like this. Let's adjourn to the lounge. I think that something to drink—"

"That's a jolly good idea!" exclaimed a voice. It came from the shadows with such abruptness that I jumped, almost as though something disembodied had spoken. The voice belonged to Dallings, whom everybody had forgotten. Peering behind the lights, we could see him sitting on the broad window seat. His air, too, was detached and disembodied, but he rose with alacrity.

Bencolin opened the door. I could not keep myself from looking back for a last glance as it closed behind us. The face of the chauffeur peered with white eyeballs round his shoulder, as though he were wishing us good night.

From the partly opened door of the porter's room across the rotunda we could hear Talbot's dry voice intoned in questioning, and the scared tones of somebody answering him. You cannot imagine how sombre that lobby looked now, the whole bleak facing of doors and the echo of hollow rooms. Apparently we were the only people present. But as we went towards the lounge we heard the whir of the descending lift. The clang of its gate reverberated up against the rotunda, and out of it hurried a tall, lank figure which stumbled and almost fell.

It was a very thin man whose angular shoulders stuck up from his dressing-gown. He had a long nose, a narrow bald skull rising high between projecting ears, and pale blue eyes set in hollowed rings. He regarded us blearily and uncomprehendingly for a moment, and then he cried:

"Can you tell me where the detective is?"

Bencolin nodded towards the door whence the voices issued. The man jerked over his shoulder, "Thanks!" He seemed to have trouble with his long legs, as though he were always tripping over an invisible sword-scabbard. Giving us a ghastly smile, he hurried over to the door.

The Frenchman seemed very surprised. He looked round the lobby, whose only other occupants were Victor, and a policeman at the door.

"Curious!" he muttered. "Who is that fellow?"

Sir John shook his head. "I don't know. I think I've seen him about now and then, though. We can find out from—"

The words stopped in a kind of grunt, like that of a man hit in the stomach. We had reached the door of the lounge. The portières were drawn back, and we all stood motionless, looking in. Presently Sir John turned and said in a querulous voice:

"Look here, Bencolin. This has got to stop! Do you hear?—It's got to stop!"

The long room was lighted only by the yellow firelight, which threw a broad unsteady glare on the carvings of the farther wall. A shadow loomed up sharp and gigantic and thin across this wall. It was the shadow of a gallows.

From the crossbeam dangled the figure of a man, swaying wry-necked on a rope.

The Woman at Chez Aladdin

"N O NEED FOR ALARM," SAID BENCOLIN. "IT'S ONLY THE toy gallows."

He pointed at the firelit table in the centre of the room.

"You see? Somebody took it out of the cabinet and put it there. The firelight…"

Sir John snapped on the lights from a switch beside the door, and we approached the table.

"There's a toy hanging on the rope," remarked the Englishman. "Gad! Look! It's a little wooden man!"

There stood the toy gallows we had seen earlier in the day. But now from the twine noose swung a little black figure. It looked to me like the same one which *somebody* had dropped on El Moulk's desk that afternoon, and which I had last seen in his hands. Now I repeated the story to Sir John.

"There's a crazy man going about here," he said, flatly.

Bencolin nodded. "Right on both points. A crazy man, if I am right in the 'inductions' you condemn. And most certainly *here*. Here in the club, without a doubt, at this moment."

"You have a theory?"

"Yes. But only in essentials. This man El Moulk is being hounded, subtly and cunningly, and probably by—. No matter. They've caught him. We had better have Victor in here."

But Victor could not help us. He came in flustered and wilted after his interview with Inspector Talbot. Expressing a modest and proper horror at what he saw, he explained that he had not been in the lounge since half-past seven. But he had been in the porter's room, off the rotunda, all evening. He was positive that nobody had gone into the lounge, at least between seven-thirty and twelve. When the body was brought in at twelve, he had left the porter's room, and could not say whether or not anybody had been here.

"Were there many people in the club tonight?" Bencolin asked.

"No, sir. The only one who came in at all was Colonel Mardale, after letters. He looked into the bar and the lounge, but he left immediately."

"Who is Colonel Mardale?"

"He's all right," interposed Sir John. "Seventy years old, stone deaf, and well down with gout. I know him. You can rule him out."

"Very well. It seems to indicate that the thing must have been hung there after twelve, in the hubbub when the body was brought in. Nobody would notice…"

He looked up. "Victor, how many people are living at the club now? Aside from servants, I mean."

"Yes, sir. You three gentlemen, of course. Mr. El Moulk. Mr. El Moulk's man, a Frenchman named Joyet, and his secretary, Mr. Graffin. Dr. Pilgrim. Seven in all, sir."

Bencolin sat down in a deep chair, rumpling his hair.

"H'm!" he muttered. "And who was the tall gentleman in the dressing-gown who came downstairs when we were crossing the lobby?"

"That was Mr. Graffin, sir; Mr. El Moulk's secretary."

"Did he go out tonight?"

"Out of the club, you mean? No, sir. He has not been out all day. His meals were sent up to him."

"And this manservant, Joyet. Is he here tonight?"

Victor's twitching lip expressed distaste. "No, sir. I believe he has gone to Paris on leave."

"Finally, this other person—what is his name?"

"Dr. Pilgrim? A very quiet gentleman, sir," replied Victor, with unction. "He went out about nine, sir. I have not seen him since."

"That's all, Victor. Thank you."

All the amber lights were on in that great room, which stretched up fully twenty-five feet to its fretted ceiling, and all the monstrosities of carving were revealed. Gargoyles, snakes, twisted columns, bats, owls, weird heads crawled up the walls, twined about the diamond panes of the windows. Skeleton figures stared out over the portraits hung there. Sitting in the deep leather chair beside that fireplace which was as tall as a gateway of stone, Bencolin stayed motionless. Sir George Falconer looked down sardonically.

"Do you know any of these people?" the detective inquired at length.

Sir John, who was bending over the gallows on the centre table, turned.

"Who?... Oh! The residents? I know Pilgrim slightly."

"The doctor?"

"Why, yes, I believe he *is* a physician. But I don't think he practises. He's an antiquarian, rather famous; written some very good things on old London. Don't care much for these modern chaps, myself," Sir John growled. "Conjuring tricks with words. Now you see it, now you don't; and then you wonder what it was, after all.—But there's meat in this man. Interesting chap, too."

"Let it go for the present. The situation is this: I have certain theories which may or may not be correct. In any case, I am convinced that the adventure which befell Mr. Dallings the other night has a bearing on this matter..."

Dallings had slumped down in a chair opposite him. Now he opened wide and ox-like eyes.

"… and I should be very much obliged if he would tell us *everything* about it."

"But, good Lord!" cried Dallings, "that was only—"

"Yes, yes, of course, a lark. I quite understand. But tell me this. I am informed that you chanced across a mysterious woman—a Frenchwoman. Was this woman fairly tall, with very dark red hair? Did she have brown eyes, set rather wide apart?"

Dallings pulled himself up to a sitting position. He demanded:

"How did you know that?"

"Merely an old friend of mine. I venture to say she refused to tell you her name? Ah yes. Well, it is Colette Laverne."

"You know this woman?" exclaimed Sir John.

"Slightly. The famous, the fascinating, the exquisite Colette! I thought we should run across her sooner or later…"

"Famous?" said Dallings, regarding him with a somewhat vapid stare. His plump, good-looking face wore an expression of acute discomfort.

"But your adventure?"

Dallings hesitated. "I say, *must* I talk about it?"

"Not to the police, I trust. But please don't refrain from telling us because of your natural gentlemanly reticence," Bencolin coughed, but his lips were twitching, "your natural gentlemanly reticence at—er—making a conquest."

"Conquest?" repeated Dallings, startled. "Aoh, no, really!"

His discomfort grew more acute.

"No, of course not," said Bencolin, in a soothing voice. "Just tell us."

"*All* of it?"

"All of it."

"But it makes me out such an ass," the other complained, uncomfortably. He regarded the detective with some suspicion. "And I don't see what right you have…" Fingering the wings of his tie, he brooded.

"All right! I'll tell you, then! It was—oh, nearly a week ago. I had arranged to go to the theatre with a friend of mine, but at the last minute she couldn't go. So I went alone.

"I had a good dinner, with quite a bit of fizz, and it rather went to my head. The play," he added, wrinkling up his eyes, "the play was one of those things where they put out the lights and scream. Jolly good, too.

"Well, I was sitting there just a bit tight, trying to light a cigarette, and having the hell of a good time. It did get on my nerves, though. Chap who goes about cutting people up with knives…"

He looked at Bencolin interrogatively, and the other nodded.

"Just when they had the lights out, and it was all dark, somebody passed a pocket lighter under my nose… for my cigarette, you see. Gad! it startled me!—I could see his face in the light from the thing. It was a man sitting behind me in the box; hadn't noticed him before. I rather think it was this Egyptian, El Moulk.

"I'd seen him before, somewhere; at Lady Possonby's, I think. I hate the damn' foreigners… Er, sorry!—that is, I mean—I didn't like his way of talking. Interesting chap, though. We had a drink between the acts, and we got to talking about night clubs. He recommended one, which he said was only for connoisseurs. Offered to give me his card. Couldn't go himself, he said.

"There really isn't much to it, you see. The club was where I met this woman. It was a queer place—artificial gardens, and hidden orchestras, and all that. There's a blue moon, and you have a table with a silver fruit growing on a tree over you. They call it 'Chez Aladdin.'… She was sitting alone, over at a table partly in the dark, with a sort of shimmery shawl around her. I can't even remember how I met her; I expect she spoke to me, because I wouldn't have—you know!"

To Bencolin, watching him in veiled amusement, it must have seemed an exceedingly naïve statement. Dallings looked round as though appealing to us. Then he went on:

"Yes, she spoke to me. Anyhow, there we were, with a bottle of champagne between us, and somebody was singing something about 'The Arabian Nights Blues'; that made me laugh, I remember. She wouldn't tell me her name; later I asked a waiter about her, but he didn't know her name. Said she was known as the lady with the bracelets. You see, she had a whole string of silver bracelets with blue stones in them. One of them was loose. I told her she was going to lose it, but she only laughed.

"She laughed a lot. She looked so *merry* when she laughed, and her eyes would dance; I imagined they could hear her all over the club. Red hair—she was lovely. I don't even remember what I said to her, except, frankly, I must have made a dreadful fool of myself. I—I wanted to be the hero of the occasion... You know how it is when it's darkish along those seats in a night club..."

He gestured.

"We got to meeting there every night. One night... well, of course, I was tight; yes, I was tight... but I was pretty hard hit. I wanted to take her home. She knew I'd make a scene if she didn't. Probably," he said, fiercely, "that was why she let me. I got a cab. She gave the address to the driver, and I didn't hear it. When we left the cab, in the fog, I didn't know where we were. And she disappeared—without a word, without telling me anything. Oh, hell! Then I wandered around in the fog, and saw that shadow of the gallows..."

Dallings sat up. He roused himself, and his lip curled.

"One thing she'd said. 'If anything happens, I'll meet you in the same place Thursday night.' Thursday night—that's tonight. That's why I was late for the play. And she wasn't there."

After a long pause he rose wearily and began to take off his overcoat. He put it down, along with his white scarf; afterwards he wandered over to the window with his hands dug into his pockets, and stared out into the fog. He added, bitterly, "If *that's* any help!"

"Thank you, Mr. Dallings. Now if you don't mind a few questions…"

"I don't," said the other, whirling suddenly, "if you'll tell me who she really is and why she let all that thing go on."

"The first part of your question is easily answered. She is a very close friend of Nezam El Moulk's—or used to be. Do you see?"

Dallings nodded. His stiff lips framed: "Oh!… Righto!"

"As to the latter part of it, I think we get into deeper waters. She did not tell you her name?"

"No."

"And gave no reason for withholding it?"

"I assumed—she was married," the other replied, sullenly. He kicked at the edge of a chair.

"Was she ever in the habit of *questioning* you?"

"I—I don't think I understand."

"About any details of your past life, for example?"

"Come to think of it," said Dallings, frowning, "she kept asking me if I had been in the army. I told her I had. Asked me if I knew some chap—I've forgotten his name, but anyway I never heard of him. She said she'd heard him mention my name."

The purport of all these questions was beyond me. But Bencolin smiled.

"Just one thing more, Mr. Dallings. That night you were wandering in the fog—between the time she left you and the time you eventually found yourself in Ryder Street, how long a time elapsed?"

"Well, the time I wandered about wasn't long. Not more than twenty minutes, though it seemed hours; but between the time I found myself in Ryder Street and the time a cab picked me up there, it was several hours."

"Then—" Bencolin was beginning, when he paused to look at the doorway. A man had pushed aside the portières.

It was the same tall, lanky man in the dressing-gown whom we had seen in the lobby awhile ago. The ears stuck out from the sides of his narrow bald head. His blue owl-eyes blinked at us slowly, and he seemed to be holding himself upright by hanging to the curtains.

"Sorry," he said in a voice of immense dignity. "Er—you gentlemen discovered *him*"—jerking his thumb over his shoulder—"didn't you?"

At Bencolin's nod he emitted a sigh of relief. He advanced into the room at a majestic and wabbly pace.

"The name is Graffin," he announced. "Lieutenant Graffin. By courtesy. I was kicked out of the service, you know," he explained, vaguely. "I'm Mr. El Moulk's secretary. Private, confidential."

He was shifting his angular shoulders under the dressing-gown, which was a very violent shade of purple, as though to adjust it. Then he sat down in a chair like a collapsing clothes-horse. He rubbed his long nose, blinked at us, and presently went on:

"All the excitement. Hang it. Hope nothing's happened to El Moulk. Hang it. I'm going to discover he wasn't a bad sort, if I know he's been done in. Ha-ha!—ha-ha-*hah!* I was his only friend, you know."

He looked at us deprecatingly, and seemed to meditate bursting into tears. A peculiar aroma began to encircle the walls. The man was quietly, dignifiedly, and villainously drunk.

"Ah!" said Bencolin. "I'm glad you came in, Lieutenant—"

"Thanks!" cried Graffin, eagerly. "Lieutenant; that's it! R. F. C."

Some hidden devil gave Dallings a poke in the ribs. Dallings was impassive now, and his accent had grown incoherent again. He raised an eyebrow. He was sleek dark laziness.

"Really?" he said, and looked at Graffin with distaste. "So was I. What—"

"Before your time, young man," Graffin interrupted, hastily. "Much. But I was. Show you records, hang it!"

"That word 'hang,'" Bencolin said, smoothly, "leads us to our subject. Sir John Landervorne here is a former official of Scotland Yard. We are conducting a sort of unofficial investigation into the death of the chauffeur, and, if you are willing, you can probably give us a great deal of assistance."

Graffin nodded profoundly, one finger at his lip. "I sh'l be most happy, sir. The inspector out in the hall is questioning all servants; *I* will not be questioned that way. He tried. Ha-ha-*haw!* Eh?... Yes, *pre*cisely; you and I, sir, are in perfect accord. I see that you agree with me." After a pause he added, "Royal Flying Corps."

"How long have you been Mr. El Moulk's secretary?"

Graffin hesitated. A crafty look pinched down one eyelid.

"Roughly," he replied, "I should say six years. I met him in Cairo. He had many establishments. We lived for a time in America. Ugh!"

"How long has he lived in London?"

"A matter of nine months now, I should say. *We* came in March."

"You are the only other person in his—household?"

"In his *immediate* household, I am happy to say. We employ Joyet, who is French. And poor Smail, who's dead; he was an American."

"You are fairly well acquainted with Mr. El Moulk's affairs, then?"

Graffin giggled as though he thought of some excellent joke.

"Then," said the detective, "do you know of any—enemies he might have had?"

"Enemies!" The other leered and clucked his tongue. He murmured in an expostulating way: "Enemies—m' dear sir! That's out of books. Nobody has enemies."

Leaning out of his chair, Bencolin said, suddenly: "Do you deny that for some time Mr. El Moulk has been the victim of a systematic persecution by somebody who is determined to take his life?"

"'Bsurd!"

The man was beating the arms of his chair with long fingers, and his voice had grown high. His wide-open eyes glared at Bencolin from a rheumy mist.

"Very well, Mr. Graffin. Where, may I ask, did you spend today?"

"In our rooms upstairs. I was indisposed. I—" He put a hand over his stomach and grimaced.

"You did not leave them at any time?"

"No."

"And you were there about six o'clock this afternoon?"

"Most 'suredly. I was in the big room—reading. There's a big room *we* have for a study."

Bencolin rose to his feet. He went to the centre table, where he detached the tiny figure from the twine noose, and took it back to hold out before Graffin.

"You were there, then," he asked, "when somebody left this on Mr. El Moulk's desk?"

Hiccoughing, Graffin bent owlish eyes on the black figure. In sudden fury he struck Bencolin's hand away.

He shrilled: "You take that away from me! *Take it away!*—" The man was flopping about in the chair like a fish out of water, and he screeched.

"Nevertheless, you were there, you say?"

"Yes," the other answered. He grew quiet. "'Z God is my judge," he announced, holding up his hand solemnly—"'z God is my judge,

I was there. I was sitting with my back to the desk, and all the doors were locked.

"I was sitting with my back to the desk, and not another soul was in the room. Then he came in from his bedroom in his dressing-gown, Nezam did, and all of a sudden he pointed to the desk.

"I turned around. And five minutes before there'd been nothing on the desk. Now—that thing was lying there."

Graffin clasped his hands together fiercely.

"And nobody'd come into the room, I tell you! Nobody'd come into the room!"

V

Mr. Jack Ketch

NOT A SOUND. BUT THE TENSITY AND HORROR OF THAT CRY still beat on our ear-drums, quivering. Graffin's pale eyes still searched our faces, fighting for belief. Then he sat back as calmly as he could.

"That, sir," he responded, "is the answer. You may believe me or not, as you choose."

Was the man lying? It was such an outlandish story that it might be true, and yet the smell of trickery was strong about Graffin's manner. His emotional outburst had been so sudden, so Drury-Laneish; and he sank back so easily into his drunken dignity, crossing his legs! There was cunning in that pinched-up right eye in the reddish face, which was mottled now in ugly patches.

I looked round. Sir John stood by the table, stroking his long lean jaw. Dallings was watching Graffin steadily, a forgotten cigarette in his hand. Only Bencolin was not in the least disturbed. He said:

"And nobody else was in the room?"

"Nobody. I sh'd have seen anybody else who entered."

"Well, well, we needn't take that up until we go over the ground... The figure seems to have appeared, anyhow. Tell me this, Lieutenant, did Mr. El Moulk go often to night clubs?"

The question was clearly the last one which Graffin expected. He merely gaped in astonishment.

"M-my dear sir!" he stammered. "*What* a notion! Night clubs, you mean? He loathed them. Queer fish, El Moulk! We went once, and they sang something like... Tra-la-*la*," chortled Graffin in his cracked voice, wagging his head with the utmost solemnity. "Tra-la-la-boom! 'When my sugar walks down the street, all the little birdies go tweet-tweet-tweet.'"

He grinned, hiccoughing on a high note. "Nezam walked out. He said: 'Pity William Wordsworth isn't alive today. He could make a fortune writing words for popular songs.' Night clubs! Really!"

"I see," murmured Bencolin. "Whatever El Moulk's other qualities may be, I have seldom heard sounder literary criticism. Did he go out often?"

"Very rarely. Ve-ry rarely. He was occupied with—studies."

"What sort of studies?"

Graffin tapped his forehead. He fell into a sort of obscure musing, talking to himself in a way that made me think he might be falling into a stupor; but for a minute he looked frightened. Once he spoke out strongly,

"Or the demons down under the sea…"

A pause. The mumbling went on: "Devilishness, I tell you! That's what he studies. You'll see, when you look at his rooms. Devilishness, and believes in it."

It was our first glimpse of the queer twisted soul of the man called Graffin. "Devilishness! Rot! All rot!"

"And where was he going when he went out tonight?" Bencolin interrupted.

The other resumed his lordly manner with a jerk.

"That, sir, I can tell you. He had a dinner engagement with a woman."

"So? Was it with Mademoiselle Laverne?"

"You know her name? That is correct, quite."

Bencolin nodded. "Something you have told us, Lieutenant, interested me greatly," he observed. "I believe you said you were his only friend. What did you mean by that?"

The lanky man had been cocking an eye at the pattern in the carpet, as though he were studying its geometric design. He roused himself.

"Did I say that? Hang it! Didn't mean to."

"Well?"

"Well, hang it, yes!" Bitterness flared behind the pale yes. "'His only friend.'... O God, that's funny!—I won't be questioned here any longer! You can't stop me. I'm going! Going... Tell you, then. He was an outcast—like me. A poor damn outcast—like me. But I'll tell you this—"

Snuffling with alcoholic tears, he stabbed a finger at Bencolin.

"—at least I had as many friends as *he* did. And if they've done the dirty rotter in, I'll weep at his grave. I'll weep at his grave. 'M leaving here! You can't stop me!"

He got up, stumbling and fearful like a child, and backed away. When he saw that we did not intend to pursue him, he bolted out of the room.

"What do you think of it?" Bencolin asked.

Dallings said he was a vulgarian.

"The man wants watching, at any rate," observed Sir John. "Personal opinion aside, I don't trust him. There's innate meanness... Well, Talbot?"

The little inspector entered gloomily, a pencil stuck behind his ear.

"Not much that's suggestive," he told us. "The doctor thinks he's been dead about four hours, possibly longer. I've collected some facts here..."

Consulting his notebook, he recited them to us. As we already knew, El Moulk had arrived in March of that year and taken the large suite of rooms on the fourth floor. Since the Brimstone cared nothing for conventions and was run in a highly eccentric way, El Moulk had little difficulty in arranging a somewhat unusual *ménage*.

His rent was princely, but his demands no less so. His attendants consisted of Graffin, a French manservant on leave now, and the chauffeur, Richard Smail, who was an American. Graffin and Joyet slept in the apartment. Nobody knew where the chauffeur lived, but the car was kept in a garage near by. At El Moulk's stipulation, none of the club servants were ever allowed inside the rooms. Sometimes he dined out, sometimes in the grill, but as a rule his meals were brought to him upstairs under the supervision of Joyet. "A particular sort of Frenchman," Talbot reported them as having said, and you gathered that Joyet had not infrequently clashed with the *chef*.

Talbot quoted the porter to the effect that El Moulk was a "quiet gentleman." Even these discreet words suggested a sneer. What about his correspondence? Were there letters? Never. Invitations? Infrequently. But parcels of some description were always arriving for him. They were all of a similar description, wrapt in brown paper and sealed with blue wax. All of them, the porter thought, bore the letter "K" stamped on the wax, and all had a London postmark. As for visitors—never one, in all the nine months.

Talbot shut up his notebook.

"I've rung up the garage," he added. "The chauffeur took out the car about ten minutes of seven. And then there's the florist's where Mr. El Moulk bought that box of flowers we found in the back. The shop is closed now, but in the morning…"

At this moment Victor slipped unobtrusively into the lounge and murmured, "Mr. Marle is wanted on the telephone."

The telephone! I looked at my watch as I left the lounge. It was half-past one. But that somebody should be ringing up at this hour did not even strike me as odd, after all the grotesqueries of the night. The telephone was just across from the door of the lounge; I took it up, stuffed with cloudy fancies…

A voice said, "Jeff!"—and a sudden shock squeezed the inside of my chest. It had been months since I had heard that voice. The whole past rose up.

I cried, "Sharon!"

Sharon Grey. Her voice, no doubt about it. Her voice, with just that quick, low slur in it. I knew then why the stirring memories had been black all day. Behind them moved this girl (damn her!) as she had moved in that evil and delicious April of the Saligny murder case.

"Is this you?" asked the voice, a little breathlessly.

"Yes. Is this you?"

"Yes. I—How are you?" I shouted, trying to talk straight.

"Fine! Er—"

There was a floundering pause, after which we both began speaking at once and had to get the sentences disentangled. I learned presently that her father (who had always figured in my mind as a kind of ogre, with a club) had gone away again on another of his eternal trips, and Sharon had come down to London from Nottinghamshire on her way to the south of France. The town house, which the Greys rarely used, had not been opened that season; but, rather than stay with friends and have her father discover she was on the loose again—until he got safely into the wilds, anyhow—she had preferred to spend a day or so in a closed house.

Listening, I scarcely understood. I was picturing her as she would be now, with her lips close against the mouthpiece of the telephone, gesturing with a cigarette while she spoke. Sharon of the amber-coloured eyes, which wandered from perplexity into dreaminess, and then looked alive and questioning with devilment. Sharon of the long black eyelashes, the eager flushed face, and the dark-gold hair. Sharon the soft and clinging, who could drink like a sailor and swear like a newspaper man. I remembered her dreaming, her jealousy, her rages and tenderness, as I had known her in the old days at Paris...

"But, Jeff," she was saying, "can you come over here now—immediately? All sorts of things are happening—!"

… and when the Saligny case was over there had been an unforgettable, hectic week in a little village along the Seine before her father, who was wild, tracked us down and broke it up. She had been literally dragged away by that old son of a what not. I had received letters which indicated real captivity. Still, there had been that week! Fortunately, Bencolin had steered her father off our track as long as possible, because Bencolin liked to see young people have a good time.

"—and I'm afraid! I heard your friend Bencolin was here in London, too, and I told Colette… Well, can you come over?"

"I certainly can! As soon as I get my hat. What's wrong?"

"Can't tell you over the phone. Do you know the address?"

She mentioned one in Mount Street. The rest of our conversation was somewhat maudlin, and, besides, I think Sharon had had a few drinks.

It was not until I had left the telephone that an uneasy premonition came to me. The premonition concerned that one word "Colette." Bencolin had used the name as that of Dallings's mysterious lady and of the woman who was entangled also with El Moulk. His mistress, one assumed. The name was a common one; it was absurd to think that the two were related or that we were all being sucked into the same whirlpool…

I tried to shake off the ridiculous notion, but it was impossible. So when I saw Bencolin come out of the door to the lounge, I told him rapidly about the call. He meditated, frowning blankly. From beyond the door I could hear Talbot's dry voice upraised.

"Her name, as I told you," said Bencolin, "is Colette Laverne. But she may not be using it now."

"Who is she?"

"Wait." He picked up the telephone directory. "It's an off chance, but then El Moulk has never been stingy with his mistresses…" The pages flicked under his fingers. "Damnation! Here it is! 'One twenty-two Mount Street, Mayfair one seven seven eight!'"

"Sharon," I pointed out, "lives right next door."

"Hurry along, then. Now listen: this may mean nothing, and again it may be very important. El Moulk started for her house tonight, we know. Whether he ever got there remains to be seen. Keep this to yourself. Talbot needn't know—yet."

"You've taken over this investigation with a vengeance, haven't you?"

"I have made a bet. I mean to win it. So go along. Tell nothing unless it is absolutely necessary; I hope I can trust you not to muddle it."

El Moulk, Dallings, the woman of the night club, Sharon: little blind gods had them and were disposing them mirthfully. Not a spinning, not a design, not an intricate doll-dance, but a cataract—blind like themselves, and roaring. The rush of waters had caught us all. I went into the lounge to get my hat and coat, and paused.

Talbot had just stopped speaking. It was such an uneasy hush that I hesitated, with my hat in my hand. He was clicking his teeth together again; he seemed like a man who has been talking at length, talking as long as possible, to avoid the matter uppermost in his mind. Standing by the table of the gallows, a stocky and dandyish figure, he cleared his throat…

There was something in the air, no doubt about it. The bright amber lamps, the weird carvings of that tall room, Talbot with dark cropped head thrust forward. Sir John said:

"What's the matter with you, Talbot?"

The inspector's opaque eyes turned towards him. Practical man! Steady-going fellow!

"I told you a while ago, sir," he began, "that Mr. El Moulk has had no visitors in all the time he has been here…"

"Yes?"

"There was one, this afternoon."

Talbot shifted from one foot to the other. He went on: "There *was* one, this afternoon. I don't know what to make of it, I'm sure. About two o'clock a man called here and inquired at the telephone switchboard for Mr. El Moulk. As a rule it's pretty dark in the lobby out there. There was a light on at the switchboard, but no lights on anywhere else, so the operator couldn't see this man's face. He was standing beyond the switchboard, in shadow.

"But he did see the man's hands. They were long, white hands, and he put them over the top of the switchboard. 'Is Mr. El Moulk in?' he asked. The operator said Mr. El Moulk had gone out… The man hesitated a second. Then he said: 'Well, here is my card. Will you tell him, please, that I will call for him soon?'"

Talbot paused, wrinkling up his eyes.

"He handed over the card. The operator didn't look at it then, but put it by to give Mr. El Moulk. He went off duty soon afterwards, and the card was never delivered. Here it is, sir."

From his notebook the inspector took a bit of pasteboard. He laid it on the table, and studied our faces as we approached to bend over it. After a quick glance Sir John turned away; his expression was too unnatural in its rigidity. I heard Bencolin's dry chuckle…

But a sickish feeling crawled in the pit of my stomach. The words came back softly, 'Will you tell him, please, that I will call for him soon?' Neatly engraved across the card was the name:

MR. JACK KETCH

VI

One Who Hanged Himself

OUTSIDE, THE FOG HAD THINNED, AND A BRIGHT NIMBUS danced round the street lamps. Pall Mall was swept clean in bitter cold. Far away, a car screamed in Piccadilly. At the corner I picked up a cruising taxi, and sank back into its cavernous depths as we mounted St. James's Street.

Jack Ketch, hangman, had presented his card; it seemed to me the most poisonously brilliant piece of madness we had yet encountered. His sly step was very close, beside us in the dark, beside—Sharon, too? Over the night-mutter of London rose the drowsy singing slosh of the tyres, and in the dark cab there were memories. They turned round in my breast, hurting damnably, but they hurt with exultation. The cab fled down the pale lights of Piccadilly, and cold lent an edge to the cry of its horn; then up Berkeley Street into quiet Mayfair.

At Barly-sur-Seine, that April, there had been whitewashed houses, and white roads, and wheelbarrows creaking along them. A dignified procession of geese went past inquiringly, like college professors. I could hear their quacks now. The streets smelt of straw and dung; they drowsed, like the lush trees in sunshine, and dimly the river sang.

At Barly-sur-Seine, I remembered, there had been a little inn where the river breeze ruffled red-and-white curtains. Sharon haunted it—Sharon's eyes and Sharon's arms, when the wick of the oil-lamp still smoked in darkness. The ache of that time, the whispers, the fights, the bickerings, the too-frequent drinks, had all blended to romance with the goblin moon of spring.

It came to me now with surprise, as it always does, that Sharon was a necessity. The cab turned to the left across Berkeley Square…

After some fumbling in the dark and cold, I found the address in that ordered street. The gears of the taxi ground away. Presently the great door was opened on a gloomy hallway where, far back, burned a muffled lamp. And it was Sharon who opened the door. She seemed even smaller than before. The low light was on her white shoulders and on the dark-gold hair; I could even see the little white line where it was parted in the middle; but her face was in shadow. When she moved it into the light, with a small tip-tilted smile and a sudden searching look, then the past rose up to choke me.

I heard myself uttering some casual and supercilious remark (as was our custom) in that immense wrenching, but anger boiled uppermost because I noticed that there was somebody else in the hallway. A man. Damn!—blurb! Our first meeting would be like this! A man. Ah, well, yes. Probably sleeping-partners were her habit. She gave me her hand. In the single clock-tick while I held it, something clicked into place in my heart and would not be moved again.

She said: "Jeff, this is Dr. Pilgrim. Dr. Pilgrim, Mr. Marle."

I drew a deep breath, and he swam distinctly across my vision. He was a tall man; lean, but giving the impression of huge bulk. And instinctively I liked the man. He had a square, shrewd, good-humoured face, with strength about the heavy jaw. It was pocked to fearful ugliness by some former disease, but lighted by a pair of cat-green eyes, whimsical and tolerant, under thick brows. His age must have been fifty, but there was no grey in his heavy black hair; and when he smiled, as he did now, he looked twenty years younger. His heavy shoulders blocked up against the light…

"Glad to meet you, Doctor," I said. Pilgrim! Pilgrim! That name!—"You're not," I inquired, "the Dr. Pilgrim who lives at the Brimstone Club?"

He looked at me in surprise.

"Why, yes, Mr. Marle," he replied, "the very same. By Jove! I've read about this sort of thing in books, but I never thought detectives really practised it! Is one permitted to ask—?"

He smiled again, inquiringly, and I groaned, for I had caught Sharon's eye past his shoulder. She was gesturing frantically, with her finger on her lip. This young lady had a quaint habit of endowing me with abilities which not even my fondest friends would have suspected. Now I had apparently been cast in the rôle of Detective; and, if I knew her genius for bragging, I was probably the Foremost Criminal Investigator of Europe.

"Ahem!" I said.

"—mud on my shoelace, or a cuff-link missing, or something?" asked Pilgrim.

I waved a deprecating hand. "It's quite simple, really. I happen to be staying there myself, and I heard your name mentioned."

"Oh!" He wrinkled his forehead quizzically. "Well, I'm glad you didn't deduce it. Must be a bit uncomfortable having those people about…"

He turned to Sharon. He was wearing an overcoat, and lifted his hat tentatively. "I think I've done all I can, Miss Grey," he told her. "She was badly frightened, but all she needed, really, was a good peg of brandy. I'll look in tomorrow, just in case. She will be able to go home tonight, of course… And now I'll say good night."

"I'm grateful to you no end, Doctor," said Sharon. "I don't know what I should have done without—"

Mustering my histrionic powers, I tried to make a face like a detective. Sharon later told me that I looked like a cherub with the toothache. I put in judicially:

"May I ask just what has happened?"

Pilgrim turned grave.

"It's a Miss Laverne, who lives next door," he answered. The cat-green eyes were reflective. "I can't tell you much about it. I was coming along Mount Street here about half an hour ago. I had been playing bridge with some friends in Grosvenor Square, and we broke up rather late. Just as I passed the house next to this one the door was thrown open and a woman came running out, screaming. Then she fell. I thought at first that she had run into the lamp-post and been knocked unconscious, but I found she had merely fainted. Miss Grey had been with her; she can probably tell you what happened. We brought her in here, at Miss Grey's suggestion, and she has recovered now. That's all, I think."

He put on his hat. A little smile twitched the corner of his lip and he studied us through half-shut eyes.

"Good night, Miss Grey. Good night, Mr. Marle. I hope you'll let me know if there are any—deductions. I'm at the Brimstone, you know."

The door closed. I looked at Sharon and said, "Grr-r-rrrr!" And then I said: "Get this female out of the house quickly. I want to talk to you."

Then we made a number of cutting remarks, inspired by the devil, and stood aloof. A hundred times I had pictured this meeting, in glowing hues, and yet I knew somehow that this would be the reality—flat and tangled and spoiled. We had so strenuously avoided sentiment that we both felt helpless. This made us angry. The light was in the searching, baffled brightness of her eyes; the lovely and mutinous lips were pressed together. It was a mess.

"Let's go and see the patient," I suggested.

"*All* right. Upstairs."

We moved through the great hallway, which smelt of portraits and ancestral virtue, and musty from lack of airing. There was ghostly shrouded furniture, white against oak panelling. I think we both felt very small. We started up a broad staircase—an immense, solid, carpeted staircase—the sort of staircase which seems exactly suited for bringing coffins down. Except for the curve, you could have slid a coffin down its handrail without danger. Below us the muffled lamp burned in a gulf, and a draught blew in our faces. Sharon paused when we were almost at the top. I remember the whitish gleam of her face, the deep lights in her black-fringed eyes, as she turned. Her head stood out against a tall dark portrait of some sinister-looking gentleman in a ruff. She looked like a child afraid of the dark, terrified beneath that towering portrait.

"I wanted to tell you," she said, "how this happened…"

It was a small, cool voice, unconvincing.

"I've been thinking," she went on, wrinkling her brows. "In all the times we've been together, do you know why we've fought and bickered, and been so suspicious and beastly? Do you?" she flung at me.

"Yes," I said, quietly.

"But you don't. That's just it; you don't know. You think I mean being in love, but I don't.—Did I ever doubt *that*? Did you? And if you say you did, you're a bloody liar."

Her fierce gaze left me and wandered up blankly into the high shadows above. Queer, baffled, tense, both of us. She beat her hands against the wall.

"Something we've left out of our crazy world, and so has everybody else. Funny people you meet—Nice, Cannes, Deauville, everywhere. Dry, hard, shiny people that cackle—hateful—*they've* left it out. Our whole generation has. It's just a little thing. I don't know whether it's true or false. I do know it's necessary. You'll see what I mean when you talk to Colette," she added. "Let's go upstairs."

"How did you come to pick up with her?"

"Oh, I've known her. I phoned you tonight at the club, and they said you'd gone to the theatre. Colette saw my light and asked me to come over; she was upset—you'll see—and then... O God! it's awful! Mess after mess! Nothing but rotten trouble all the time!" she burst out, clenching her hands. "Why am I always the one who gets mixed up in these things?"

"You're not here entirely alone?"

"Yes. And burgled a window to get in, at that. If my old man knew..."

It was only a flash, this brooding against the dark portrait, as in the high and draughty places of hell. Sharon the gallant, Sharon the debonair, had come back inscrutably when she opened the door of her little sitting-room overlooking Mount Street.

"You are a long time, my little girl," a voice said, querulously.

In a winged chair before the fire, which gave the only light in the room, sat Colette Laverne. Her voice was flat, tinged with a French accent, and clicked the syllables as though each word were a separate sentence. She turned her head only slightly at our entrance.

The wood in the fireplace hissed and smoked in pale bluish flame, throwing a weird light on the brass andirons and on the woman's face. She sat very straight between the tall wings of the chair, and drew about her a blue quilted robe which must have belonged to Sharon, for it was much too small.

Her features were cold, flawless, and petulant. Hers was a smooth white hardness of skin, on which the lip-salved mouth stood out like a bruise. The eyes were dark brown, with whites that seemed luminous—chill and level eyes, supremely logical, under straight brows. Her dark red hair was coiled in a knot at the nape of her neck. I think she was the most beautiful woman I have ever seen, and also one of the least attractive. She was tall, and of a figure which mirrors the lecherous mind of man, now only too obvious under the blue quilted robe; but this very voluptuousness was hard and metallic, as unyielding as her face. Again it suggested logic. The very shadows beneath her nostrils were business-like, so business-like that they shadowed her whole face.

"So you are the detective," she said, and her voice chinked the syllables. "My God! but you are young!" She laughed suddenly and loudly, showing all her fine white teeth. "Do not take offence. Sit down beside me, and then we will talk."

She patted the sofa near her. She seemed merry, but her eyes were level and appraising, and bad temper lurked at the too-firm jaw. When she put out her exquisite arm, it jingled with many silver bracelets set with turquoises. I knew her sort; one sees immediately the Riviera, where they are to be found. They love the tables, and sit there for hours, blindly absorbed; but they are small, crafty gamblers. Their wild affection is for Pekinese dogs (those things one always wants to kick), which they dandle in the air fondly, and their loud laughter rings under the palms of white promenades. They wear gowns by Patou, and dubious pearls. They are dazzling, ignorant, intelligent, superstitious, and cold as cobras.

Colette Laverne addressed Sharon abstractedly. "Dear," she said, "go like one good girl and bring me more of the good brandy. And the Abdulla cigarettes. I will talk with the nice young man."

Sharon stiffened, and her face looked as though she were saying, "Oh, really?" But the other woman seemed to have forgotten her. Dislike of Colette Laverne was hardening in me. I was not going to enlighten her. She thought me the detective; *ergo*, I would be the detective, and with all those cards up my sleeve from tonight I would play the hand for all it was worth.

And the woman was frightened. She laughed, she was business-like, but she had been given a terrific fright by something. Staring into the fire, she said:

"You are not of the official police?"

"No."

"Then I can tell you. I am in trouble. Bad trouble, but I would not tell you if you were police. Sharon says I can trust you." Slowly she turned round the level brown eyes. Her lips seemed to be uttering inaudible curses. Her eyes smouldered deeply; all of a sudden she beat the chair arms with her flat palms, and her curses beat forth now with metallic bitterness. They were against Nezam El Moulk. Her bracelets jingled in time.

"—but you would not know," she broke off. "I mus' tell you.

"I live next door. The man who keeps me is an Egyptian, very wealthy. You understand? What happened happened ten years ago. I am dumb, but I know it was this.

"Nezam—his name is Nezam—lived in Paris then. It was November, this month, just after the war was finished. We had one gay crowd. I did not live wit' him yet, but he spent much money. Always he spends much money," she said, reflectively. "Well! Besides Nezam, there were two others who liked me, you understand? One was French. His name was De Lavateur. He was vehry nice, but"— she shrugged her shoulders—"he had not much money, and he was cripple from the war. The other, he was English.

"He was one big, tall young man, and he laughed a lot. He was *aviateur* in the war, and they shot down his *avion*, and they thought he was dead, but he was in the hospital in Paris. He used the name of 'Keane.' I don' know why, because he told me that was not his real name; he said it was the name he had written a book under, once.

"But he said he was goin' to use the name 'Keane' because if his family knew he was alive they'd want him home, and he didn' want to go home just yet."

She laughed, showing all her teeth again.

"Ha! He used to say to me, 'Bettee' (he called me Bettee), 'are you my little girl?' And I say, 'Yes, I am your little girl, but please take your hands off my hair.'" She lifted her shoulders again in a broad, angry gesture, lower lip thrust forward. "Nezam, he was one damn-God fool. He thought De Lavateur and Keane were favourites of mine, instead of him. Ha! I was not such a damn-God fool, you bet! But Nezam, that is what he thought. He was so stupeed!—*Eh bien*, Nezam had bought one big house near the Bois…"

She grew reflective.

"Sixty-four rhooms it had. And he gave pahr-ties. Such pahr-ties! What they cost him!—one hundred thousand francs for the orchestre alone, once! And he would hire a ballet to dance. Then everybody get dhrunk.

"One night (it was the night of the seventeent' of November, tomorrow), he gave an Egyptian dance, or somet'ing like it, with everybody in costume. Magnificent! Three hundred thou— No matter. Nezam looked—funnier—more strange—that night than I ever saw him. He was wild-looking, and he wore on his fore'ead something like one snake."

She paused as Sharon came into the firelight with a carafe of brandy and a silver cigarette-box, which she put down on a little table beside the woman's chair. Then Sharon sat down beside me on the sofa.

I stared into the yellow-blue flames that hissed round the logs, and monstrous shapes began to take form on the borderland of my brain. "Something like a snake"—the royal diadem, the emblem of Pharaoh! It would go well on the brow of Nezam El Moulk. With a feeling as though somebody had yanked my spine sideways, I remembered those words Bencolin had spoken in the afternoon. "The Paris police found in the woods at dawn a man in the sandals and gold robes of an Egyptian nobleman. He had been shot through the head…"

Colette Laverne raised her hand to light a cigarette, so that the glimmering bracelets slid tinkling down her arm. A little curl of smoke drifted out of her lips, up past motionless glazed eyes.

Stretching herself sinuously, she sat back between the wings of the chair, and her extended fingers crisped round the arms of it. Cold, dead, watchful was her face. The dark brown eyes were narrowed. Over white teeth her bruised lip lifted slowly, and a tiny wisp of paper from the cigarette adhered to it.

"Nezam reads things I do not understand," she told me suddenly. "Me, I am dumb. There are things...

"That night it was one brawl. I will not tell you what happened. I looked for De Lavateur and Keane, but I could not find them. Towards the morning, one of my friends came in. He shake all over, for he was not so dhrunk as the rest, and he could not make nobody understand because they were so dhrunk, all lying round in t'e flowers. He stand and yell, 'Somebody has shot De Lavateur. They are looking for Keane.'"

A pause, while the fire crackled.

"They find De Lavateur in the Bois, dead. They have trace' Keane to his rhooms in the Avenue Marceau, and he is lying dead dhrunk on his bed, with a revolver in his hand. And Nezam, he is smiling."

Another pause. She whisked up her hand and took a deep draw at the cigarette.

"When Keane is sober, he start to cry. He says that he has fought one duel with De Lavateur. The police ask, Where is the other pistol? Because they have not find any pistol except the one Keane have. Keane says that *Nezam* have supplied the pistols, and that Nezam said he would go with them when they fight the duel, and that he gave the word to fire. Keane said Nezam would tell them this was true.

"Nezam just smile and smile, and shrug his shoulders. He says it is all one lie..."

She crossed her long silk-clad legs. She reached out, poured herself a glass of brandy, and sank back inscrutably into the chair.

VII

A Hand Knocks by Night

S HE WAVED HER GLASS WITH GAY FEROCITY, HOLDING ONE shoulder high.

"This amuse' you, does it not, darling?" she asked Sharon. Some of the brandy spilled out on the blue robe, and she became poutingly contrite. "Oh! I am so sorry, darling! It is one nice... *Alors, revenons à nos moutons!*"

Sharon gave me a smile over her shoulder.

"Ah," said Colette, "it is so pretty!—The little English girl and the ghreat detective! But we have business."

Subtle, shifty, her jaw grew more square.

"I was tellin' you," she continued, puffing at the cigarette. "Keane, you understand, Keane was so dhrunk he didn' remember much of anything... He says he remember arranging to fight one duel with De Lavateur, he remembers shooting at him, but he don' think he hit him at all.

"He says all he remembers was Nezam patting him on t'e back and telling him he have shot De Lavateur, and to go home, because it is one bad business. That's all.

"Nezam deny all this. He say he have overhear Keane threaten De Lavateur, and he say prob'ly Keane just take De Lavateur out in the Bois and shoot him. He says he can prove *he* never left the house all evening. So he prove it by me, because nobody else was sober enough to know; and I am to testify he never left t'e house..."

"And did he?"

She regarded me speculatively. At length a little smile twisted round her lips, and she shrugged her heavy shoulders.

"Me? How should I know? I don' pay attention to all he does. And I get one nice Hispaño-Suiza car from him, so what do you want?"

She spoke with such surprise that I nodded.

"I see. Go on, please."

"Yes. I am glad you are one nice man and see that... Well, Keane went on trial for murder, and Nezam talked in the court, and so did I. Keane said he didn' give damn about t'e penalty; he jus' wanted to prove it was duel, and he was not coward enough to shoot a man unarmed. *Ça, c'est rigolo, hein? Ces anglais, ils sont très, très droles!*" She laughed, taking a drink, hesitated, and laughed again at the drollery of such conduct. Suddenly she became grave.

"Keane he was sentenced to prison for life. But he didn' go. He hanged himself in his cell."

She sat back in her chair. Somewhere down in the vast house a clock chimed half-past two.

"I was nervous till it was finished," she admitted, reflectively. "There was one man I know, jus' one, I was afraid of. You wouldn' know him. His name it is Bencolin. *Ce chameau, ce sale fils de putain!*" she swore, clenching her hands. "He laugh and laugh all the time. He don' believe nothing at all. But he was in t'e war, and he wasn't back at Paris for the trial, so he couldn' do nothing after it was all over. And then one day he knock at my door, and he come in, all vehry elegant, wit' gloves and the high hat, and he smile, and say, 'Good afternoon, mademoiselle.' And I say, 'What you mean? I don' know you!' And he say, 'Ah no, mademoiselle,' and smile again. 'But sometime you may. I jus' wanted to tell you, mademoiselle, sometime you may.'

"And then he walk out. I am scared of the police. They are not stupid. Every time I think of the police, I think of him—and I wouldn' dare go to the police. But you—you are different, my frien'."

The blind gods weaving! Death, chance, and Sharon's braggadocio, all conspiring to produce this tale from a woman who would not have told it to the police! By the merest accident I had been prevented from telling her the truth. And it meant—what?

"You are wondering," she resumed, "why I tell you all this. All right. I told you I never knew what 'Keane's' real name was. All right. *Somebody does know it. Somebody think Nezam and I we send Keane to death, and somebody want to kill both of us.*"

She regarded me with terrible intentness, bending forward.

"And this person is—?" I asked.

"I don' know! That's what I want you to find out! It is horribl'! The way he sneak around, I can' stand it."

I must be careful now not to betray what I knew; the sinister design was almost complete, and I could hardly stifle a triumphant exclamation.

"And you think somebody who knew Keane, some friend of his, is planning an elaborate vengeance?"

"Yes."

"But all this occurred ten years ago. You mean somebody has been persecuting you"—watch out, now!—"for all that time?"

"No, no, no! it is not for the ten years. Only since we are in London. Only since a few months. And it is Nezam he have persecute' mostly. I was not in it until a few weeks ago that he got after me. That's what I'm goin' to tell you. I don' care about Nezam. It's *me*, you understand? I don' care if they kill Nezam; there is one nice will that take care of me. But if this man want to kill me, too..." She flung out her arms.

"I see," I said, dryly. "And what reasons have you for thinking you are being—persecuted, or that these attentions are the result of Keane's death?"

"Oh, Nezam, he know. He don' tell me much, and he is so queer.

He rave. He say his death is on him, and he *know*." She stressed the word, striking the chair arm with a large hand. Superstition was in her eyes. "He say no use to call police, and he use some funny words I don' understand. But he is a man very, very instructed, and he know. But I don' tell you what happened to him; I'm goin' to tell you what happened to *me*."

She paused to visualize the thing in her mind, drained her glass, and put it down.

"For a long time Nezam have told me about somebody scaring him, all the time, with things he got sent to him, you see? But I jus' laugh. And then, O my God! *I* get a letter! I haven' got it here; it's over in my house; but I know what it said. All the time I am reading it! I tell you jus' what it say, every word."

Holding up her finger, she spoke slowly. "It say, 'My dear Miss Laverne,' it say, 'I have recently learn' you were instrumental in t'e death of a young man named J. G. Keane in Paris. I am not sure you deserve t'e full punishment for this, but one had better be sure. The seventeent' of November will be the tenth anniversary of his death, and I think this will be one memorable occasion for both you and Mr. Nezam El Moulk. Sincerely yours'—"

She paused, swallowing hard.

"Well?" I said.

"'Jack Ketch,'" she concluded.

Now the shadow that was to darken our nights with horror had risen up fully, and in fancy I saw the white hands of Jack Ketch drooping over the back of Colette Laverne's chair as they had hung over the telephone desk at the Brimstone Club.

She sat motionless in the pale firelight, *her* hands gripped together.

"I asked Nezam who it was. He say Jack Ketch is only—pen name, name of man who used to hang people in London. Executioner."

"And what did you do?"

"Well, at first—when Nezam was so nervous—he wanted me help him find out who was doing this. But me, *je m'en fiche!* What did I care? Then, naturally, when *I* got the letter, I was scared. I was willing to help, then, naturally."

She lit another cigarette from the stub of her first.

"And Nezam said he had one clue…"

"What sort of clue?"

"I don' know, except it was like this: Keane never said much about himself, you see? But once Nezam had heard him use somebody's name—somebody Keane must have know—and Nezam, he never forget. He spoke 'bout a man, a friend of his, whose name was Dallings."

"Oh!"

"And Nezam thought we might find out from Dallings who 'Keane' really was, you see? Because if Keane spoke about Dallings, Dallings must know him, eh? And if we find out who Keane was, then maybe we know who is behind all this…

"But that Dallings he is such a funny boy!" She laughed suddenly again, and her eyes were bright with reminiscence. "Ha! The English, they are one funny people. I think Mr. Dallings is a goof, hah? No, no. I will tell you. Nezam waylaid him, and he send him to one night club where I make his acquaintance. The other night he get vehry dhrunk, and he say he is going come home with me. What good is *he* to me? I fool him, and send cab away, and he don' know my name or my address…

"We don' dare go straight to him and ask him if he knew Keane; we got to be careful; we don' dare let him know what we want, because—"

"Because you think he may be Jack Ketch?"

She regarded me with surprise.

"That one?" she said, contemptuously. "Ha, that man! He is like a fish. No, no, no! Besides, you think I thrust myself in the taxi with him if I think he is Jack Ketch? Ha! Do I look like one such a damn-God fool, my frien'? No, no. We thought he might know Keane, that's all."

She moved with impatience.

"But he don' know nothing! I told Nezam he wouldn't. How is he goin' to know Keane's real name, if 'Keane' is one assumed name? How is he goin' to know *who* Keane really is, if we can' tell him any more than just the assumed name? Bah! He's got lots of frien's. *Voilà*."

"You have no picture of Keane? No snapshot, or anything of the sort?"

"No."

"And nobody ever learned who he was, even at the trial?"

"No. He say, 'If I'm goin' die, why bring disgrace on anybody?' And they couldn' find out; he tore up his papers, all of the papers. 'I'm just goin' disappear,' he say."

"Well, what did he look like?"

"Plouf!" She wagged her head. "I don' know. Was tall, with the dark hair and the grey eyes. I don' know. Might be anybody. Might be *you*. But now I'm goin' tell you what happened tonight."

Shivering, Sharon rose from the sofa and went forward to stir up the fire. The sizzling logs turned over in a gust of flame, but it was very cold in the room. I could feel my heart beating heavily.

"Mr. Marle, Jack Ketch has got Nezam!"

This announcement of Colette Laverne did not create the sensation she expected. I merely nodded, and asked, "How do you know?"

"Early this afternoon he phone' me. He have a cold in the head, and he is excited, but he say he is coming around tonight in his car and we go out to dinner. I say all right, because I have give' both my maid and my cook the night off. He say he will be at my house by eight, likely.

"Well, this night I dress myself and get ready. But he don' come. I wait and wait, all dressed, but still he don' come. I am all alone in the house, and all of a sudden I think, My God! suppose something has happen'? I go round and turn on all the lights in the house, and I keep looking out the window, and every time I hear a car in the street I open the door, but he does not come. I phone to the club where he live. They tell me has gone an hour before. Then I think, Have Jack Ketch got him? Is he comin' get me, too? I am frantic!"

Her mouth was working. She looked at Sharon.

"Darling, where is the dress I have take' off to put this on? I left something with it. Quick!"

"On the chair behind you," answered Sharon.

The woman rose. She was even taller than I had thought. Her tense muscles emphasized the sensuous lines of her body, superb breast and hips under the scanty blue robe, and the sheer black-silk stockings rolled above the knees. But there was nothing awkward in that tall figure (how she must have dwarfed El Moulk!) as she moved beyond into shadows. I saw her pick up something from a crumpled gown across a chair, and, as she bent, her red coiled hair glowed lustrously. The eyes darted sideways at us. Then she returned to the chair, holding something in the palm of her hand.

"There was another hour pass', and then I knew something had happen'. I sat by the window. I saw a policeman pass, and I was so scared I tried to get him to come and talk to me, but he wouldn'! He wouldn' at all!" she snarled.

"I didn' want to go out, and I was afraid of the house. Then I saw a light up *here*, and I remembered I had seen Miss Grey come in this afternoon, and said she was alone. I rang t'e bell, and I said, 'For God's sake, darling, come over and stay wit' me in the house for a while; I am afraid.'

"She had been trying to get you on the telephone, but you were out. So we sat upstairs, and we drank, and we talked, and she told me how you had done all t'e great detective work in Paris last spring…"

I glanced sideways at Sharon. Her eyes were turned steadily away, and her face was flushed.

"… so it got more, more late, and Nezam did not come, and she said, 'I must be going'; but I said, 'No, no, no! Please, you mus' not go! You must stay here with me tonight, because I am alone.'

"Then, after while, some one knock at the door."

A chill crawled through me at those words. Her eyes were fixed on me with stricken appeal.

"It go, Knock, knock, knock—just like that, down at the street door. Knock, knock, knock." She raised her hand slowly and imitated a knocking in the air. "I say to myself, *Is it Nezam?* But he always ring. And at first I am afraid to go down. I say to Sharon, 'Darling you mus' go, too.'

"All the lights are on. I go downstairs, and I am so scared I am choked, and still it is going knock, knock, knock.

"I open the door. And there is nobody there. I look out in the fog, and then I see somebody have left a calling-card on the doorstep. I bend over to pick it up, and all of a sudden *somebody tap me on the shoulder*."

She flung out one arm. The lips were wide over her clenched teeth, and she sobbed.

"I have just pick' up the card when a finger tap me on the shoulder from behind. I can stand it no longer. I scream. I start to run, and then I don' remember anything more. When I am recover', here I am on that sofa, and I have the card in my hand."

She held it out now. I knew what it would be. Dim in the firelight, I read those ominous words, MR. JACK KETCH. And on the edge of the card was a smear of blood.

A long silence…

"You were not attacked?" I asked.

"No. I think it was a—a warning. I don' think he's ready…"

"And the person who tapped you on the shoulder?"

"I didn' see—*anybody*."

I turned to Sharon. "You were there when this occurred?"

"I was right behind her," Sharon replied, staring ahead with a pinched face. "And *I* didn't see anybody…"

"What happened then?"

"She fainted out by the street lamp. I saw a man coming along, and both of us stooped over her. I said, 'We ought to have a doctor,' and he said, 'I am a doctor.' We brought her in. She wouldn't go back afterwards."

"Go back to that house?" shrilled the woman. "You think I am crazy?"

"Please, not so loud. When did this occur?"

"I know when it was," said Colette, swallowing hard, "because always I was watch' the clock. It was fifteen minutes after one."

The problem was stated. The pieces were before us, in their subtle and ghoulish pattern. I hesitated before them. "Tell nothing," Bencolin had said. I wondered what questions I dared ask.

"So I couldn' stand it no longer," she said. "I remembered what Miss Grey had said, and I told her to call you…"

(And she had to make good her bluff, eh? Incidentally, so had I.)

"Tell me, then, Mr. Marle, you t'ink I am in danger?"

"Yes."

"And you think he has caught Nezam?"

"Yes." I could speak with conviction on *that* score. Curious how easy it is to sit judicially and look wise when everybody gives one credit for enormous penetration; I stroked my chin and scowled, feeling rather like the President of the United States.

"We must—go into the psychology of this thing," I said, shaking my head.

(That is always a safe statement when you don't know what the hell it's all about.)

"But what am I going to do, I ask you?"

"Do?" I inquired. I slapped my knees decisively, rose, and gathered words for speech in the approved fashion. "A very pretty little problem, Miss Laverne. I shall want to think it over. Let me communicate with you tomorrow. In the meantime I shall just keep this card, if you don't mind... Also, I should like to see that letter you received. You are going back to your house tonight?"

"No! I am going to stay here, with Sharon. We will lock ourselves in one room, with a gun."

She had coolly assumed charge, and there was no dissuading her. There was much more talk, which got us nowhere, because I had to be very cautious in questioning her. Several times I was tempted to come out with the whole truth; but now, at this drugged and hysterical hour of the morning, it could do no good. What a scare one could throw into this self-possessed lady by the casual mention of Bencolin's name! "I don't know," I fancied myself saying; "I must talk it over with my colleague. His name—"

And so I took my leave, studying her from the doorway.

"There is no other person," I asked, finally, "who might have some idea as to the identity of Keane?"

"Oh yes!" was her surprising reply.

"What!"

She had been staring into the low fire abstractedly; but now she roused herself. I read her eyes in that flash. Her eyes said she had made a blunder. She responded in a hard voice: "Yes, there is. But there's no way to make *him* tell."

"Who? What do you mean?"

"I'm not goin' argue with you," she said, flatly. "There is some-body. But we won' learn from him. You don' know why, but I tell you we won'—that's enough."

It was all I could get out of her. She shut her lips hard and took refuge in shrill irrelevant abuse of El Moulk. Yes, she had made an error in saying what she had; but of the nature of that error I had no idea. More puzzles! They raced about after Dallings in the hope he might know Keane's name; yet here, if she were telling the truth, must be somebody who did know it, and they dismissed him with a shrug. Anyhow, nothing came of my efforts to persuade her to talk.

And, to top it all off, Sharon had got herself into a perverse mood. We descended the broad stairway together, shivering. The house was even more dismal in that bleak hour of morning. Things were all snarled, and nobody could ever tell why or when they would get snarled. Why not give it up? Any attempt to get along reasonably with Sharon was hopeless, as I should have discovered. She was a pretty little spoiled child. To add to it, she was illogical. She held open the front door while I put on my hat and coat. The chill struck through my bones; the fog had lifted and a frozen moon shone down on Mount Street. Romance! Drowsiness smarted on my eyelids.

"Good night, Mr. Marle," she said in a frigid voice, "and thank you for getting me into this mess."

A row of exclamation points. "May I remind you," I said, gently, "that it was your own clever tactics which brought *me* into it?"

Silver and corpse-white the whole scene was. She stood look-ing up at the moon, with the smoke of her breath drifting up; but, though she trembled in the chill, the stare of those blind bright eyes did not waver.

"Go inside," I said. "You'll catch cold." Romance! The wind before dawn blew out of London's sleeping spaces, stirring uneas-ily. My footfalls echoed on the pavement. Far away, an electric horn muttered on waking, and I heard the clop-clop of hoofs. The street lamps drowsed in pale light...

It was past four when I reached the Brimstone, for I could not find a cab. There was a dim light in the bay window of the lounge, but everything else was thick with darkness. The revolving door swished with startling loudness. Peering through the black lobby, down the passage at the left, I saw the gleam through the curtains of the lounge door. And I knew who was awake—the man whose curse was that he could not sleep unless he drugged himself.

Bencolin did not hear me when I entered. He sat in a deep chair before the great fireplace, sprawled, with an open book across his knees. A lamp burned at his elbow, but the rest of the tall room was in darkness. A glass dangled from his hand, and he stared fathoms deep into a low fire.

His chin was sunk on his breast and he did not turn; but presently he spoke:

"Long nights, Jeff. Long nights..."

Then he passed a hand vaguely across his eyes, saw that there was a little whisky left in his glass, and emptied it. He smiled at the fire furtively, as at one who shares a secret.

"I've learned a lot on this one," I told him. "Listen! Do you know—"

"Yes, I know," he said. "I know what you've learned; *I* knew it, too, you see. But drop it, please. I don't care to talk about—"

"Don't you want to hear—!" I protested, and paused as I saw the book he had put on the table; then I said, "Why, what the devil, Bencolin! '*The Murders at Whispering House*, by J. J. Ackroyd...'"

He looked at the book gravely, and nodded. I thought he was drunk.

"It's very good, too," he assured me, speaking French. "That detective—I admire him tremendously! I am not yet sure who is guilty, but then I haven't reached the middle of the book..." He broke off, grinning. *"Tiens!* Jeff, you should see yourself! You look very funny!"

"With a real murder before you, you sit and read—"

"Ah! But you miss the point altogether, *mon vieux!* You see before you," he explained, tapping the scarlet jacket of the book, "the only way in which an intelligent man can find diversion in this eminently dull world. I feel myself becoming philosophical..."

"This," I said, "from the most eminent detective in Europe! It is out of character. Truth, I may remind you, is stranger than—"

"Please," he urged, "please, I beg of you, spare me that tedious lie! You are quoting the only paradox which unimaginative people ever succeeded in inventing. And it is not true. It is insidious propaganda, Jeff, on the part of cheerless souls who want to make fiction as dull as truth. It is probably the only ancient maxim which nobody thinks of doubting in this sceptical world, and what we need is some fearless iconoclast who will come out boldly against this damnable tyranny, saying, 'Fiction is stranger than truth.'"

"Have another drink," I said.

"But, Jeff, the harm it has done! We taunt fiction-writers with that obscene jeer—and then we fall into a great state of rage when they write something strange to answer us. We challenge them to a wrestling-match, no holds barred, and then we cry 'Unfair!' the moment they enter the ring. We think it very bad, by some twisted process of logic, that fiction should fulfil its manifest purpose. By the use of the word 'improbable' we try to scare away writers from any dangerous use of their imaginations... And yet, of course, truth will always be inferior in interest to fiction. When we want to pay any tale of fact a particularly high compliment, we say 'It is as thrilling as a novel.'"

"Science," I said, oracularly, "has demonstrated that the wildest flights of fancy are not so queer as the intricacies of the human mind—"

He shook his head sadly. "I grieve, Jeff, to hear you talking like a publisher's blurb... Do you believe in dragons and sea serpents? Well, I find them very fascinating when they are hunted in spacious tales of knights on war horses, but snaring dragons in my own brain cells is apt to bore me. It is too much like slapping at mosquitoes in a dark room. Dr. Freud's night-shirt tournaments lack some of the excitement of those other fabled fights at Camelot..."

"But you," I said, "who have been in some of the worst criminal cases—"

"Like most people," he interrupted, yawning, "I am most unutterably bored. Hence *The Murders at Whispering House*. It is the only sort of fiction to which I can safely turn. War stories, in which I used to delight, are now devoted to demonstrating how much the French loved the Germans, and the Germans loved the French, and by what a narrow margin cruel rich men prevented everybody from dancing round a May pole in No Man's Land. Stories of fleshly lust and love (which I likewise enjoyed immoderately) have now become solemn, ponderous tracts designed to prove that a man and his mistress may do anything they like, provided only that they do not presume to enjoy it. And our 'vital,' 'important,' 'significant' books—ah, God! Their authors all try to write like a bad translation from another language..."

He broke off to look at me gaily.

"Being a chivalrous person, Jeff," he continued, "I do not like to see a lady seduced with words of one syllable. It is not fair to her modesty. One is reminded of that ingenious invention of the young man from Racine in the limerick... But here at Whispering House I am not deceived. My fine nightmare is not bounded by any dull probability, nor yet by the discouraging fact that it really happened. The detective never errs, which is exactly what I want. I could never understand why writers wanted to make their detectives human beings, patient workers, liable to error, but through sheer dogged-ness—*bah*! The reason, of course, is that they have not the wit to create a really clever character, and so they must try to bulldoze us with makeshifts..."

"How long," I asked, "is this sermonizing to continue?"

"... in brief, life lacks all the fascination, the drama, the tidy work-ing out of plot which I find here. In reply to your last question, I may say that you had better go on up to bed. I want to finish my tale."

"But the *real* case—?"

"My dear Jeff, there is nothing very puzzling about the real case. If the butcher or the baker or the candlestick-maker commits a crime, rest assured I will catch him; but please do not ask me to be interested in him. For I find 'people' eminently dull. You shall have the solution to your real case any time you like... Meanwhile, I confess I am most damnably puzzled over the identity of the killer at Whispering House..."

I left him absorbed in the book, bent over it with knitted brows, while the hands of the clock crawled towards five.

VIII

The Blue Seals

B R-R-R-R-RING-BRR-RR-RRRRING! AN INCESSANT DINNING through the mists of sleep.

"Telephone, sir," said the voice of Thomas.

I sat up foggily in bed and reached for it. Murder, but the place was cold! Fog again, or was it rain? A cup of tea steamed on a table beside my bed. "Hello!" I said to the telephone.

"Jeff?" replied Sharon's voice, and I snapped alert. "Jeff, she left this morning."

"Oh?"

"Jeff, you knew all about that last night! I've seen the papers."

"Oh?"

"I'm leaving today."

"You *are* not. I'll make them hold you as accessory or something… Shut that window, you Eskimo," I said to Thomas.

So Sharon and I arranged to have tea that afternoon, and I promised to tell her all about the case. When I had drunk the tea and taken off a little of the chill, Thomas told me that the gentlemen from the police were waiting at breakfast downstairs. I tabulated the events of the night as I dressed. At least we had a partial explanation of Jack Ketch, and of Dallings's adventure with the mysterious lady of the night club. Now for it!—Bencolin and Sir John sat at breakfast in a deserted dining-room, which was dark except for the lamp at their table. Inspector Talbot had come in a few minutes before, and accepted a cup of coffee.

After breakfast, when we had lighted cigarettes and felt more comfortable, I told my story from beginning to end. Talbot made no comment, but his eyes widened, his teeth clicked, and his pencil was very busy with the notebook. At the conclusion Sir John frowned, knocking out his pipe on the edge of his plate.

"Do you think," he said, "it was altogether sporting to—?"

"If you had talked to that woman ten minutes," I declared, "the word 'sporting' would be lost to your vocabulary. You'd have precious little sympathy for her."

"Jeff is a great believer in the Victorian woman," said Bencolin. "Still, Colette *can* be irritating."

"Besides," I said, "she as much as admitted she had helped railroad that poor devil Keane… There really was a duel, it would seem." Sir John pursed his lips, frowning. "Still, I don't think you quite understand the law, Mr. Marle. The mere fact of a duel would have made no difference in Keane's conviction, you know. The law recognizes no mitigating circumstances. Any intent to take life constitutes murder in the first degree, particularly in a duel, where the intent to take life is the most obvious thing of all. Keane was guilty of murder… On the other hand, El Moulk, if he had been party to this affair *in any way*, was also guilty of murder. In the eyes of the law, he was as guilty as Keane. He merely seems to have been clearing his own skirts, rather than 'railroading' Keane. Not a very honourable way of doing it, but—"

"You mean," I said, "that if you and Bencolin, for example, decide to fight a duel, and Inspector Talbot and I are merely your seconds, we are guilty of murder if one of you gets killed?"

"Exactly."

"And then El Moulk may have had no animus against Keane!"

"One moment, please!" interposed Bencolin. He smiled quizzically. "You are talking about the law of England, Sir John."

"Isn't it the same in France?"

"Theoretically, yes. But the decision rests with the jury entirely; it is up to their discretion, the law rules, and the judge may not instruct them to bring in a verdict of guilty... And you know, I think, how the duel is looked on in France? It is believed (and I share the view) a perfectly straightforward, decent, honourable affair, much more sane than dragging a dispute through the law courts to have one's wounded heart healed with franc notes."

Sir John waved an impatient hand. "Yes," he growled. "Duels! Truth, then, is determined in a duel by which of the contestants is a better pistol-shot."

"Or," said Bencolin, "it is determined in court by which of the contestants is a better liar. The conditions are equally fair."

"Melodrama, nevertheless. Can't you see how foolish it is? 'Sir, you have insulted me; therefore I will have your life.'"

"Whereas," said Bencolin, thoughtfully, "nowadays they merely say: 'Sir, you have insulted me; therefore I will have your pocket-book.' I am not sure which is the more reasonable, but it seems fairly clear which must be the more sincere... At any rate, I was endeavouring to tell you our own state of mind on the matter. It is most unlikely that any French jury would send a man to prison for life for fighting a duel while drunk, particularly if somebody got up and made a flowery speech about *l'amour*. I am certain they would never have given El Moulk any sentence at all merely for having been there. No. El Moulk's actions were deliberate, cunning, and vindictive. I think he planned that duel himself, stirred up the feeling between the two while they were drunk and he was sober; I think he even suggested it, supplied the pistols—"

Inspector Talbot had been moving impatiently.

"The point is, sir," he put in, "that you knew about this all along, didn't you? You knew it last night."

"I suspected it last night, yes. But I wanted to make sure these events were all connected... Let me finish. Finally, I don't think Keane ever shot De Lavateur at all."

"Ah!" Talbot muttered. He nodded. "Yes, I'd thought of that, too."

"I arrived on the scene too late to do anything," continued Bencolin, "but I saw the evidence. De Lavateur was shot in exactly the centre of the forehead, and there were powder-marks. Not even a drunkard's duel is fought at such short range. Of course, this was splendid evidence for the prosecution that there had been no duel—and that De Lavateur had been killed deliberately by Keane with a weapon held close to his head. I agreed that the shooting was deliberate, but not as to the identity of the killer. For the present, there is no need to go into my reasons. I have no evidence."

He paused.

"But I am convinced that El Moulk shot De Lavateur with Keane's pistol. And, gentlemen, Jack Ketch knows it."

Through a window beside the table I could see cold needle-points of rain pricking up puddles in a grey courtyard of shuttered windows. The lamplight at our table was bright on the strained faces of the men around it. Bencolin was lounging back, a cigarette unlighted in his fingers. Talbot swallowed cold coffee at a gulp.

"You seriously maintain, then," Sir John said, weighing a spoon in his hand, "that some maniac is avenging a crime ten years old?"

"I fear so. And he is the super-criminal—ruthless, shrewd, naïve, and infinitely patient."

"But why hasn't he acted before, then? Ten years—"

"Well, obviously because he has only learned within the last year the identity of Keane. He said as much in his letter to Mademoiselle Laverne. And when he did learn it, he set out on his vengeance without hurry. He was endlessly patient along one small crazy line. He may have taken months to fashion that perfect little gallows, toiling with secret and delighted diligence. He may even have learned the use of the engraver's tools, lovingly to labour on his own evil calling-card. He could go on for months or years, tirelessly wearing down his victim to a bag of nerves, until El Moulk was ready to scream at a shadow. He is working on some prearranged plan—and that plan is not yet complete...

"Tonight," he added, "will be the tenth anniversary of the crime, as he said."

"You mean, sir," observed Talbot, without the least flurry, "that Mr. El Moulk may not be dead—yet?"

"Just that! Isn't it what the horrible clarity of this man's logic indicates? He has been working to just that end for nearly a year, and all things move irresistibly towards it—the climax, the infernal crown of his vengeance! And we know it. He has let us know it. He has hidden his victim in a street the police can't find."

Sir John put down the spoon with which he had been toying. His thin dark brows were high over cold eyes, and his taut nostrils quivered. He ran a hand over his silver hair as though he were fighting off cobwebs.

"And do you fall in with this nonsense, Talbot?" he asked, in a suppressed voice.

"Well, sir, where *is* Ruination Street? And where *is* Mr. El Moulk?" asked the inspector, looking blankly at the table. "H'm! The fact that it's nonsense doesn't mean it isn't true. There! I've said it." His opaque stare turned towards Bencolin. "You think, then, that Jack Ketch caught Mr. El Moulk on his way to Miss Laverne's, and that he is being held now in—in Ruination Street, to be dealt with at the right time?"

"What do *you* think, Inspector?"

Talbot meditated. From the chair beside him he took three articles—an ebony stick, a flower-box, and a pair of white gloves, which he laid with precision on the table.

"I go by the evidence only, sir," he stated. "We can take it up from the very beginning. Before starting out, I have ascertained at the garage, the limousine was cleaned and overhauled thoroughly, and the tank filled with petrol. Mr. El Moulk left here at shortly after seven. The postmortem on the chauffeur indicates that he must have been killed not very much later than that—about seven-thirty, say; though we can't be sure. His throat was cut and he was stabbed through the heart with some sharp instrument like a very long knife—evidently a surprise attack, for he seems to have shown no fight."

He paused, groping in his mind to arrange the facts properly.

"When we examined it after the murder, the front of the car bore no fingerprints except those of the dead man on the wheel. The wheel, however, was smeared with blood in such a way that somebody other than Smail must have been driving it with gloved hands. In the seat beside the chauffeur there were blood smears to show somebody had been sitting there, and the top of the emergency brake was bloodstained..."

Grisly scene! Worse than an invisible driver, this picture of the murderer riding round London with the dead man beside him!

"How do you explain the fact that we saw nobody beside the dead chauffeur?" asked Sir John.

"The fog, maybe," suggested Talbot. Then he smiled in that slow way of his, which cracked the dusty impassiveness. "I don't know, sir. I for one—well, I don't know. I'm giving facts, that's all..."

"He leaned across the body of the dead man, then, with his hands on the wheel?" Bencolin questioned.

"So it seems. He must have driven about quite a long time, for the petrol-tank was nearly empty."

"It would account for the space of several hours between the death of the chauffeur and the time we saw the car," mused

Bencolin. "Round and round, up streets and down, joy riding. Mad, Inspector!"

Talbot nodded. "As you say, sir, mad. But true. That's why— Never mind. In the rear of the car," he went on, squaring himself in his chair, "there were no fingerprints at all. No signs of disorder. Nor were there any prints on the gold head of the stick. Mr. El Moulk must have worn these white gloves when he handled it—"

He paused as Bencolin picked up the gloves. The detective examined them carefully, holding them close under the lamp. His eyes widened, and then narrowed with sudden attention as he looked at the palm of the right-hand glove. It was of an excellent grade of kid, lined with chamois. It was smudged with black dust along the tips of the fingers, the thumb, and in a broad band across the centre of the palm.

Bencolin looked up. His gaze was fixed on something remote and startling, and his mouth drooped open. "Damnation!" he said. "I wonder if it's possible—!"

"What, sir?"

"I've no reason for believing there might be one," Bencolin was muttering to himself; "and yet it's the only thing that could have made these marks. Yes, it all fits! Even the shadow fits!" He whirled to me. "Think, Jeff! Was El Moulk wearing these gloves when he left the club last night?"

"Yes," I said. "Yes, I remember; he was."

"And did you notice whether the right one was stained?"

I visualized the scene; I remembered El Moulk holding up his hand in that curious gesture of protest in which he had exposed the palm of his right glove...

"No," I answered. "It was perfectly clean."

"What's all this, sir?" demanded Talbot.

"Patience, Inspector; I don't know I'm right yet. El Moulk was wearing his gloves! Of course he was. That's the glory of it. O blessed fashion-plate. O sublime dandy! He was wearing his gloves!"

He tossed the glove on the table and sat back, nodding in a pleased way.

"No, Inspector! Not one word shall you hear until I have proved or disproved it; and you, Sir John, shall buy me the best dinner in all London... Now, then, Inspector: have we more facts?"

Talbot was regarding him suspiciously, and the muscles were drawn tight in his square cheeks; even the shine of his broken nose was suspicious.

"Over *here*, sir," he announced, gravely, "we don't approve of that sort of..." He checked himself. "Very well, then. There is the flower-box—"

"By the way," murmured Bencolin, "what is in the flower-box?"

"I suppose it's too far fetched to say flowers?" asked Sir John.

"Yes, I know; but has anybody bothered to look inside?"

With a table knife Talbot cut the strings in a rather hurried manner. There was a rustle of tissue-paper; then the inspector sat back with a jerk of relief, pushing the box towards Bencolin.

"Flowers," he said.

"In fact, orchids," said Bencolin, tilting the box. "The South American type called 'The Golden Butterfly.'—Diable! it's a corsage!"

There was a pause while he looked curiously at the contents.

Sir John inquired: "Well, what about it? What's wrong?"

"There speaks the recluse! My own social activities are not many, but when I order a corsage for a lady, I most certainly have the flower shop send it to her. I do not carry it myself. There's something very wrong here..." He snapped his fingers. "And it fits, also! Did you call at the shop, Talbot?"

"Yes. They remembered about it. Mr. El Moulk telephoned early yesterday afternoon and ordered the corsage. They thought it was odd, too—about not sending them—but he just said, 'Damn it, man, do as I tell you,' or something like that. They said he spoke as though he had a cold."

"Did he call for the orchids, then?"

"Somebody did. They don't remember who it was. Only one or two of them know Mr. El Moulk by sight. Supposed it was a servant. 'A tall man with his collar turned up.' He came about two o'clock or two-fifteen."

"Not El Moulk, anyway. H'm!... Have you asked the servants about this?"

"Nobody in the club was sent on such an errand, unless it was some one in Mr. El Moulk's household," the inspector answered. "The porter swears to that. Might have been Graffin."

"What about the French valet?"

"He left for Paris yesterday morning early." Bencolin nodded, smiling in a curious fashion. "Yes," he murmured, "yes. We had better have Graffin in here for a moment…"

The man must have been in one of the downstairs rooms, for when we sent the waiter after him he appeared almost immediately. He was very nearly sober. His head wavered atop that long, scrawny neck which was horribly like a turkey's. His face was mottled, and his hands twitched.

"Good morning, gentlemen," he said in a husky croak. His bleary eyes would meet our gaze and then fall, meet it and fall again. He was trembling in a way that set one's teeth on edge; but he tried to disguise it by holding tight to the edges of his chair.

"We have just been discussing the points of this case," Bencolin said, "and there are things we should like more information about…"

Graffin's shoulders jumped. It was unnerving. He murmured, "C-certainly," and his eyes were spongily staring. "B-bit indisposed." (Jump!)

"Were you by any chance sent on an errand yesterday by Mr. El Moulk?"

"S-sir?" cried Graffin. He tried to be dignified, but the neck twitched his head sideways.

"To a florist's shop in Cockspur Street?"

"N-no. Was in my room—all day. All day!"

"Between two and two thirty, you are sure?"

"I am s-sure. Yes! I can prove it. Waiter brought my lunch about t-that time."

It was rather pathetic, this helplessness of his. He looked as though at any moment he might scream out, and his eyes were fixed with glassy regard on Bencolin while he twitched. The detective said, pleasantly:

"You have seen nothing of Mr. El Moulk yet, I take it?"

"No!"

"He didn't come in last night, by any chance?"

The man grabbed at the edge of the chair. He said rapidly, "O my God! what are you asking me that for? No!"

"And you still maintain he was not the victim of any persecution?"

There was a silence. Graffin's head sank lower; the life washed out of him and he moved his neck in a contorted way as though he were trying to swallow hot soup. At last he said, in a whisper, very humbly:

"Sorry, gentlemen. Afraid I must have... a little drink..."

When the whisky was brought, he took it noisily, and after a time of heavy breathing his shaking quieted. But he was getting crafty and truculent, glaring from the mottled face.

"I am going to repeat, my friend, a question I asked you last night, and see whether you don't wish to reconsider your reply. How long did you say you had been in Mr. El Moulk's employ?"

"I know," the man said, cunningly. "Trip me up, eh? Righto. Told you last night it was for six years; said it was in Cairo. *You*—you'll look up army rolls, won't you? Find out I've been out of service ten years and never was in Cairo. Well, it was in Paris I took up with him. I lied to you last night."

"Strange! Why did you tell us that?"

"None y'r business," mumbled Graffin into his glass. One red eye opened over the glass's rim.

"Your secretarial duties were not heavy, I presume?"

The other laughed boisterously.

"But Mr. El Moulk has never been disposed to regret this—ah—added expense in his household, I fancy," said Bencolin, in a musing voice…

Graffin set down his glass with such a curious motion that for a moment I thought he had been stricken sober. He stared. A nerve twitched beside his cheek-bone.

"I gave satisfaction, my dear sir," he answered, after a pause. The voice was humble.

"Well, well, I shan't detain you, my friend. There is just one other point. You knew, of course, that Mr. El Moulk has been taking precautions against an attack on his life?"

"Oh… oh yes."

"But you have no idea as to the source of his fear?"

"Absolutely *none!*" Graffin leaned forward intently. "I swear—!"

"Hm, yes… By the way, was the chauffeur armed?"

"Armed? Oh! Oh, you mean—weapons? Yes, I know, because El Moulk gave him a pistol that had belonged to me. It was a Smith and Wesson revolver. A forty-five, long barrel, with an ivory handle. Smail was quite proud of it; used to delight in keeping the nickel polished."

Now I was sitting where I could see Bencolin with the light of the table lamp full on his face. At this remark the muscles tightened round his bearded jaw, his pouched eyes drooped lazily, and he began to tap softly with his fingers on the tablecloth…

"Thank you. May I suggest, Lieutenant, that you remain here in the club for a time? We may have to take steps to go over Mr. El Moulk's rooms, and we should like your assistance."

Graffin nodded and rose. His bleary blue eyes blinked once or twice, but he said nothing more except to explain that he was taking over arrangements for the funeral of the chauffeur. Then he lurched out.

"I thought of that," remarked Talbot, gloomily—"about going over his rooms—if it's permissible—"

"Graffin!" Bencolin was muttering. "Why is he so insistent that El Moulk is the victim of no undue attentions on the part of Jack Ketch? Why won't he tell us anything about these mysterious packages with the blue seals? The blue seals, with 'K' stamped on them—Jack Ketch's monogram! The blue-sealed packages El Moulk was forever receiving? Why did he lie about the time he met El Moulk? Why does a man keep as private secretary a drunkard who is not only unfit for work, but even boasts of neglecting his duties? What use had El Moulk for a secretary, anyhow? Do you see, Inspector?" he demanded of Talbot. "There's your key. And then he nearly jumped out of his wits when I asked him…"

With an obscure smile, Bencolin nodded. "Bit by bit the pieces click into place. And the only weak piece in Jack Ketch's whole intricate plan is—Graffin; is Graffin himself."

Talbot sat up straight.

"You mean… Don't try to confuse me, sir!" he snapped. "Things appear in Mr. El Moulk's room when Graffin is the only one there. He swears they come out of the air, which is nonsense. We've decided that Jack Ketch must be somebody living at this club. If we can break down his alibi that he was at the club all evening—"

"And if you can, Inspector, what then? Where did he go? It brings us right round in a circle again to the old question, the really important question, *Where is Ruination Street?*"

Talbot put his hands to his forehead and rested his elbows on the table.

"There's no such street in the whole directory," he said, like a man holding hard to reason. "No such street! And it's the only clue we've got as to where, in all London, that car might have gone…"

He was still sitting there, brooding, when the porter came in to tell us that Joyet, El Moulk's manservant, had just come back from Paris and would like to see us as soon as possible.

"Murder, Considered as One of the Fine Arts"

"**S**END HIM INTO THE LOUNGE," GROWLED TALBOT. "SEND him some place. Anyhow, tell him to wait…"

The little man's face was screwed up ferociously. He looked like a malevolent gnome. And then he spoke, thus:

"I'll carry on. But I want you to know, gentlemen, that in this business I'm out of my depth, and I know it. I've worked my way up. I started as a police constable in K division—and that means Limehouse, in case you don't know it. As far as crooks are concerned, just now I've got the swell mob at the tips of my fingers. But this thing! It's not a murder case; it's a nightmare." He made a futile gesture. "There's nothing to *hold* to. I've just got to let go, and try to be as dotty as the case is, and then, maybe—

"See here. A practical man would say that this Ruination Street is all tosh. But Jack Ketch says he'll do things, and he does them. He says there's a Ruination Street, and I'd just as soon take his word as the word of all these so-called respectable people who tell us crazier things than he does."

He looked defiantly round our group. "We've got to find it. It's our only hope. I think you know how London is mapped out. Well, I've put a corps of men to work. We know that at present there is no street by that name; the only alternative is that some street was formerly called Ruination. With all the alterations that have been made in London, it's very likely. Maybe five, maybe fifteen, maybe fifty years ago—"

"Or perhaps a hundred and fifty," observed Sir John. "*If* it exists. You'll want a whole college of antiquarians, Talbot. And you've only the word of a telephone message…"

"All right, sir. All right. Admit it. But I've questioned servants, I've looked up records—and I get nowhere. It's time to try something else. And grant the street may have had its name changed a hundred and fifty years ago. Doesn't this Jack Ketch sound the sort of person who'd call a street by its eighteenth-century name? Isn't the name Jack Ketch itself from the eighteenth century?"

"Seventeenth," corrected Bencolin. "I'm up on that sort of literature, you see. The hangman at Tyburn was nicknamed Jack Ketch from a man called Richard Jacquett, who owned Tyburn manor in 1678."

"Moreover," persisted Talbot, "the phone message said 'hanged on the gallows in Ruination Street.' If we look for old streets that had gibbets on them in the old days… There's Tyburn itself, for example; it stood there around the beginning of Edgeware Road, didn't it—?"

"Damn it all, man," said Sir John, irascibly, "you don't think he was hanged from the Marble Arch?"

"I don't think anything, sir! And that story of Mr. Dallings's I've been hearing about—*he* saw that queer shadow of the gallows, and it's *too* insane to suppose casual people are sitting up all over London amusing themselves with gibbets at one o'clock in the morning. He must have seen it. And since he took the Laverne woman home, it might be within a very short distance of Mount Street itself. In that direction, at least. And there's all the more reason for supposing this is true, because Mr. El Moulk was starting in that very direction when he was waylaid."

Rather embarrassed at his own eloquence, Talbot sat back with folded arms. I was watching Bencolin during this speech, and I could have sworn I saw the faintest flicker of a smile on his lips.

"Bravo, Inspector!" he murmured. "I'm afraid there's one little thing you're overlooking; but if I pointed it out to you right now, we should be even deeper into the dense, dark soup."

Sir John regarded Talbot with a sort of remote speculation. Then his long, lean jaw relaxed in a smile, and the wrinkles round his eyes deepened in amusement.

"I congratulate you, Talbot," he said, whimsically. "You follow our friend Bencolin's lead with remarkable aptitude. Superintendent Mason will be delighted. 'Scotland Yard in Cap and Gown.' Every newspaper in London, as Bencolin would say, will graciously present us with The Bird."

"Can't help that, sir. It's our only chance. And I was thinking this: I've learned something about this Dr. Daniel Pilgrim who lives at the club. He's one of the foremost authorities on old London we have, so they tell me… Why not get a bit of help from him?"

"Not a bad idea," said Bencolin. "I'm rather curious to meet this gentleman, from what Jeff tells us… What do you know about him, Sir John?"

"Pilgrim?" The other shook his head. "Not much. Just what I told you last night. Knocked about the world quite a bit, I believe. One book of his made a stir some years ago. They called him 'the detective of history.'"

"The detective of history?"

"Yes. He took some famous murder stories—historical facts they've never properly explained—and worked them out, with evidence, just like modern police-court records. Exciting stuff, some of it, pinning guilt on dead men. Nearly got himself kicked out of some historical society for it, I believe…"

"I know," murmured Bencolin; "according to that brilliant principle of historians which decrees that anything really interesting must be either unimportant or wrong. From what they tell us of English life in the Middle Ages, I think they must be under the impression that English life today is just one long speech in the House of Commons… Ah, well. Let's go in and talk to this valet of El Moulk's."

Joyet was warming his hands by the lounge fire when we entered. He was a short, very stout man, with a red face heavy in jowl, and a big head across which a few hairs were plastered in the semblance of a dandyish curl. A whole map of wrinkles surrounded bulging blue eyes, always wide with astonishment. Under a bulbous nose he wore a most enormous moustache with an intricate and comical curl at each point. At first glance he seemed all stomach, watch chain, and wheezes.

"Ah, messieurs!" he cried in a voice which issued from deep in that stomach. His eyes bulged; he puffed with excitement and flicked his moustache: "But it is bad—hah? I have just come from Par-*is*!"

The apparition was bowing as though in a minuet. Then he made a huge gesture. "I don' speak English good—hah? You see?"

"Speak French," said Bencolin, in that language.

Now a whole range of upheavals began to animate Joyet's stomach. He was chuckling capaciously, and the wrinkles livened his beaming face.

"That's good; that's fine, monsieur. I want to talk, and here I get choked up because I can't. Eh? But this…" He became mournful, and then swore excitedly. "Last night I receive' a telegram to return—"

"What's he saying?" asked Talbot.

"Did you send him a telegram to return here?"

Talbot eyed the man with distaste. He nodded. A hostile gleam appeared in Joyet's blue and expressive eye.

"Had his address from Graffin," explained the inspector. Joyet seemed on the point of exploding with excitement. He resumed:

"My wife says: 'Marcel, you are on leave. Here you can smoke your pipe and walk in your garden.' You should see my garden; the beautiful flowers—it's like a first-class burial. In summer, of course. But I say, 'No! I go to London immediately.'"

The man's energy, the power of those eager naïve eyes, swept us all back a little. It was no wonder the club servants considered him difficult. He had something of a Napoleonic swagger; we were dealing, obviously, with one of those democratic French servants who give the best service in the world for being treated as fellow men. Therefore Bencolin said:

"Have a cigar."

Sir John stared, but said nothing. Bencolin took a cigar himself, and he had no more than lifted it when, by some staggering sleight-of-hand, Joyet had a match before it. His regard was fixed tensely.

"There is an art in lighting cigars," he announced, moving the match with care; "the fire should be *just* distributed—so, monsieur!" With a sigh he blew it out. "And now, monsieur?"

"And now, Joyet, you know what has happened?"

"I surmise it, monsieur, from what I know already, and from what I read in the newspaper this morning. It has happened, then? What he feared?"

"You know about it?"

"Oh yes, monsieur; a great deal."

Bencolin translated rapidly to Talbot. We were all staring at Joyet. *He* knew about it, and Graffin didn't. Bencolin motioned Joyet to a chair; the questioning was interrupted by translations of each query and answer for Talbot's benefit, which I shall not include. Joyet was puffing at his cigar between pursed lips, rather in the fashion of a child sucking a stick of candy. With a huge hand he slapped at intervals on the chair arm.

"You ought to know, monsieur, that for some months past Monsieur El Moulk has been undergoing a sort of—persecution. Every so often (sometimes a month, sometimes a week, sometimes only a few days) there would come a package in the post, or something left at the apartment. You understand?"

"What do you mean, something left at the apartment?"

"Why, monsieur, this man had the damned impudence to come right in—to leave things on the table—and his card with them, too. While we were out, of course. I don't know how he got in. The rooms were always locked."

"The club servants never saw anyone."

"These English! What do you expect? No!" Joyet gave a ferocious twist to his moustache and made scornful noises.

"Hm!… Lieutenant Graffin knew of these things?"

"Plouf! *that* man!—he is always drunk! Always, always, always, always!—Why, naturally he knew about it. He just laughed… I said to monsieur, 'Me, I'd find out who it is and wring his neck.'" A fist was shaken out of furious gusts of cigar smoke.

"You were fond of your employer?"

"Ah!" said Joyet. "Like this—like that." He wagged his head deprecatingly. "He was always in the apples. And he had a bad temper. Sometimes he was terrible. But me, why should I mind? Good salary, good quarters—and besides, how that man knew food! Tck!—how that man knew food! Yes, he had his redeeming points. The secret of life, monsieur, is logic."

Having delivered himself of this sentiment, leaning forward with a finger beside his red nose and his face screwed into an expression of the utmost profundity, Joyet settled back with beaming complacence.

"You have no idea as to the origin of these threats?"

"No, monsieur. He never told me much; I generally had to ask him pointblank."

"Who were his friends here? In London, I mean."

"Ah, that is easy. He had none. The theatre, the concert, his studies (and what studies!)—that occupied him. Sometimes he went to see Mademoiselle Laverne. Eh? Yes, yes; it is natural. I have seen him talking to Dr. Pilgrim, the gentleman who lives here. *And*"—Joyet lowered his voice dramatically; his lifted finger was portentous—"I say *I* had no idea about the person who was threatening him. But I think he had. I think he had just learned about it."

"What do you mean?"

"Well, it was like this. He'd been worried. He couldn't sleep, you understand. Some nights I would look into his big room, and he'd stand there with the firelight on his face, in the middle of all those ornaments of his—just shaking. He couldn't rest, he couldn't even read. And M. Graffin would drink whisky and play the piano, and sit there laughing at him. You know, monsieur, I read in the journal that Monsieur El Moulk had disappeared. But, the devil!—it seemed to me that if anybody were to disappear, or get killed, it would be more likely to be Monsieur Graffin. I have seen monsieur just holding his own hands together to keep from flying at Monsieur Graffin's throat. So furious, you understand! But he never did anything…"

Joyet's recital took form in the dusty room with blurred shades of terror, but at the time (to me at least) it had no significance. Before many hours we were to recall it in the revelation of its sinister import.

"But," Joyet continued, "just before I left I spoke to monsieur, who was hopping with delight. 'A word for you, Joyet,' he said; 'if things work out, I am going to trap this Jack Ketch. I'm going to trap him at work!' I inquire, 'But how, monsieur?' He replies, 'Ah, but I've found a helper right here at the club.'—And there! That's all I know."

Bencolin nodded absently.

"Yes," he muttered. "That would be it, of course. Did you know what he meant?"

"Alas! no, monsieur! I'm afraid not."

"Now, tell me. *You* saw these packages with the blue seals, didn't you?"

"Oh yes. Every one."

"And what did they contain?"

"Allow me to think, monsieur. Ah yes. For one thing, there was a pair of glass duelling-pistols—exquisite! And one of those jars you put ashes in when you are cremated. Always something!"

Bencolin chuckled. "No lovelorn swain ever exercised more careful selection than Jack Ketch. It's so elaborate that it becomes comical. Now, Joyet, these things that were found in the apartment, the ones he brought himself—"

"We always knew where to look for them, monsieur. They were always in the same place—on the centre table of the big room."

"Always in the same place?" repeated Bencolin. Suddenly he rose from his chair. "Always—you are sure of that, Joyet?" he demanded, tensely. "Never in the hallway, never—"

"Never, monsieur! Once we found a long coil of rope there. And books—many books." Bencolin swung round with a flourish, drooping a lazy eyelid towards Sir John. The cloven hoof peeped out suavely; his slow smile was delighted.

"You understood that, didn't you?" he asked. "It is most suggestive. The little toy gallows was sent by the post, but the wooden man left on the desk…" He paused. A pleased expression twitched up one eyebrow. "*Tiens*! in English it scans!

> "The little toy gallows was sent by the post,
> But the wooden man left on the desk—"

He stood blankly, running it over as though he were trying to finish the verse. "Tut, man! Don't look so furious. Besides, I can't think of anything that rhymes with 'desk.' Do you know the secret of being a poet? You always start out with some thought in mind, and the exigencies of rhyme force you to say something entirely different—which is always much better than your original senti-ment. This is called inspiration.—Come along, Joyet; if you will conduct us, we are going up now to have a look at Mr. El Moulk's rooms."

The four of us went out across the lobby and into the lift, Sir John coldly silent, Talbot glum, and Bencolin thoughtful. The lift-gate clanged at the fourth floor. Rounding the turn of the stair which descended near it, I saw Dr. Pilgrim just going down. He was in shapeless tweeds and had a pipe in his mouth. He took it out, and the shrewd, humorous, cat-green eyes ran over us appraisingly.

"Good morning, Sir John," he greeted. "Good morning, Mr. Marle. I was just going up to see you, and found you weren't in. I wanted to tell you: Went round to see our—our patient this morning, and she has quite recovered. You're still making deductions, I hope?"

Introductions were made. Talbot went to the point at once.

"Shall you be inside for a time, Doctor?" he asked. "We've a little mission here, but afterwards I should like to have a talk with you about—last night and other things."

Pilgrim was studying Bencolin covertly. "By all means, Inspector. My professional duties are—not pressing. In case you come down within the next half-hour, I shall be in the lounge."

His eyes asked questions, but he said nothing. He stepped into the lift. He knew I was no detective, or did he? The pocked face was a genial but fathomless enigma, and he seemed interested chiefly in the bowl of his pipe...

After he had descended, Bencolin stood looking round the long passage. No lights were on, and its sombre arch was full of shadows. The detective passed to the front, under walls that had once been gilded, and drew back the massive draperies before a bay window. For a time he stared down into the sleety drizzle at the thin chimney stacks of St. James's Palace, blurring away across from us and beyond.

In silence we heard sleet pattering on the roof, and the multitudinous voices of the wind...

Suddenly he jumped round, and the hearts in us jumped too.

Talbot blurted: *"My God! What is it?"*

We were still quivering to the echo of a cry—a horrible childish scream from the depths of the passage. It was muffled; but, no doubt about it, the cry had come from beyond the pointed archway leading to El Moulk's rooms. Again that voice shrieked out; something fell with a clank of metal. And as we stared at the curtains of the archway a figure bolted through.

It ran for the staircase, screaming once more; then it tripped, and seized the balustrade just in time to avoid pitching down. For a moment it clung there—a dwarf, a white-faced child, breathing hard—then, staring with great eyes in the gloom, it saw us. And it ran straight to Sir John, babbling something I could not understand.

After that momentary shock I collected my wits. This was no goblin, though in that first plunge it had seemed imp-like and devilish; it was only Teddy, with his witless stare, his pounding little fists, and his shrill treble, crying: "I seen it! Ow, gory, I seen it!" He pointed at the archway; he was drooling with terror... Teddy was one of those ugly curiosities, a child stunted during the war. His body was a child's and his mind a baby's, though his pulpy face had wrinkles and his carroty hair was always thick with brilliantine. I had seen him often about the club; they gave him a place to sleep and a little pocket money, with which he bought cigars. He served as errand-boy and drudge, and you would see him struggling through the passages with a coal scuttle, singing some bawdy song they had taught him as a joke. Sir John was, I think, one of the few people who had been kind to him...

"What's the matter, Teddy? Come out of it, now!" Sir John said, sharply. He shook the little shoulders, and Teddy's usual witless grin came back, though his voice went on cracked and shrill.

"Teddy don' mean nothing!" he whined, and he shifted from one leg to the other and looked at us furtively, still with that cut grin. "Teddy don' mean nothin!—Just a-going to lay the fire, like I alwis do."

"You say you saw something in there?"

"'M." After a pause he added in terror: "Dunno. Ain't sure!"

"I thought none of the servants were allowed in there," Talbot put in.

Teddy capered. "That's it! That's it! Nobody but me. Mr. Moulk don' mind me; don' mind Teddy. Gave me a bob once, 'e did. Yerce."

"Come now," continued Sir John, "what's in there? Was somebody trying to scare you?... They've frightened the life out of him in the kitchen," he told us, angrily. "Tell him tales about ghosts, and savages in strange lands."

Teddy's fear had returned; he clutched at Sir John's coat. But he was stubborn. He had seen nothing. He grew hysterical; coaxings, cajolery, even threats could draw nothing out of him. When Sir John offered him a gold penknife, with his name on it, his eyes gleamed with horrid cupidity, and with his chubby hands he pulled at his hair until the brilliantine oozed down his face—but he had received such a shock that he would not speak. 'Cos things 'u'd get him, he pointed out. There wos things as reely gotcher, 'cos cook said so. Yerce. He, Teddy, was averse to the things as gotcher. All the same, he would like the penknife with his name on it. Finally we released him, and he scampered down the stairs at his curious hopping gait, singing one of the most obscene songs I have ever heard.

Bencolin made no comment on the boy. He merely asked Joyet:

"The rooms are not kept locked, then?"

"They were kept locked when monsieur was here. Of course, he never minded the half-wit. But now that Monsieur Graffin is in charge... This way, messieurs."

He walked down and raised the curtain of the archway. Beyond it a bare passage ran some fifteen feet to a heavy, pointed door, which was standing ajar. We passed through it into a huge and grotesque room, vaulted to a height of twenty feet. Four lanterns of hammered brass hung on chains from iron hooks in the ceiling, but the room was lighted only by a gas-lamp with a green globe on the centre table... We stood a moment in the doorway, looking at its curious decorations.

In the wall to the left, an old mantelpiece of black marble with a coal fire laid in the grate. On the mantel-shelf stood four *canopes*, vases of blue enamelled earthenware with lids in the form of armed heads; I judged them, from an imperfect knowledge of Egyptian pottery, to be of the second Theban dynasty. Above the mantel stretched a large mural in hollowed wood (the *cavo-rilievo* which is distinctive of the New Kingdom), depicting the Judgment of the Soul. The colours were amazingly preserved: on a pale background, the god Horus, with the black hawk's head and yellow body, was weighing in immense scales the heart against the truth; Maat, white-clad goddess of truth, watched from her throne, and Thoth of the ibis head, the gods' scribe, stood by recording the judgment... Bookshelves, with curtains in dull green damask, rose high along the same wall on either side of the fireplace to a door at each extremity... In the wall opposite us were three tall windows, shrouded in thick drapes of the same dusty green, and with gilded cabinets between. It was difficult to make out more than shapes, because the light burnt green and dim in the globed lamp. But more curtained shelves stretched to the ceiling on the right hand; before them stood a massive grand piano, and the light caught dull colours on a painted sarcophagus standing upright in the corner.

We walked into this colossal room over the dark-green carpet, very soft and deep, which covered a floor laid in squares of black and white marble. The chairs were of black carven wood, with much tarnished gilding. This whole place was oppressive with the smell of dead flowers—I could see withered stalks in vases of red porphyry—of dust, parchment, spices, and that indescribable embalming reek which clings to the tombs at Abydos.

It was a room of death. Talbot suddenly kicked over a coal-scuttle which lay in the centre of the floor; its clatter jarred harshly on the thickness of scented and decaying peace, and the four brass lanterns tingled in gloom above our heads. I do not know what any of us expected to find. Our steps fell deep and noiseless, and we moved, without a word, over towards the table of the lamp. It was a long table, stacked with books and papers, so that we did not at first see what lay behind...

Talbot sat down in a gilded chair, his notebook on his knee. Sir John remained standing, fingers on the table and head forward, studying Bencolin from under shadowed brows. Bencolin began to walk about the room. He paused before the door at the left of the fireplace as we faced it; that is to say, at the corner of the room.

"To where does this door lead, Joyet?" he asked.

"To monsieur's sleeping-apartment, by way of a passage. There are three doors beyond it; one to monsieur's room, one to a dining-room, and one to the rooms occupied by M. Graffin and myself... The suite, you see, occupies the entire back of the house."

"And this other door?" He indicated the corresponding one, in the corner towards the right of the fireplace.

"To an outside staircase—enclosed, of course. It goes down, with a landing on each floor, to a rear door of the house. There's an alley below."

"The main rear entrance, then?"

"Oh no. The service door is farther up, beside the kitchens. This is just a sort of private stair. We keep it locked; Monsieur El Moulk never used it. It's not lighted, you see."

"So, then, if a—an unwelcome visitor wished to come in here and leave a Jack Ketch souvenir, he might enter without being seen by anybody in the club?"

Joyet pursed his lips and heaved elaborate flippers in a shrug. "Ah, as to that, monsieur—no. Monsieur El Moulk thought of that. It is always locked and bolted. Besides, you would need a key to the alley door. Monsieur had special locks fitted up, and he has the only keys himself."

"Wherever he is now," the detective commented. After a pause he drew a long breath and went on: "I should like to see those sleeping-rooms, Joyet, if you'll show me around... Coming, Inspector?"

Talbot hurried after him. Sir John remained standing by the table, motionless, his brows drawn down. In this atmosphere I felt uneasy and oppressed. The mere closing of the door caused echoes to tremble in this hollow vault; it seemed that the green curtains stirred, the vases shook in faint uncertain quiverings, and even the brass lanterns murmured with an answering clink. Here one could not hear the wind or sleet, or the friendly ticking of any clock. Teddy thought that he saw something in this room. He had trudged in here—whistling, probably, and swinging his scuttle of coal, with his head carried on one side in his own cocky way. He laid the fire, still whistling. Then I fancied I could see the little, pulpy, wrinkled face turned over his shoulder, slowly, as he knelt by the hearth; the sudden stare, the jump of his carroty eyebrows, and the mouth pulled square like a Greek mask. Kicking over his coal-scuttle, he screeched and ran—from what?

My eyes travelled to the right wall, that immense reach of cur-tained shelves. The keys of the piano were whitish blurs. Beyond them, in the corner, loomed the dusky gold, orange, black, and ochre of the painted mummy-case, whose countenance grew with each moment into a more staring likeness of the face of Nezam El Moulk.

It was no illusion; the damned thing really resembled him. Painted in rings of black, the round brown eyes wore a fixity of blank idiocy, like those faces which are so horrible when they bend over us in the grey corridors of nightmare... Above the sarcophagus hung relics: the leather gauntlet of the Pharaoh, worn in his battle-chariot when he handled the bow or reins; a cuirass of quilted leather; the terrible war-axe, the lance, the dagger, and the sling.

I approached the sarcophagus, stared up into the painted face, and wondered why my heart beat with such heavy, thudding blows. Then it seemed to me that I saw the damask drapery move before the nearest window, so that I turned sharply and drew it aside. There was only a great barred window, through whose glass I looked down into the mud of an alley far below. It ran in from St. James's Street on my left, and ended in a *cul-de-sac*. I glanced across at the bleak walls and shuttered windows of the building opposite me, whose back gave on the alley, as ours did, before I let fall the curtain.

"Who is smoking in here?" asked Sir John.

His voice seemed to come from a great distance. I turned, and saw him looking at the centre table. This table I saw now from the other side, so that it was unobscured by the top-heavy piles of books.

"Nobody," I said...

He pointed a bony finger at the large desk-blotter. I had not realized that the crisp and solid Sir John Landervorne had eyes that could be so unnerving to look upon. In his grey face the high cheek-bones and thin dark brows accentuated them—they stared unwinking at me from over the lamp, an ugly grey-green. His gaunt shoulders were so hunched that he seemed to have no neck. He still pointed at the blotter.

It had been swept clean of rubbish. A book lay open upon it, and the chair had been pushed back as though someone had been interrupted at his reading. Beside the book stood a shallow bronze ash-tray, and in one of its grooves a smouldering cigarette sent up a straight line of smoke. Again as if someone had been interrupted at his reading...

I walked slowly to the desk and looked down. Not an echo, not a murmur in that vault, or a flicker of the green lamp. The cigarette was an Abdulla, smoked half through. The open book was a copy of De Quincey's *Murder, Considered as One of the Fine Arts*.

Sir John's pointing finger dropped. He turned away from the table.

X

Lord of the Diadems

I LOOKED LONG AT THE SUGGESTIVE VOLUME, UNTIL ITS TYPE grew blurred and meaningless, and the ash of the cigarette overbalanced, so that it fell into the bronze tray. Then I looked towards my right, at the door to the outside stair.

"We've been fools," I said, "not to investigate that door..."

Sir John only said: "Have we? I don't know."

I hurried over to it, and found what I expected to find. The bolt was drawn back, the door stood closed but unlocked, and the key was in the outside. Beyond lay a dark landing, dusty and airless, with a crazy balustrade meandering down beside the steps, and walls papered in dirty yellow. This being the top floor and the termination of the staircase, there was at my left only a ladder mounting to a trap in the roof. At the right was a window.

When I looked back, Bencolin had come out of the door to the sleeping-rooms. He stood with his hand on the knob, Talbot peering round his shoulder.

"I saw it, Jeff, a while ago," he told me. "For the moment, you needn't trouble; I don't think you'll find anything."

"But you haven't seen the table," I said. "And certainly somebody was here a moment ago... What luck in the rooms?"

Talbot answered me. "Not a thing. It's a queer enough place, but all in order. We *did* find the mummy out of that thing," he indicated the sarcophagus, "beside the man's bed."

Hands in his pockets, Bencolin was looking down at the desk

blotter. Once he leaned over, picked up the vellum-bound book, examined it back and front, and tossed it on the table again.

"Bah! Stage-setting," he snapped. "The pages aren't cut." He tapped the back of the book. "What a magnificent title to dignify the clumsy crimes of John Williams!—Jack Ketch will get few tips from it. Hello!"

One of the drawers in the table was slightly open, and his eye had caught the glitter inside. He flipped the handkerchief out of his breast pocket, wound it round his fingers, and pulled out the shining drawer...

Inside, spread on a red bandana handkerchief, lay a long-barrelled revolver with an ivory handle, some large glass buttons, a couple of gilded tassels, and a trumpery watch.

"The murderer," said Bencolin, "has returned his loot."

Talbot bustled past him and glared into the drawer. "Why— those—they belong to the *chauffeur*—!" he muttered. He stuffed the notebook into his pocket, like a man who has come on despair.

Gingerly Bencolin lifted one corner of the red bandana, which was soiled on the outside with blackish dust. Under it lay a large photograph. It was a picture of Smail, the dead man, wearing boxing-gloves and fighter's trunks. His face was snarling and a little self-conscious; the black muscles gleamed in their strained crouch behind the gloves. Across one corner a sprawling hand had written, "Yrs. truly, Dick (Killer) Smail, New York, Aug., '27."

"His bodyguard," Bencolin murmured, "was a boxer—"

The detective paused. Abruptly he stiffened; the fingers of his hand clenched in a spasmodic gesture, and into his eyes flashed that terrifying light of revelation which I had seen so often. It was gone in a moment, and he shrugged his shoulders in easy fashion and turned away with a wry smile. But there, beside the table of the green lamp, I knew that Bencolin had solved his case.

"I'll take care of these," said Talbot. Wrapping the articles carefully in the bandana, he lifted them from the drawer. The little inspector went on with something like ferocity: "It means one thing. The murderer has got Mr. El Moulk, and he's got the keys, and he can come through the alley door up here whenever he likes. But why, *why*? If we had come in here sooner—"

Bencolin shook his head thoughtfully. "I'm not sure we should have been in time, Inspector. At any rate…"

He ran his eye over the desk, and then turned to regard the sarcophagus. He walked over to it, ran his hands along the ancient wood, and as though on impulse wrenched off the heavy lid.

"There's nothing inside," he said, fitting back the lid. He turned with a satiric grin. "I knew there wouldn't be, but I wanted your minds to be set at rest. Yes, yes. Whenever a sarcophagus appears, fiction-tainted imaginations immediately suspect the presence of some nice fresh corpse inside. In fact, they suspect the presence of every conceivable thing except a mummy."

He meditated, looking about the room. Then his eyes wandered up to the nearest of the four brass lanterns which hung fully fifteen feet over our heads.

"Joyet," he said, craning his neck, "do you happen to have a stepladder on the premises?"

"Pardon?" exclaimed Joyet.

Bencolin pointed to the lantern. "That," he announced, with the relish of a connoisseur, "is an exquisite example of rare old Whagoolian-Kynwitz brass from the post-vertigo period. I want to examine it more closely. Get me a stepladder."

"Man, this is getting past a joke!" cried Sir John. "We've stood for your foolery all day. Now would you mind stopping that gibberish and—"

"You know I'm not joking," the detective replied, mildly. "Besides, if you're not interested in Whagoolian-Kynwitz brass, I am."

Joyet had disappeared in the direction of the bedroom, and presently emerged, trundling a gigantic and shaky stepladder. He set it up beneath the lantern and held its base while Bencolin mounted. Far up there in the gloom, where it was difficult to see anything at all, we could hear him tapping the lantern and emitting a series of amazed clucks.

"Very rare," he announced, and continued with a lecture of elaborate nonsense; but when he descended the stepladder his face was very grave. While Joyet removed the ladder he went to the table again, where he began ransacking the drawers and going through their litter. There were some papyri, framed between sealed sheets of glass. I saw the fragments of a clay seal, smeared in blue ink; a magnifying glass; a little camel's head of carven ivory; pens, ink, and erasers. Thrown carelessly into a pile of theatre programmes lay a pendant of gold cloisonné enamel and lapis-lazuli. Bencolin found at the very bottom a portfolio of leather, from which he drew some neatly written sheets of manuscript.

"Our friend El Moulk has been doing some translating from the papyri, I think," he remarked. "English, too…"

The others were not paying much attention, but I glanced over his shoulder when he looked at the conclusion of the second sheet. On it was written in the same copper-plate hand:

This is the completed writing of the account of Nezam Kha. em.uast, and of Uba-Aner, and speaks concerning the curse of strangling which was (put?) upon Nezam Kha.em.uast, nephew of the mighty King User.maat.ra. Written in the month Tybi by Anena, the owner of this roll. He who speaks against this roll, may Tahuti smite him.

"I think I shall just keep this," he muttered. "Wait! There's a book in the portfolio."

He drew it out. It was a slim volume in dark-blue leather, bearing in gold characters the title, *Tales of the Lost Land*. And the author's name was J. L. Keane. Bencolin looked at me and nodded. I remembered Colette Laverne's words: "Keane was the pen-name under which he had written a book once…" Its date was 1913, and it was privately printed, which would make very difficult any attempt to trace it. *Tales of the Lost Land* contained translations from the papyri in the British Museum: the Harris and Anastasi papyri, selections from the Tell Amarna tablets, and some unclassified matter.

"Another Jack Ketch souvenir, I suppose," the detective commented. "Now—just one thing more."

While Talbot took up the portfolio he searched in the shelves near the staircase door until he found a candle in a bronze holder. Lighting the candle, he held it high and walked out on the landing. As I approached the door, I saw him halfway down the first flight. He was descending backwards, very slowly, and moving the flame of the candle along the bannister at my left. The strong light was reflected in his narrow, cruel eyes. All else was shadow, except for the yellow light on that malignant face. Wind rattled dimly the casement of the window at my right. Silently the face receded down the stair; silently it turned the corner and was lost, so that I saw only a flickering gleam in the depths of the well. But once I heard him laugh.

… Talbot had drawn up a chair before the table and he was examining the contents of the portfolio. Sir John was seated in a chair over near the door to the bedrooms, where I could make out only his dim shape. The vast vault was very still. I leaned against one of the curio cabinets, and the tides of death and silence bore me into murky realms.

"Nezam Kha.em.uast, nephew of the mighty User.maat.ra!"— that is, of Rameses the Great. I remembered that tablet of stone under the fierce blue sky, on the route to the Nubian gold-mines: "Rich in years, strong in victories, Lord of the Diadems, Mighty in Truth of Ra, King of Upper and Lower Egypt, Rameses Beloved of Amen." And I remembered ruined Karnak, sticky with brooding heat, when bats were wheeling in a lemon-coloured sky at dusk, and torches grew bright along the Nile…

Now did Nezam El Moulk, in this year of grace, fancy in himself a likeness to that first Nezam of the papyrus? The books, the ornaments, even the sarcophagus, bore out this whispered reference to the "curse of strangling" upon the sons of the first Nezam. What fancies, then, were hidden in the skull of El Moulk? A vision of the sun on painted columns, of flowers and the flutes of Thebes—so that he ran screaming from a hangman in London fog?

I have heard people say that no man really believes in reincarnation, and I know that they are wrong. Buried with the kings is a weird and potent magic, which turns the student's brain as on a colossal wheel. It blinds and befuddles him, so that whispering voices murmur round the lamp of his study. Where Talbot sat now behind the green-globed lamp, I fancied El Moulk sitting at his papyri, brooding, through the long flute-haunted night. "Lord of the Diadems, Mighty in Truth of Ra, King of Upper and Lower Egypt, Rameses Beloved of Amen!"—How those rolling words echoed in cymbal-crash, in the rapid shrill plaudits of the trumpet! "And the rumble of his battle-chariots is as the noise of rain and thunder, and sweepeth as the dark hurricane of the desert; and upright in his chariot of silver he weareth the armour of bronze, and on his brow the royal diadem of the snake; with his right hand he hurleth the dart, and his left is for the sword wherewith he smote the Khita, and none may prevail against him."

Still the dark figures of my companions did not move, occupied with, I wondered, what such mill-wheel speculations as my own. For

I was listening to ghostly bugles in old wars—bugles that woke the coloured halls of Karnak, and then went crying through the streets of Thebes. And as I thought of Ra's Chosen lashing his two Arab horses, Victory-in-Thebes and Nura-is-Satisfied, in triumph up the Avenue of Sphinxes, I turned my eyes naturally to the collection of weapons which hung above the sarcophagus.

Leaning against the curio cabinet, I studied them. It was, as I have mentioned before, an almost complete equipment of fighting-gear. Stay!—There was something subtly wrong about the placing, some peculiarity in their arrangement on the wall. Between the dagger and the mace was a large gap which cried aloud for some trophy to balance them. For a second time I approached the sarcophagus and examined narrowly the wall above it, but the light was too dim. Then I drew up a carven chair beside the mummy-case. Standing on the chair, I snapped open my cigarette-lighter and moved its flame along the unfilled space between. The plaster walls were kalsomined in light green, and very dusty; I saw clearly an outline where there was no dust. Something *had* hung there. Something in the shape of a broad-bladed short sword with a long handle. Just above the outline was the nail by which the sword had hung. If I deduced correctly, it was the evil double-edged blade which the scribe Meremapt calls "the throat-cutter." A vision of the chauffeur's gaping throat swam across my mind…

"What the devil does this mean?" snarled a voice.

I turned, startled, to see Lieutenant Graffin standing in the doorway. His red and truculent eye moved from Talbot to me; he had not seen Sir John. He was leaning against the doorjamb, fingers hooked in his waistcoat pockets, and he seemed at the stage where he would presently offer to fight somebody. I looked him up and down while he glared at me, turned without appearing to see him, and continued my scrutiny of the wall.

Talbot said, sternly: "We've had little enough help from you, sir. These rooms want looking into, and that's what we intend doing. We'll do it with your assistance or without it, but I advise you to keep quiet—for your own good."

The other's voice grew high:

"You'll threaten me, will you?" he shrilled. "You'll—" The loud voice cracked; there was a sound like a choking cry, and a sudden jarring crash from the chords of the piano. I whirled about. Graffin had stumbled. His hand was on the piano keys. Then he straightened, making frantic motions towards the staircase door. He cried drunkenly, "Go back, you damn fool; go back—!"

Bencolin stepped through the door, shifting the candle so that it now illumined his face. Graffin stared as though he could not believe his eyes, and put shaking fingers before them. "Oh!" he said; "oh!…"

Now the little inspector was touched with a repressed ferocity; his brown jaw came forward squarely, and he walked with jerky steps over to Graffin. "Yes, that's M. Bencolin," he snapped. "Well—whom did you think it was? By God, I *will* have some sense out of this!"

Graffin looked at him loftily, wrinkling his long nose. He said:

"My dear fellow… nerves. Most unfortunate, you see. Nerves." He sat down shakily on the piano bench.

Talbot regarded Bencolin as though to say, despairingly, "He's lying—but what can I do about it?" There might be, I thought then, some merit in the good old-fashioned third degree. In the meantime I saw through the door that Bencolin had blown out the candle and put it carelessly on the newel-post. Now Graffin had made out the dim figure of Sir John, and he moistened his lips as though to speak, when the bedroom door opened to disclose Joyet. The lieutenant was growing more and more flustered.

"Hullo! Er—you back, Joyet? I—er—hardly expected it. Thought you were in Paris…"

Joyet ventured into English. "I am return'," he replied, belliger-
ently. "It surprise you, hah?"

"Tell me, Monsieur Graffin," Bencolin said, picking up the portfolio on the desk, "was anybody ever in the habit of making use of
that staircase, to your knowledge?"

Graffin's lip was twisted back. He hiccoughed in a way that shook
his whole body. "Thinking about the souvenirs Jack Ketch left us, eh?"
he demanded. The owlish eye regarded Joyet craftily. "Don't know,
I'm sure. Maybe *he* can tell you about it. He had a quaint habit of
locking me in my room at night."

"Sohnovabeesh!" yelled Joyet, whose face had become the colour
of boiling lava. "Sohnovabeesh! I lock him in 'is rhoom, for he get
so drunk he make trouble, and can't do noting with 'im. He get
drunk and he—"

"Really? Ah, well," murmured Graffin, with overdone laziness,
"not wishing to contradict the word of a servant—"

"Sohnovabeesh!" Joyet shouted again. "I punch your goddam
face, hah?"

"Quiet!" said Bencolin, seizing Joyet's arm. He addressed a few
rapid words to the Frenchman, who stood glowering and dusting the
arms of his coat with apoplectic energy. Homicidal words rumbled
beneath his curled moustache.

"What vul—garity!" said Graffin, hiccoughing. His wandering
eye fixed itself intently on a corner of the mantelpiece. "At any rate,
I have heard voices out here at night…"

"Voices?"

"Voy'z," agreed Graffin, and nodded. "Now, gentlemen, I have
finished."

He turned away with dignity, and would not listen, for he began to
play selections from "Aïda" on the piano. The man had swift, supple
fingers, with a magnificent touch. When Talbot tried to interrupt,

he said that he was flight-commander and would brook no insubordination in the army of Egypt. When we presently left him, the stately thunder of the grand march followed us out into the passage.

"It's no good," Talbot muttered. "That place is a madhouse."

He glanced back at the weird green light in the doorway, and then he added, "I can't see that we've learned anything of material importance. Short of arresting the man and grilling him, there's no way to get at any truth. That's what I shall have to do... What were you doing on the staircase, sir? Did you find anything?"

Bencolin hesitated. "Yes," he answered after a pause—"yes, I found something. I was not looking for it, but I found it. And it explains much. I suggest, Inspector, a little interview with Mademoiselle Laverne."

Taking his hand from his pocket, he held it out to Talbot, and his gaze wandered slowly up to meet the inspector's. During another pause we heard the great march crash to its climax in the room behind.

Talbot said grimly, "I see."

The light was very dim, but in his palm glowed a coil of turquoise and silver. It was a woman's bracelet. Talbot opened the red bandana wherein he was carrying the trophies we had found in the desk, and wrapped up the bracelet inside. We walked in terrible silence to the lift.

X I

A Light on the Stairs

THE REMAINING EVENTS OF THAT MORNING AND EARLY AFTER-
noon would make tedious telling. Looking back over my notes,
I see that nothing was brought to light which had any material
importance on the subsequent investigation. An inquest on the dead
chauffeur was held at one-thirty, but it was as dull as most inquests,
and determined merely that Richard Smail had met his death at the
hands of a person or persons unknown. The only revelation was the
admirable way in which the press cooperated with Talbot. We got
none of your tabloid sensations. The barest and most unadorned
accounts had already appeared: one Nezam El Moulk was not to
be found, and his chauffeur was dead. The subsequent events were
suppressed. At Talbot's suggestion, the whole affair was not even
given first-page space. It would, I reflected, have broken the heart
of any American city editor; but such is the power of Scotland Yard.

After the inquest, Talbot was called in for a conference with
Superintendent Mason, which Bencolin attended. The divisional
inspector, I knew, wished to work independently for the present,
without the assistance of any of the special force from the Yard, but
with Bencolin as a sort of unofficial partner. The famous Parisian
detective was as well known at the grim building above Westminster
Pier as he was in that other building on the quai des Orfèvres, and
Talbot anticipated little difficulty.

Pursuing his theory about lost streets, he had already referred
the matter to the Ordnance Survey, under the Controller of H. M.
Stationery Office, the British Museum, and the Library of the House

of Commons. London would unquestionably be ransacked. He had a talk with Dr. Pilgrim on this subject, and, though the doctor was dubious, he promised his assistance. At three o'clock Talbot and Bencolin left for Scotland Yard, followed shortly by Sir John. Pilgrim and I were left chatting at one of the low red-topped tables in the bar. It was a snug room, with low red-plush chairs, lights in great inverted bowls, and curtains drawn against the thickening fog. We had a pipe and a bottle of Bass, for the Brimstone Club never observed hours. Since Talbot had communicated a good deal of the story to Pilgrim, I told him as much more as I thought discreet. His big ugly face was puckered as he listened, and he cocked an eye thoughtfully down the stem of his pipe. At length he shook his head.

"I'm no detective, of course," he remarked, "though I do believe that a historian who reconstructs past events must have the detective faculty rather highly developed. He hunts his meagre evidence through a hundred libraries, on the slenderest clues; he fits together fragments and weighs testimony, to solve a puzzle which is forgotten or to track down a murderer who has been dead five hundred years. The crimes of Jack the Ripper, I assure you, require not half so much skill at unravelling as the crimes of the Borgia." The widow's peak was drawn down on his wrinkled forehead, and his mouth pursed up. Again he shook his head. "I'm bound to say I don't favour Inspector Talbot's theory... Ruination Street. Hm! yes. Ruination Street. No, I don't believe I shall find it in my maps..."

He looked up.

"But I may be able to give you a bit of help. Are you doing anything in particular at the moment, Mr. Marle?"

"Why, no! I've a tea engagement later..."

"Possibly, then, you might care to step round with me to my offices? They're pretty much a sham, but they let me study in quiet. It's just round the corner in St. James's Street."

"Certainly. Your maps are there?"

He paused, opening his tobacco-pouch, and contemplated me from under shaggy eyebrows. "My maps are there, yes. But that isn't what I meant. You detective chaps like to—go over the ground, don't you, or whatever the term is? The window of my back room overlooks the alley behind the club here. From that window I can see straight across into the windows of this man El Moulk's apartment…"

I sat upright.

"Mind, I don't say it means anything!" said Pilgrim, raising his hand. "I didn't know until now that those *were* his rooms. But when I heard all these things I remembered… Shall we start?"

Taking our hats and coats from the hallway, we went down the steps into Pall Mall. Pilgrim, a bulky figure in slouch hat and curious box-caped cloak, strode beside me with enormous steps. He was strung with nervous energy; he kept chewing his pipe stem, and darting glances from right to left as we walked. It was bitter weather. Street lamps made weird and distorted blurs in the fog, the sidewalks were treacherous with ice, and in this chaos the noise of all auto horns had joined in one infernal tooting uproar. Phantoms crowded us close in the streaky glow of St. James's Street. The jut of Pilgrim's jaw, the angle of his pipe, and the curve of his hat brim were all poked forward, like the confident snuffing of a dog; and his gigantic lope had carried him well ahead of me when we stopped. It was a sedate-looking building, rather like a club. We ascended, round several dimly lighted landings, to the fourth floor.

"Those are my offices," Pilgrim said, sardonically, indicating a ground-glass door. We blundered through a couple of dark rooms; at length he snapped on a light and closed the door behind him.

It was a bare brown room, furnished with odds and ends of shelves, ranks of decrepit bottles, chemical apparatus, and a bewildering array of books and maps. The desk, on which stood a lamp with a lopsided shade, resembled an architect's work-table; its litter of pens, triangles, rules and coloured inks stood just beneath the window.

"Hm!" said Pilgrim, knocking the ashes from his pipe on the top of an ink-bottle. "My workroom… Have a drink?"

After the amenities, he drew back the curtain of the window. "Now, Mr. Marle, I'm going to turn out the light. If the fog isn't too thick, you shall see it as I saw. Ready?"

The room went dark. Wisps of fog curled past the window, but I could see clearly the windows of the opposite building—particularly those three significant barred ones of El Moulk's study. These were on a level with us not more than twenty feet away. Two of them showed mere greenish cracks of light through closed drapes. But the third—the one on my extreme left—had its drapes pulled back. In the green light I saw the gilded shape of the mummy-case, and above it a section of the weapons on the wall.

"I often work here all night," continued the doctor, "and generally I keep my curtain drawn. But the other night—it was five days ago, to be exact—I was preparing to leave, and I had turned out my light, when I thought to open the window and air the room a bit.

"It was a foggy night, but one of those moving, spotty fogs which sometimes shift and allow you a perfectly clear view. I say night; rather it was one o'clock in the morning, for I heard Big Ben strike. There wasn't a light opposite. I leaned out of the window. And then I heard somebody walking in the alley below."

Pilgrim, that tireless smoker, lighted his pipe again. The match flame showed the pocks and creases in his square face as he sucked at the stem. The eyelids were raised briefly; two luminous greenish eyes studied me momentarily before a film veiled them, and the match went out.

"It was too foggy to distinguish any figure down there, but the footfalls continued to that rear door across the way. Then I heard the sound of a key in a lock; the door opened and closed. You tell me those windows, one above the other beside the study windows, give on the landings of a rear stair. Well, I saw the light of a candle spring up and mount past each window, disappearing as the person rounded the turn of each landing. Curiously enough, there was a partial rift in the fog which gave me rather a good view. Once the candle-flame stopped, and for an instant I thought I saw a shadow so thin and tall that it seemed horrible…

"Just then another light attracted my attention. It was that green lamp in the room opposite. Perhaps the curtains had been too tightly drawn for me to see it before, or perhaps it had just been lighted; in any case, the curtains of one window were drawn away, and I saw silhouetted the figure of a man who seemed to be peering out. It was only for an instant—that shadow against the green light. The curtain fell again. Still the candle continued its march up the stairs. There was something so uncanny about those noiseless shapes, and the colours of their flitting lights, that—I tell you, Mr. Marle I was too fascinated to move. It seemed to me like a ghastly little marionette show. You know"—I saw his rugged profile a moment on the grey of the window, and he leaned over to tap me on the arm—"you know, to me there is something inexpressibly dreadful about those Punch and Judy shows, where the children sit and laugh while Punch clubs everybody to death—the puppets' squeaky voices, and the *thwack* of the club on wooden heads—until Punch is finally carried off by Jack Ketch. Silly of me, but I used to think what a dark and horrible world lay inside the box of a Punch and Judy show."

He laughed softly.

"Even the faces are hideous on those murderous dolls… But no matter! I grew to calling that my little marionette theatre, and to wondering what shameful act might be played there. I had to rag myself out of it; I laughed at the fancy, I kept my curtain resolutely drawn, until yesterday afternoon."

I had not realized until I attempted speech that my own voice was not steady. I said, "You mean the afternoon—before the murder?"

"Yesterday, yes. I had come back here (it was about five o'clock), and I thought to myself, 'My dolls don't appear in the afternoon. I'll chance a look.'

"It was rather foggy, if you remember, but the distance here is short. Look there! That was what I saw!—that same window lighted, as it is lighted now. I saw the mummy-case, and the weapons above it; they were very blurred by the fog, but I saw them. I was about to turn away, when I noticed a *hand*."

"A hand?"

"Yes. It was a small hand—a woman's, it seemed to me—but I cannot be sure because of the fog. For a moment I thought my eyes were playing tricks. The hand hovered directly over the top of the sarcophagus; it was as ghostly as those other presences in the green light. It seemed to be disembodied, until I realized that its owner must be standing on a chair in the very corner, hidden by a corner of the drapery. It remained poised, as though hesitant, with fingers uplifted before a collection of weapons there. Then it took down—"

"A very short-bladed sword, with a curved haft."

The doctor's start was so very slight that the glowing coal in his pipe hardly quivered. I could not see his face well, but I knew that he was examining me hard. After a pause he asked, quietly:

"How did you know that?"

"Saw its outline in the dust. Not very mysterious, really."

"Well, you gave me a turn," confessed Pilgrim, chuckling wryly. "It sounded like something out of a book—not that I read 'em. Yes, you're quite right, Mr. Marle: it was a short sword or long dagger, though at this distance I saw no curved haft. Just as the hand took it down, this person seemed to be aware of the open curtain. And again the curtain fell... End of my marionette show! I am not sure I want the little puppets to dance again.—What do you think of it?"

"Look here, Doctor. You really ought to have seen Talbot about this. It may be of the utmost importance."

The glowing bowl brightened and darkened steadily now. "My dear fellow, of course I shall. I only realized its bearing when I learnt about the whole matter from you awhile ago—I didn't know those rooms belonged to El Moulk." He shrugged. "Besides, it might have been a mere vagary of mine. We get this way sometimes. So I hesitated. But, see here..." He snapped on the light again. When the bleak and dusty room was again revealed, I felt more comfortable. Pilgrim threw himself into a creaky desk chair, and with extended foot he hooked out another chair by the rung and motioned me to it. Sprawled there, with his greatcoat collar still turned up, pipe dangling loosely between strong teeth, he stared hard at the litter on his desk.

"... see here, Mr. Marle, I'm not one of your detective chaps who go about finding cuff-links and things in dead people's hands. But I flatter myself that I have conducted some pretty shrewd investigations on clues several hundred years old, as I told you. There was King William Rufus, for example, mysteriously slain in the New Forest. The case has every feature of an up-to-date thriller. A man with a hundred enemies, a drunken hunting-party, a haunted wood with blue lights at night, and then the big red-bearded devil lying in the underbrush at dawn with an arrow through his chest. Who killed him?—Yes, every feature of an up-to-date thriller, except that it all occurred in the twelfth century. I think, Mr. Marle, that I could name his murderer. Well, and who really blew up Kirk o'Field on the night poor Darnley's throat was cut? What was the name of the sombre gentleman in the iron mask (which wasn't iron, by the way)? That is the sort of case *I* get. Here in my ghostly Scotland Yard I can track my criminal beyond the very tomb, and extradite murderers from the happy country of hell."

He quirked a shaggy eyebrow, and the big ugly face was lighted by a smile. He did not raise his chin from his breast when he went on:

"That is by way of tedious preface for some theories of mine which are doubtless all nonsense. Nevertheless…"

Scowling, he kicked moodily at the edge of the desk. "Nevertheless, suppose El Moulk isn't dead?"

"I beg your pardon."

"I said, 'Suppose El Moulk isn't dead,'" repeated the doctor, sitting up with abrupt energy. "Suppose, in short, the whole thing is an elaborate bit of hocus-pocus, staged by El Moulk himself?"

"The idea is—novel."

"It's novel, right enough. But see here," said Pilgrim, earnestly. "There's something dashed funny in the whole affair. According to the evidence, El Moulk travels in a bullet-proof car, puts bars on his windows and double locks on his doors, and never allows anybody in his rooms. What protection does it give him? Apparently this Jack Ketch is able to stroll into the rooms whenever he likes, leave a souvenir, and depart without being hindered by locks or seen by any servants. They just seem to take it as casually as though he were the postman. El Moulk, for his part, takes good care that every time he receives a threatening parcel somebody sees him in a fit of gibbering terror… Reasonable so far?"

"Yes."

"Next item! That enclosed staircase with the locked door, which everybody says is never used, has all the appearances of a public highway. At least, somebody is in the habit of using it for visits at one o'clock in the morning—with a key to the alley door, mind you. While the visitor is going up somebody is awake in the apartment, as I saw it, and obviously lets the visitor in…"

"Hold on! That doesn't necessarily follow."

"Well, I can tell you I watched the place for an hour after the person went in, and nobody came out. Unless he was camping outside the door, it looks very like collusion. It looks as though he *lived* there, and somebody in the apartment was waiting up for him. What about El Moulk himself, coming in late? You told me yourself that this afternoon, when Graffin was there and Monsieur Bencolin walked through that door holding up a candle, Graffin mistook him for somebody else and yelled, 'Go back, you fool,' or something like that. Doesn't it smell strongly of collusion between the inmates? If we suppose that El Moulk planned his own fake murder, doesn't it explain everything?"

The man's memory was amazing; he seemed to recall the smallest point I had mentioned, and the points dovetailed with devilish plausibility. I said:

"Everything except *why* anybody would plan a hoax on such a terrific scale… As I understand it, you are assuming that the 'persecution' was El Moulk's conniving; that there is no hidden enemy, no Jack Ketch, and no Ruination Street; that El Moulk himself killed the chauffeur, with a weapon from his own rooms, and is at present in hiding; in short, that the whole case is one complete tissue of lies from beginning to end. Ee-God!" I said, "Let me get my breath!"

Pilgrim's eyes were shining with excitement, though he tried to remain very calm and very judicial. He poured himself a little brandy, turning the thing over in his mind.

"In hiding," he agreed, nodding vigorously, "close to his own rooms; perhaps *in* his rooms—"

"That's no good. We searched them."

"All right. I have it! What about those other suites at the back of the club? There are three corresponding ones, one on each floor over the other, and each must give on the private stair. I'll just lay you a fiver that at least one of them is unoccupied..."

"Two, as a matter of fact. Sir John has the one on the ground floor. But the suite under El Moulk is empty—"

"Ah, now you see a use for that private stair, don't you? He has a hideaway under his own rooms, and a means of communication with the outside free from all surveillance. It explains how those trinkets from the dead man might have been returned to the table; it explains Graffin's consternation when he thought El Moulk had blundered from hiding, and also what frightened the kid. Some mad idea of gibbets and vengeance must have come to El Moulk from brooding over his papyri, and this is the result."

I stared at the faded brown curtain hanging before the window, while Pilgrim watched me carefully from over the rim of his glass. Unquestionably, in its accounting for details, the theory was so startling and so perfect that I found myself believing it. And yet! And yet some stubborn sense of *wrongness* obtruded itself...

"It's ingenious," I said. "It's damnably ingenious, Doctor. Nevertheless! It makes sense of all the parts, but nonsense of the whole. You explain the facts by demonstrating that the real El Moulk must be a thousand times crazier than the mythical Jack Ketch. You produce thoroughly credible reasons to account for wildly incredible conduct... Why should El Moulk do all these fantastic things? I can believe that Jack Ketch killed the chauffeur in order to kill El Moulk. But I can't believe that El Moulk killed the chauffeur in order to play a joke."

Pilgrim laughed.

"Oh, come, Mr. Marle! I don't profess to be able to explain everything. I was merely suggesting a line of thought. But, take my word for it, there's a good reason behind El Moulk's conduct—a very good reason for this seeming lunacy. And you can scarcely blame me if I am unable to hand you El Moulk's signed confession in the course of one afternoon... No, really, does it sound a worth-while lead?"

I rose. "So worth-while, doctor, that if you've a telephone here I want to ring up Talbot at the Yard and have him look into those vacant rooms at once..."

Opening the door to his consulting-room, Pilgrim turned on the light and indicated the phone. It was a bare, monastic place, with a green-shaded drop-lamp over a closed roll-top desk, and smelt of medicine. I sat down before the phone, which was attached to the desk. Talbot, undoubtedly, would still be with the superintendent. Courteously and in rapid succession I was connected with Gerrard 4223, Central 5091, Royal 8550, and Holborn 336; but, being used to Paris telephones where you get no answer at all, I was encouraged. While engaged in correcting the impression of some gentleman at City 1041 that I wished to engage a table at Wilkinson's Boiled Beef House, I noticed that the doctor had closed the door communicating with his workroom. I could hear him walking about rapidly, and once I saw his shadow fall across the ground-glass panel... Presently I was put through to Scotland Yard. Superintendent Mason told me that Bencolin and Talbot had just left.

I pondered. They had intended going to see the Laverne woman, and in all probability I should be able to catch them there. On an impulse I asked for the Mount Street number, and this time I was answered almost immediately by a girl's pleasant voice.

"May I speak to Miss Laverne, please?"

"Miss Laverne is out at present. This is her maid speaking. Is there any message?"

"No-o. Can you tell me where she went?"

A pause. The voice asked my name. Finally it replied: "Why, yes, sir. She went to Scotland Yard early this afternoon with the gentleman who called here for her."

I rang off. Rejoining the doctor, who was sprawled in the swivel-chair as though he had not moved, I explained matters, and added:

"Lord knows where they are now. But if you're at the club about dinner-time, I'm sure we can find them. And if you see any more manifestations—"

"Righto. Glad to give you any help I can."

He conducted me to the door of his office, and I blundered down the dimlit stairs to St. James's Street. Before going to Sharon's, it might be just as well to drop in at the Brimstone and leave a note for them in case they turned up. What Colette Laverne had said under examination at Scotland Yard might be very interesting indeed, especially if she talked to somebody who really understood cross-examination.

But there was no need for a note. I ran into them in the lobby; they wore coats and hats and were just going out.

"Well!" said Bencolin. "I thought you were going over to see Miss Grey?"

"I am. But listen! There's news—important evidence—"

"Walk along with us, then, and let's hear it. We're going to pay a call on Colette Laverne and have a talk with her."

I looked at him in surprise.

"On Colette Laverne? Didn't you see her at Scotland Yard?"

Inspector Talbot opened his eyes wide. Bencolin's hand paused in turning up his coat collar. He snapped, "What do you mean, Jeff?"

"Well, didn't you send a man to take her to Scotland Yard this afternoon? Her maid told me—"

"O my God!" Talbot said, in a toneless voice. Under the bright lights of the lobby his dusty face was white, and a horrible fear smote into me. Suddenly he stamped his feet on the ground like a man distracted.

"Nobody was sent after her! And, anyway, she wouldn't have been taken to Scotland Yard; she would have been taken to Vine Street. Quick! when did this happen?"

"I don't know. I just talked to her maid on the telephone; she said it was early this afternoon—"

Talbot spread out his hands toward Bencolin. "He's got her," said the inspector; "Jack Ketch. And I posted a man there this morning to watch the house! What was the matter with him? *What?*"

Before Bencolin could reply, Victor appeared from the passage towards the lounge. He said,

"Inspector Talbot is wanted on the telephone…"

Victor's smug face blurred before me. The evil possibilities of those words crystallized into one monstrous shape—a crossbeam and a noose. Talbot looked blankly before him for an instant, and then he almost ran towards the telephone, while Bencolin and I stood motionless in the chill bright lobby. In a few minutes Talbot came back. He walked slowly. His eyes lifted slowly also.

"'Colette Laverne has been hanged on the gallows in Ruination Street.'" Then his voice broke in fury. "Get a cab—quick! Hurry! We're going to Mount Street!"

XII

The Mirth of the Murderer

WE WERE IN A CAB AND RACING UP ST. JAMES'S STREET before Talbot spoke again.

"They got the message at Vine Street not five minutes ago," he explained. "They shot through orders to trace the call, and found it came from a public call-box in the Burlington Arcade. Two men were sent out at once, but I doubt they'll find anything when they get there. I don't suppose there's any question—?"

Bencolin shook his head.

"It's Jack Ketch, Inspector. But, as suspicious as she was, how did he get her to accompany him? Well! There's no use theorizing now..." I was full of the story I had got from Pilgrim; but, in the stress of this new and ghastly twist of the deviltry, I was silent until we should learn what it meant. Another person had walked out into the fog to be swallowed up in Ruination Street.

"The thing I want to know is," said Talbot, "what happened to Bronson? He's one of my oldest and best men. I set him watching the house this morning; and he had orders to stop everybody who went into the place and find out their business. I thought that was protection enough for her..."

He said no more until our cab stopped before the house in Mount Street. A street lamp near the door threw dim light through the fog on its cloistered and embalmed dignity; its polished door-knobs, its areaway, its glow behind drawn shades. It was sedate, it was—

"We'd better look for Bronson," Talbot muttered, gruffly. The same thought was in all of us as we stared about. Bencolin went to the areaway, where he peered down the steps. No lights showed at the basement level. We heard the scrape of his feet on the stone stairs, and the presentiment of horror choked me like that raw fog...

"Better come down here," he said from the depths. "I just walked on somebody's foot."

A damp chill ground into us as we descended, groping. Then *I* walked on somebody's foot—a foot with a stiff leg, whose shoe seemed to hook into my own. Through fog and gloom a tiny glow appeared. It was Bencolin's cigar-lighter. He was moving it low along the stone floor at the bottom of the stairs. It shone dully on a figure.

The man lay on his back, his head twisted to an upright position against the wall, so that his chin was on his breast in a hideous, broken-necked fashion. He was a young man, and his red hair was sodden with moisture. So were his clothes. One leg was drawn up at the knee, as though he were trying to rise, and his arms crumpled back. All this I saw piece by piece as Bencolin moved the light along him. He wore a light tan overcoat, so that one noted distinctly the scorched black hole over the heart. There was no sign of his hat. And as Bencolin tried to lift his stiff head, I could see on the dead man's face an expression of the most profound surprise.

"Shot," the detective murmured. "Dead for hours."

An automobile whirred past on Mount Street. He had lain alone in this damp little areaway; the assassin had simply jammed the weapon against his chest and pulled the trigger, so that he had slipped down without fuss, and with that mild look of surprise. His hair, I saw again, was of that very pale red which one associates with young people, and I shuddered.

"This is Bronson, I suppose?" Bencolin inquired.

Talbot was still staring at the fallen figure, bent forward on his knees. The inspector rose stiffly. He nodded and blinked.

"Poor devil!" was all he said. He turned, and walked with slow steps back up to the street. Almost immediately we heard a vicious ringing at the door-bell.

The door was opened by a trim, very pretty little brunette in maid's cap and apron. Her eyes were dark blue and had long lashes, and her lips were opened in a slight inquiring smile. The inspector did not waste words.

"I am Inspector Talbot, from Vine Street," he said. "There's a dead man in your areaway. Come down and see if you know him."

For a second she stared at him...

"Come down," snapped Talbot.

She screamed when she saw the thing, screamed and started to run up the stairs, but Talbot held her firmly by the arm.

"Let me be!" she sobbed in the gloom. "I can't!—I—"

"Do you know him? Ever see him before?"

"No!"

We went up into the house. And the moment we passed the threshold we walked into France. It was a Frenchwoman's dwelling, every line of that hallway. The glass chandelier, lighted palely; the mirrors; the white panelling; even that curious odour which is a blending of waxed floors, old coffee, and curtained stuffiness. Backing away from us, the maid shuddered and pressed her hands over her eyes.

"Where is the telephone?" Talbot asked.

"At—at the back of the hall, sir. I'll show—"

"I'll find it. Take these gentlemen in somewhere; we want to talk to you."

She led us into a drawing-room, rather badly lighted, which had the usual dubious oils on the wall and some faded Empire furniture in red. Yes, a *very* pretty girl: black bobbed hair, eyes that were a mixture of blankness and appeal; cool and slim-bodied. Talbot's treatment of her was infamous. I said, "Look here, sit down!" But she only started, and smiled in a vague horrified way as though I had suggested something else entirely, saying, "Oh no, sir!... Let me take your hats."

"We shan't bother with the formalities," said Bencolin. "What is your name?"

"Selden, sir."

"Selden, we want you to tell us everything that happened today."

"I—I don't understand, sir. About what?"

"Everything Miss Laverne did."

She was perfectly calm now, in a waxen, half-smiling way. Her eyes wandered past us to the mantelpiece, but foreboding was in them. The foreboding deepened, and she glanced at us in sudden alarm.

"Yes, sir; of course. I—I had the night off last night, and I was a bit late in getting here this morning. Miss Laverne seemed upset—"

"At what time did you arrive?"

"At a little past nine. She told me she had spent the night with Miss Grey next door. She had come over here early, and she was dressed much earlier than usual. I took up her breakfast. She was—upset." Selden's brows wrinkled slightly, and she smiled in a deprecating way.

"Do you know why she was upset?"

"Oh no, sir!... About half-past ten a Dr. Pilgrim called, and talked with her for a time upstairs—"

She paused as Talbot reappeared through the portières. The death of Bronson had come home sharply to the little inspector, and he showed it.

"Carry on," he said, gruffly. There were creases round his down-pulled mouth; he stood before the door as though he were preparing against a rush.

"She asked for all the morning papers, sir, and sat upstairs, reading them. She—stormed at me a bit, and had a dreadful headache. I could hear her walking about, and she cried. Cook prepared her a lunch, but she simply wouldn't eat it... I—I hope nothing's wrong, sir?" Selden burst out. Then she caught herself up, and continued: "Oh yes! I almost forgot. Early this afternoon there was a telephone call—"

"From whom?"

The girl's eyes shifted; she looked embarrassed and flushed a little.

"Well, sir"—she looked up steadily, and her round lower lip was thrust forward a little—"well, sir, he didn't give his name, but I knew who it was. It was Mr. Nezam El Moulk."

An enormous roaring silence was in the room...

Talbot took his hands out of his pockets slowly, and his eyes took on a wild, witless, despairing stare. Bencolin, who was standing by the table, idly running his finger over it, shot a sideways glance at the girl.

"You are sure of that?" he asked, without surprise.

"Yes, sir. I—I've heard it before. I— Well, I *am* sure!"

Clearly her worry was for the domestic arrangements, and her mind had jumped to that explanation when she saw Scotland Yard— Scotland Yard pointing a stern and virtuous finger at her mistress's morals, and possibly sending them all to jail. This lady was either extraordinarily naïve or else a thorough hypocrite.

"Selden," said Bencolin, musingly, "have you by any chance seen the newspapers today?"

"No, sir; I'm afraid not."

"Or talked to anybody except Miss Laverne?"

"No, sir. Nobody but cook, that is." She was growing more frightened.

"Very well. Miss Laverne spoke to Mr. El Moulk, then. Do you know what was said?"

"Oh *no*, sir!—That is, of course, I did catch a few words, because Miss Laverne was very much excited and talked quite loudly—"

"Ah yes. And what did you catch?"

"Really, sir, nothing that would interest the police!—She just said, 'Yes, I'll go! I'll go with him.' That's all I remember, sir, truly! Afterwards she was quite excited and had ever so much colour in her face, and she sang. She seemed very pleased. So much different from earlier."

"Go on."

"A bit later"—Selden reflected, her blank blue eyes very earnest—"a gentleman called to see Miss Laverne—a Mr. George Dallings, sir. But she wouldn't see him. She yelled—she yelled *rude* things downstairs, if I may say so, sir." A defiant flash rose in the girl.

"I see. And what did Mr. Dallings do?"

"Why, why—he just stood in the hallway, sir. He looked straight ahead of him for a while, and he looked so queer. Then he said, 'Oh! Righto!' and turned around and put on his hat and went out. But then he stopped a second, and looked at me queerer still, and said, 'I say, how long have you lived here? Miss Laverne, I mean?' I told him several months, and he went out as though he couldn't understand something, sir."

"And then?"

"I was helping Miss Laverne dress. She said, 'Selden, there will be a caller here for me, a detective from Scotland Yard. I am going there with him.' She—was *laughing* so much, sir! She said that she would be downstairs, and if the bell rang, for me not to go to the door; she would answer it. But just then the bell *did* ring, and I answered it…"

Talbot's hands clenched. He bent forward involuntarily. The only one of us whom the tensity of that moment did not string to the breaking-point was Selden; but she caught it in our faces, and hesitated.

"Well?" Talbot demanded, hoarsely.

"Why, sir, it was only Miss Grey from next door. Miss Laverne came downstairs, and I left them talking together in here. That's all I know, sir!"

"You didn't see Miss Laverne again?"

"No, sir! I'd brought her wraps down, and—and I went belowstairs, with cook. I didn't see her leave, but I heard the front door close, and I knew she must have gone."

"Did you hear the door-bell again?"

"Oh yes, sir. But she had told me not to answer it, you see."

Bencolin remained unruffled, tracing little designs with his finger on the table. "And at what time did you hear the door-bell then?"

"I don't know, sir, I swear! Three o'clock—three-thirty—I don't know. Maybe cook can tell you."

Talbot put in: "You heard the closing of the street door. Did you hear any sound like a shot?"

"A shot, sir?" Selden was growing hysterical. She hesitated, motioned towards the street with sudden knowledge, and said, "You—you mean the poor gentleman who's *dead*? No! No, sir. I— We did hear a sound, that is, once, and cook said, 'Somebody's blown out a tyre…'"

"All right," said Talbot. "Go and get this cook now. Send her up here."

Sharp now in the street rose the crying of a police car. There was a thud of feet on the pavement, and a long peal from the door-bell.

"Go and get Miss Grey," Bencolin told me. "Bring her over immediately."

When I went down the steps, grim figures in the fog were directing the smoky rays of bull's-eye lanterns down the areaway. Feet scraped on the stairs, and I heard smothered curses. A voice said, "Somebody go and unlock this area door from the inside…"

Sharon opened the door of the other house before I could reach for the bell. She wore blue, as became her; the expression of the amber eyes was a look of fear, and I knew she had noticed the tumult.

"Jeff," she said, "something's *happened*, hasn't it?"

I told her rapidly. Her flushed cheek went pale and she clenched her hands in a baffled way. "Something," she muttered, "always something!" From her look faded the dreaming of the firelight by which she had been sitting; her perfume, the exquisite wave of her hair, seemed futile, like the tête-à-tête we had arranged. A whiff of fog swirled into that low-lit interior which suggested deep sofas and the intimacy of old blue china. Raw dampness withered it, as it might wither the fragile hues of a painting on silk. From the next house jarred the creak of an opening door. A voice said, "Take him easy, boys…"

"Do you know anything?" I asked.

"But I saw him!—the man she went with!"

"And you recognized him?"

"How should I recognize him? Besides, I didn't see his face. Come along; let's get this over. Nice quiet meetings we always have!"

We hurried over. As we entered the door of the drawing-room, a red-faced woman of ample proportions, apparently the cook, was just stamping out in a huff. We found Bencolin seated in a chair, staring at the head of his stick as he twirled it between grey-gloved hands. Talbot stood by the mantelpiece, making notes. By the doorway Selden was hesitating…

Sharon's frigid and easy grace dominated that red-hung room. Her face was quite expressionless now, and the black eyelashes flickered over cool, impersonal eyes. She became a thing of clean wind and light; that is the only way it can be described. Taking a cigarette from a silver box on a tabouret, very calmly, she lighted it and closed the lid of the box with a snap. Her quick eye wandered to Selden, measured her in an instant, and showed a faint flash of calculation as she turned away.

She laughed. "We have a habit of meeting at murders, monsieur," she said to Bencolin. Sharon on parade! The Sharon of iced flesh, who mocked.

"I have a recollection," said Bencolin, lifting a thoughtful eyebrow, "that mademoiselle is the perfect hostess, even to a corpse. The gentleman opposite you is Inspector Talbot. Be so good as to tell him what happened when you were here this afternoon."

She dropped into a chair.

"Not much, really. I came over here about three-thirty—possibly a bit earlier. Colette was just coming downstairs. We sat in this room for a while and talked. Afterwards someone called for her, and she went out with him. That's all... Oh yes! On the doorstep I was stopped by a young man who said he was a detective from Vine Street, and wanted to know what I was doing there."

"Be a little more explicit, if you please," suggested Bencolin. "She seemed in good spirits?"

"In very good spirits? Oh, rather! I've never seen her look so happy—which," murmured Sharon, looking sideways at her cigarette, "is an achievement for Colette. She kept hinting at some mysterious thing she had just learned."

"Did she tell you what it was?"

"Oh no! I gathered that her precious Egyptian was safe and sound, that's all." She shrugged, and her sulky mouth was compressed. "While we were talking, the door-bell rang... I'm forgetting something. Just a bit before that we heard a noise; that must have been the shot. I jumped, and said, 'That sounded like a shot,' but she said: 'Ba-a-a-h, darling, you have got the nerves.'... Of course, when *she* had nerves, she must get ever so much sym-pa-thee, darling. I remember the time; it was twenty-five minutes to four."

Overdoing it, she stifled a yawn.

"She answered the bell, and I heard her talking to somebody outside. The portières were drawn, so I couldn't see who it was, and, anyway, the light in the hallway was very dim. I heard her laughing. Then she put her head through the curtains and said she must go...

"She was out on the sidewalk when I started down the steps, and she called to me to close the door. There was a man standing near the street lamp in the fog…"

The simulation of laziness left Sharon. Her eyes were fixed.

"He was a tall man with his collar turned up. I couldn't see him very well. He was hailing a taxi then. As I started down she waved her hand to me. She was laughing hard, and all of a sudden the man joined in her laughter. He—he took hold of her arm, still laughing.

"As the cab stopped, she looked down, and there was a man's hat lying in the middle of the sidewalk…"

Across my mind drifted the memory of that sprawled hatless corpse lying at the foot of the areaway, its pale-red hair shining dully and the scorch of black powder-burns over its heart. Lying there, its hat on the sidewalk, while Colette Laverne and her laughing, merry-hearted companion waited for their cab… The echo of evil jollity coiled round this silent room where Sharon sat with one hand pressed to her temple, staring…

"And," she continued, "when Colette saw it, she said something like: 'Oooo, look! Somebody has left his old hat here!' And the man said in a low voice, speaking French, 'He probably doesn't need it any more, mademoiselle.' She only laughed and gave the hat a kick, and it rolled out into the gutter. They got into the cab and drove away."

XIII

The Turquoise Bracelet

O F ALL THE GHOULISH MIRTH IN THIS CASE, IT REQUIRED only that last little pleasantry to climax the horror. It was so diabolically typical of the shadowy man we pursued, and so typical of the woman who was his victim. It remained in my mind long after Sharon had ceased to speak; even long after she had left the house.

There was much more talk, and questioning which lasted a long time; but we learned nothing new.

"We are going to have a little council of war here," Bencolin had said. "I suggest, Jeff, that you arrange to go out for dinner with Miss Grey, or something of the sort, and then forget her for the next hour or so."

I took her back to the house, so shaken and bewildered that not even Sharon seemed real. When I rejoined them, Talbot and Bencolin were the only ones in the room. Bencolin closed the folding-doors to the hall, pointing to chairs.

"You had better sit down," he suggested, grimly. "We are going to clear up a few points in this case now. Since the murderer has forced my hand—"

Pilgrim's theories, pushed to the back of my mind, rushed over me now in an incoherent flood. I told them everything I had heard, with the doctor's interpretation. Previously I had given it scant credence. But now that we heard Miss Laverne had received a telephone call coming from El Moulk—or somebody the maid swore was El Moulk—the ugly plausibility of it all emerged in sharp colours of truth.

Bencolin listened without comment, sitting back, shading his eyes with his hand. Only when I mentioned the weapon on the wall, the short sword taken down by the inexplicable hand, did he snatch his hand away in excitement.

"The weapon!" he cried. "Yes, of course... it would be something like that. Good, Jeff! Excellent! The actuality of it escaped me. Though, of course, it makes no difference to the sequence of events. A kitchen knife would have served just as well..."

"And Pilgrim's theory?"

"Oh, as to that—beautiful, my friend, beautiful. And not a word of truth in it from start to finish."

Talbot stared at him. An uneasy expression had been pinching down his eyelids while I spoke; it was clear that he more than half believed Pilgrim's to be the true explanation.

"But, see here, sir," he said, dubiously, "now we learn that Mr. El Moulk *seems* to be alive—!"

The thin lines tightened down past Bencolin's moustache and pointed beard. His narrow eyes glittered under their hooked brows. He slapped the arm of the chair impatiently.

"Of course he is! When did I ever deny it? Isn't that exactly what I've been trying to tell you all day? It's the trend of Jack Ketch's game; his monstrous sacrifice; his fine, balanced, rounded vengeance! El Moulk spoke over that telephone. He spoke with Jack Ketch's gun at his heart, and drew that woman to Ruination Street. And now that they have both been lured into the same trap, they are trussed and ready for the sacrifice in Ruination Street. Remember that the executioner in the old days did more than merely *hang* his victims. There were some delicate disembowellings before death..."

Talbot sat down slowly, lowering himself with the utmost care. There was sweat on his forehead.

"God in heaven!" he said, quietly, as though he prayed. "And to think they're somewhere in this city and we haven't the faintest trace—"

"Oh, nonsense!" said Bencolin. "I know where they are."

"You—you—*know*—?"

"Certainly."

"And yet you sit there like a damned dummy—!" Talbot caught himself up, the veins swelling on his dusty forehead. "I—I beg your pardon, sir," he muttered, and swallowed the blast that choked him. "All the *same*…"

Bencolin did not even blink. He sat regarding Talbot sideways out of his long, gleaming, inscrutable eyes, elbow on the chair arm and fingers at his temple. From the mantelpiece, the ticking of a rockwork clock was as drops falling into a fountain…

"Inspector," Bencolin said, thoughtfully, after a long pause, "you liked this man Bronson, didn't you?"

"We—we all rather liked him, sir."

"And when you go into the Old Bailey to testify against his murderer, you want to be sure that his murderer goes to the gallows, don't you?"

"Yes."

"Ah yes!" Bencolin shifted the position of his arm slightly. He shrugged. "Not that it makes the slightest difference to me. Call out your flying squad, if you like, and in less time than that"—he snapped his fingers—"I'll have you in Ruination Street… But if you do, Inspector, I assure you that you will never take Jack Ketch. Moreover, even when you know who he is you will never convict him of murder. He has not harmed the people who can testify against him, do you see? The only ones he has harmed are Bronson and the chauffeur. I haven't my Sûreté laboratory here, unfortunately, and I cannot promise to convict him of *their* murders."

He paused.

"I believe that for some hours yet the lives of El Moulk and the woman are as safe as though you had them under your protection. Tonight, as Jack Ketch told you, is the anniversary of that shooting ten years ago. At just the right time, to the very minute and not before then, he will tighten the noose. On that belief I want you to stake three lives."

"*Three* lives?"

The detective chuckled. "You don't see it yet, do you, Talbot?" he asked, musingly. "Yes, three lives. There is to be another victim."

After a silence Talbot sat back and drew out his notebook.

"You said a moment ago you were going to clear up some points in this case. Well—I am listening."

"Very well," murmured Bencolin, nodding. He frowned across at the mantelpiece. "I do not think I have ever known a case into which every detail fitted so evenly to form a central pattern. They did not lead us astray, these details. They were simply presented to us with each person's opinion attached, and, besides fitting the detail itself into the design, everybody tried to fit in the opinion also. The result was a nightmare.

"Let us take up Pilgrim's ingenious hypothesis first, because it is the very beginning of the whole affair. We can demolish it by simply restating his evidence combined with evidence which we all know."

He took out a cigar, but he did not light it.

"We know, first of all, that El Moulk and the Laverne woman were working together to discover the identity of Jack Ketch. In pursuit of this end, they were endeavouring to worm out of Dallings evidence which they thought Dallings possessed. This was very obvious from the very story Dallings told us at the beginning—the glaringly crude way he had been accosted by El Moulk, the pick up at the night club, the clear evidence of collusion between the Laverne woman and El

Moulk; and, of course, it was the reason why I asked Dallings whether he had been 'questioned' by her.

"Last Monday night—five nights ago, you recall—Dallings got drunk and insisted on going home with her. She eluded him, he lost himself in the fog, and had his various adventures, finding himself at length in Ryder Street. You may recall that I asked him *how long* this whole process had taken. His reply was startling, for he said, 'Not more than twenty minutes.' In other words, on a foggy night, when he must grope his way slowly, when he has no idea where he is going and blunders round in circles most of the time—under these circumstances, is it possible to believe that he walked all the way from this house to Ryder Street, *a distance of several miles*, in twenty minutes? More than this, he would have had to pass one of the most brilliantly lighted sections of London on the way, and he would be sure to run into crowds… It means, Inspector, that he never brought her to this house at all."

Bencolin lighted his cigar and puffed at it for a few moments.

"Dallings himself realized the absurdity of this when today, for the first time, he learned that her home was in Mount Street. That was why he was puzzled when he called this afternoon, and why he asked that inane question of the maid, 'I say, have you always lived here?'—The truth is that he must have let her out of the cab, all unwittingly, at some point very close to Ryder Street, where he eventually found himself.

"He let her out of the cab five nights ago at one o'clock. Five nights ago at one o'clock, we have learned, Dr. Pilgrim from his window hears some one come along the alley and open the alley door of the Brimstone Club with a key…"

Talbot suddenly smote his fist into his palm.

"It was Colette Laverne, of course," said Bencolin. "I found her turquoise bracelet on that rear staircase, as you remember. Dallings told her she was going to lose it, and she did. She had merely arranged to go up and report progress to El Moulk, who let her in. But clearly she couldn't let Dallings know where she was going, or the game would have been spoiled. Dallings, as you will be able to see now, simply walked from St. James's corner up to Ryder Street—a distance of several hundred yards. And if you still entertain any doubt on the point, have the maid in here and ask whether our friend Colette came home on Monday night."

We knew what the result would be. Selden, when we summoned her, confirmed the statement. Afterwards Talbot grinned.

"That's clever, all right," he admitted. "I *was* a proper ass…"

"There's nothing clever about it," said Bencolin, testily. "I simply arranged well-known facts in consecutive order. Have you ever heard, Inspector, that two and two equal four? It is a fairly familiar observation. I doubt that even the American Mr. Coolidge could get much credit for sly humour if he tossed it off in his droll and whimsical way. But that is precisely the trap: knowing that they equal four, we become quite unable to put them together. We hang one 2 on the chandelier and throw the other under the sofa. The difficulty is not in adding them, but in performing that strange, mystic, and terrible operation of putting them together."

"But look here!" I put in. "Why didn't she tell me last night, then, when she mentioned the matter, that Dallings hadn't brought her home here?"

Bencolin raised his eyebrows.

"You must consider, Jeff," he returned, "the clear and unsullied simplicity of our lady's mind. I don't think it ever occurred to her that it was in any way important—which, incidentally, it wasn't. It didn't matter to her whether she spent the night with El Moulk here or in his rooms, so why mention it to you? No, no. It is important to *us*, as you will see before this case is over, but never to her."

"But what about the hand Pilgrim saw taking down the sword?" demanded Talbot.

"A different matter altogether. Of course, you jumped to the conclusion that the person who entered El Moulk's back door with a key was connected with the person who took down the sword. What basis had you for assuming that? Only Pilgrim's poetic theories, which tried to show El Moulk practising a huge and deadly hoax. No, no, no! Colette Laverne's midnight visits were a part of El Moulk's protection of himself; the hand which took down the sword was a part of the elaborate design *against* him…"

He rose and took a turn about the room. He was watching Talbot, and suddenly he snapped:

"Well? Don't you see what all this means? Never mind Pilgrim's ideas; but if you grant that Dallings really took her to the alley behind the Brimstone Club, and that he later walked up St. James's Street to Ryder Street, what follows? The significant point is that during this very short walk along St. James's Street up as far as Ryder he saw the shadow of the gallows!—And, as you yourself pointed out, it is too monstrous to assume that casual people are sitting up all over London, amusing themselves with gibbets at one o'clock in the morning—"

"It means," said Talbot, slowly, "that we have narrowed the search for Ruination Street down to a few hundred square yards."

Bencolin swept him a great bow.

"Bravo, Inspector! That is it, exactly. Which, of course, suggests the inference that… No, no; you shall make it for yourself."

Talbot scratched the back of his neck with his notebook. He was plunged in profound and wryly humorous meditation.

"Blast it!" he said. "That's clear enough. You knew this all the time?"

"Naturally."

"Well, then, why not speak out, sir? Why let me make an ass of myself chasing all over London for lost streets?"

"Because," Bencolin answered, "I didn't want the murderer to be warned. I wanted to let him think we were wildly searching for these lost streets in every quarter except the one where he has his lair."

"But if you know who the murderer is—!"

The cigar-smoke left Bencolin's nostrils in two thin streams. He turned from the window, where he had been staring out into Mount Street.

"And the only evidence I have against him," he said, touching his forehead, "is *here*. If I had Dr. Bayle with me! If I had Sannoy and Disslart, and their assistants in the laboratory! I should simply say, 'Messieurs, this is the truth. Now prove it for me.' Then lights would go on over their microscopes, and shiny test-tubes bubble for them; so that presently my gnomes would come smiling out of their cavern, and, *voilà!*—on somebody's neck the knife of the Red Widow would fall. You remember, Jeff, how they confirmed each statement I made in the Saligny case? But I haven't got them. And so I must snare my murderer in another way. I must lay a trap for him, and when he goes after his third victim—"

"You've said that before. Who *is* his third victim?"

"Why, Lieutenant Graffin, of course!... Surely you saw that?"

Talbot made little clucking noises. He spread out his hands.

"If it's so obvious as you seem to think," he observed, sourly, "I suppose I should have seen it. But—excuse me!—I didn't. *Graffin!* Why Graffin, of all people?"

"Because Graffin knows who Jack Ketch is. More than that, he... I had better tell you, I suppose."

"By all means do," said Talbot, in a sugary voice. He mopped his forehead again.

"I asked you this morning, Inspector, a number of questions, and hoped they would lead you in the right direction. There are several sinister queries to be answered about this man Graffin. Why does El Moulk, a recluse, without an occupation and without social duties, keep a 'private secretary'? Above all, why does he employ Graffin? The man is a drunkard, not only unfit for his duties, but even boasting about his neglect of them. He lies around in a half-stupor all the time—he laughs at El Moulk, taunts him, enrages him, and altogether drives him to such a fury that the Egyptian has great difficulty in keeping his hands from Graffin's throat. Yet in spite of this, El Moulk endures every insult and actually coddles Graffin! Does our Egyptian strike you as a very sentimental or tender-hearted sort of person? No, no, Inspector. There is only one answer to it, and the answer is—blackmail."

Bencolin struck his fist against the back of the chair.

"Blackmail, then; but about what? About a matter so serious that the headstrong, violent, callous El Moulk does not dare protest, even when he is offered insults which might ordinarily drive him to murder. Blackmail about a crime, no less. El Moulk has no position to lose, no reputation to be wrecked, by some minor scandal. He is guilty of a crime, and Graffin holds the proofs. Obviously they are legal and tangible proofs, which need no support from the word of a disgraced and besotted officer. Obviously, too, they are not kept about the person of a man who is generally in a stupor. They have been left with somebody, under seal, and with a note 'to be opened in case of my death.' Otherwise I can hardly fancy Graffin trusting himself alone with our charming Egyptian.

"I ask you again, Why did Graffin lie about the length of time he had been with El Moulk? When he saw he might be trapped, he admitted that he became attached to El Moulk *just ten years ago in Paris*—but why did he first lie, about *that particular time and that particular place*? When we remember what doubtful event occurred in the Egyptian's life at that time, we can understand what Graffin's drunken cunning was trying to conceal."

Talbot nodded, drawing a long breath.

"Yes," he replied, "yes. He knows the truth about who shot Keane."

"Precisely! You recall how he went pale when I asked, 'El Moulk has never had cause to regret this—extra expense, has he?' That struck home! Our wild and sottish lieutenant now emerges in more sinister colours. But consider now to what this assumption must lead us…"

Throwing open his coat, Bencolin sat down on the arm of the chair. He pointed his cigar at the little inspector.

"Jack Ketch's persecution of El Moulk began just after the Egyptian came to London, a little over nine months ago. Not in all those years before, but *only then* did Jack Ketch learn the real truth about Keane. Until then he undoubtedly thought that somebody he knew had been killed during the war; he never suspected that this unknown Englishman, 'Keane,' was in reality that very somebody he believed killed in action—until he was told the truth nine months ago. And the only man who knew the facts was Graffin.

"Then Graffin told him. Graffin told him deliberately. Perhaps our lieutenant's cupidity got the better of him, or perhaps his hatred of El Moulk. He was bleeding El Moulk; why not sell his secret to somebody else and bleed both of them? He could pit them against each other. He could still draw gold from El Moulk, all the while he was sitting off and laughing at the Egyptian's agonies. A pleasant fellow, our friend Graffin!

"Anyhow, he told Jack Ketch. It follows, then, that he had known the real identity of Keane, since he was able to pick out the avenger. And if you want further proof, think back!"

Staring before me, I saw those red and rheumy eyes, the scrawny red neck, the drunken leer of Graffin, metamorphosed now into a thing chuckling and leprous. Bencolin went on:

"Do you remember last night, when we were crossing the lobby of the Brimstone after we had looked at the chauffeur in the billiard-room?... Graffin, we know, had been upstairs all day. How could he possibly have known what had happened? But down he came flying in his dressing-gown, calling out, '*Can you tell me where the detective is?*' That was a horrible mistake. No signs of anything wrong in the lobby; no disturbance whatever; merely a policeman standing by the door. But he had been waiting upstairs in those gloomy rooms for news of the outrage, and, finally, when he was unable to restrain his fear and curiosity any longer, he came downstairs. Seeing one policeman in the hall, he knew that what he expected had happened—and he blurted out those damning words."

There was a silence. Talbot beat his knuckles against his forehead.

"I see! Oh yes, I see now. Then Graffin knows who Jack Ketch is..."

Bencolin laughed. It was that deep, shaking, almost soundless mirth which convulsed him when he had pinned somebody like a butterfly to a card.

"Of course he does, Inspector. Examine his conduct now in the light of that fact. His jeers at El Moulk when the Egyptian was receiving those packages by the post. His wild denials to us that El Moulk was the victim of any persecution; his too great insistence that he had *no* idea of the source of the threats. The man is endowed with a species of low, mean cunning which would not deceive a child. Examine, in short, everything that he said or did, and see if it does not bear me out. Recall his outburst, 'Go back, you damn fool; go back'—that exclamation so ingeniously and wrongly explained by Dr. Pilgrim—when he saw me come out of the staircase door with a candle. He would never have mistaken me for El Moulk; I am at least ten inches too tall. He did mistake me for the murderer... Finally, and conclusively, recall Mademoiselle Laverne's remark that *somebody* knew the identity of Jack Ketch, but could not be persuaded to tell. She knew, naturally, that Graffin knew; but she knew that trying to learn from him was useless."

The clock struck six-thirty as Talbot sat with his head down, brooding.

"Yes, of course," he said. "He blackmailed Mr. El Moulk, and now he's blackmailing somebody else..."

"A dangerous thing," said Bencolin, "to try on Jack Ketch. Moreover, do you see that Graffin is his logical next victim? It will complete the gay trio: El Moulk, who committed the crime; Colette Laverne, who abetted it; and Graffin, who concealed it..."

He paused as Talbot rose decisively.

"I think I shall have a little talk with Mr. Graffin," he murmured, in a chilly voice.

"Sit down, Inspector!" Bencolin snapped. "Sit—down! If you are advised by me, you will do nothing of the sort. Graffin is our bait for Jack Ketch. I am going to outline to you a plan which will go into operation tonight. If you will have dinner with me, we can talk it over. Jeff, you are going out with Miss Grey, but let me beg of you, at all costs be back at the Brimstone by midnight. There will be work. Tonight, I assure you, Jack Ketch will be prowling to kill."

He rose from the arm of the chair, buttoning up his overcoat. It was the hungry hour when one begins to think of lights and cocktails and black clothes laid ready. Energy is new-born; traffic sinks to a more leisurely roar; and in tall restaurants there is a warning *plink* of tuned fiddles. Already, outside the theatres, the long gallery queues would be forming, jostling, cracking jokes, and eating, with maybe some coins for a street performer who amused them while they waited. But *we* awaited the time when the little curtain should fly up on a Punch and Judy show. Even now we could hear those ugly puppets flopping about in their box, ready for the swampy dark where they would cackle and chase and kill...

"We close in on him, Inspector," said Bencolin. "A few more hours—"

Smiling, he drew patterns on the carpet with his stick. "In the meantime, I think our friend Graffin needs to taste fear. In a moment of bad judgment he sold his secret to Jack Ketch. At this moment, I imagine, he is beating his head against a wall. The celebrated Mr. Frankenstein had nothing on him. *He* created this monster; *he* endowed Jack Ketch with life. And now he is running about in circles, for he sees, to his horror, that the grisly thing has turned on him... Should you care, Inspector, to look back and see that face over your shoulder while you ran?"

Over swamps and around trees, a darting pursuit for our little show-box, with Jack Ketch's hooded head bent in full cry! I could see Graffin's red-mottled face; and again the red-draped room was full of the detective's laughter. Immaculate, he stood beside the table and prodded on the carpet with his stick, as though he menaced some ant hurrying about there. He raised a delighted eyebrow at the inspector...

Talbot had gone over and thrown open the folding-doors. The orchestra! A trampling of feet echoed at the back of the hallway, and in the cold twilight they carried Bronson's body out to the waiting automobile. 'Cellos, horns, and fiddles mingled an overture in the noise of those feet. There was a curious expression on the little inspector's face. He squinted past his broken nose; and suddenly he cleared his throat.

"I think, sir," said Talbot, "that it might be bad enough to be chased by Jack Ketch... But if *I* had committed a crime, I would rather have the devil after me than Henri Bencolin."

He threw the doors wide.

XIV

How the Glove of the Dead Man Beckoned

"—No one to talk with,
    All by myself,
No one to walk with,
    But I'm happy on the shelf:
Ain't misbehavin'!—"

UNDER SLIGHTLY NIGHTMARISH LIGHTS, A NIGHTMARISH VOICE protested in this fashion over a vast shuffling of feet; the voice strained groggily on a high note, and was drowned by the amorous crying of seduced cornets. Round in the gloom of the dance floor wriggled the hot and coloured centipede of which I was two legs. We were packed in tightly, so that heat waves quivered up past the collar and mingled in the brain with a crackle of drums and champagne. But I could look down and catch the line of Sharon's eyelash as we danced, and the expression of her eyes as we were pressed together; and I hoped (for more than one reason) that the music would not stop too suddenly…

All evening, after dinner, we had been wandering round to supper clubs; that is to say, you bought a supper consisting of three sand-wiches, each one inch square, so that you might drink champagne until the waiter yanked it out of your hands. It all commenced, of course, when Sharon had insisted on dining at one of London's unspoiled places.

Now if there is one lesson which a normally intelligent person learns in Paris, it is to beware of people who want to take you to quaint restaurants which nobody knows about. They are exactly the restaurants everybody knows about. The smaller they are, the more obscure and hard to find in a labyrinth of back alleys, then the greater your assurance that they will be shrieking infernos, jammed to suffocation by a mob of eager Columbuses. When visitors to Paris ask me to take them to some quaint and unspoiled place, I always suggest the Ritz. A good dinner has three essentials: food, wine, and privacy. The dinner table, in short, is the place for talk and philosophy, but nobody can feel quite so uncomfortable as a philosopher overheard. Those crowded Parisian wall-seats, where you are jammed elbow to elbow with every noisy stabber, and forced (even worse!) to overhear your neighbours as well as be heard by them! The yells, the struggling waiters, the blatter of noise! There are now in Paris just three restaurants one may enjoy, and these are bearable because they are so celebrated that nobody ever goes to them.

But Sharon's romantic soul was set on an unspoiled place, and we went. To my surprise, it was only moderately jammed with evening gowns and white ties, and I was deeply obliged to Sharon because it specialized in that noblest of all drinks, beer. Lovely and fastidious ladies like Sharon will drink beer only at unspoiled places… And Sharon was in fine feather that night when she drank Pilsener out of a pewter mug, and her bright gown glowed against the dark oak panelling. Her eyes, I told her truthfully, were just the colour of that matchless beverage; they had the softness, the promise, the exquisite soul-shaking lure of Pilsener beer; but somehow she did not appear to think this sentiment very lyrical.

Afterwards she wanted to dance, and so we began the customary round. We danced to "Ain't Misbehavin'"; we danced to various tunes in various places, until I bethought myself of Chez Aladdin. I was curious about this place. And Dallings had correctly described it.

There was blue moonlight on the white globules of mosque spires, shot with twinkling gleams. The tables were hidden in the shadow of dwarf trees with silver fruit, and the shadow was alive with starched shirts and jewelled flesh. But for the low murmuring and an occasional laugh, you might have thought the place deserted. A whiff of jazz music deepened and boomed from invisible players; a spotlight opened in blue gloom and picked out some gentleman in a red fez, alone in an acre of polished floor. He wore baggy shimmering trousers, and sang plaintively of his mammy in Baghdad.

Sharon and I sat far back in a corner, redolent of thick spices, against many-hued rugs in shadow. The tablecloth was ghastly white; dim reflections touched the edges of our glasses and the dark-gold shimmer of her hair. We talked, as the swathed bottle tilted in a warmer mist, and they played old waltzes which make men dream. These waltzes creep swinging out of twilight, low at first, then rising through the breast in aching volume; they are pale and cloaked mummers, and they kindle witch-lights in the closed places of the heart... I saw Sharon's white face; I knew her quick breathing, and the searching brightness of her eyes, and the tiny half-smile that curved ever so slightly her soft sullen lips. All things had a dim roar as of a waterfall far away. And the dream was even more unreal when we said, quite simply, what we had never said before—that we loved each other. But now the witch-light fell fully on her face, and I think we both felt a mighty mad exultation as at the breaking of fetters, a heavy heart-beat that was ecstasy.

Ecstasy. I write the word again, but it does not convey the singing and the fire. These people—these funny little people—had been too vain, too stupid, too suspicious for sentiment; and now that sentiment had come, it loosed stirring tentacles which clung and sealed each to the other, fiercely. Tomorrow we would go away together, and we would not be separated again. Now we did not speak at all, for fierce waves went through us at the locked pressure of mouths; bewilderment, joy smashing free, and flight through chaos. And the waltz-tune died away down its dark stream. And one watching the shadow which enclosed us would have seen only two glowing ends of cigarettes drop unheeded in the dark and smoulder out on the floor.

But this, I remember, is a tale of murder...

I shivered with the cold when I went up the steps of the Brimstone Club at close on midnight. The fog had cleared into a black, moonless night, and the lights shone out on a few lazy flakes of snow. Under one window close against the balustrade I noticed a man standing motionless...

The lobby was deserted. Even in this dreary place there is generally *some* noise—voices in the lounge, the click of billiard balls, or glasses clinking in the bar. But now there was not a sound, or the trace of any person. The lift was down, but without anybody to operate it. My footfalls echoed on the marble of the floor, and the bleak globes of the wall-brackets tingled in time to them. I looked up at the inscriptions which are graven like a frieze high up around the rotunda. "From the hag and the hungry goblin—"

A low fire smouldered on the hearth in the lounge. A few red gleams shone in the dark. No lights, nobody here, either. I was about to drop the curtain when I thought I could see, dimly outlined against the window, the profile of a man. It did not move. Some faint and pale illumination fell into the room from a street lamp, and the man appeared to be smiling.

There was something so uncanny about that still, smiling, shadowy form that I had an impulse to switch on the lights. But one ceases to wonder at the foibles of members in this curious club. If somebody chooses to sit in the dark, that is his own affair; and yet, after seeing that other figure by the steps, I felt that I had strayed into a world of ghosts.

Dropping the curtain, I went back into the lobby. Nobody at the desk—damnation! Bencolin might have left some word. I called for the lift-boy, but my own words came reverberating back without a reply. I explored the other downstairs rooms, finding them likewise deserted. Finally I glanced into the deserted billiard-room, where last night we had laid the body of the chauffeur. A tiny pale flicker moved outside its windows, showing in dim outline the shape of the table, and the place was dank with musty cold. Closing the door again, I hesitated momentarily to look back. Was that another of the silent figures, sitting on the window seat?

I stood straining my eyes. For an instant I could have sworn I caught the movement of a smiling face turned towards me from the window. Nonsense! It was certainly the deceptive swinging of a light outside... I closed the door. Perhaps Bencolin was up in his room, waiting for me. I recrossed the lobby and mounted the stairs to the second floor, where I groped along a dark passage until I found his door. My tumultuous knocking echoed back, unanswered.

They might at least have left lights on in this place! The musty smell of the passage was oppressive. Blundering up the staircase, I fought down a growing uneasiness. In any case, I could go up to my own room, sit by a good fire, and talk to Thomas until some word from Bencolin arrived. I was almost to the top floor when I remembered I had given Thomas the night off to visit some relatives in Tooting. Curiously enough, there were lights in the passage of the top floor.

Every flaring gas-globe was illuminated, bringing out the harsh and tawdry decoration. You could see clearly those begrimed murals, invisible except in full light, which once had been a scandal to the side-whiskered gentlemen of the 'eighties. I remembered then hearing once that El Moulk's rooms had been inhabited by the ill-starred

Lord Rayle, who shot himself for love of Kitty Darkins. A breath of all that lace-paper parade blew back, as of old cupboards opened, and an echo of the gallants who called for madder music and for stronger wine...

I opened the door of my bedroom on darkness. Was it possible that I should see, sitting by the window, another of those smiling white-faced things? But when I struck a match everything seemed in order. I lighted the gas-lamp on the table beside the fireplace. The dusty cream-and-gold panels of that tall room took form as the glow rose up. I saw the mantelpiece of white marble, the gilded mirrors whose surfaces were tarnished with mist, the twining legs of the bedpost with their monstrous canopy, the long draperies of white velvet at the window. I locked the door to the sitting-room. Any feeling of uneasiness was nonsense. Everything just as usual—suit-case under the window, big canopied bed, clothes hung up in the closet—like old Scrooge, I thought, this peering about. "Nobody in his dressing-gown, which was hanging in a suspicious attitude on the wall." I put it on, tossing my jacket and wet overcoat across a chair. They had neglected to lay a fire and the room was freezing. Annoyance blazed almost to fury in me. I pressed the bell savagely, ringing it a long time, and then sat down in an armchair before the cold grate.

Was that the sound of somebody *hammering*? I jerked up my head from contemplation of the grate, and listened again for that faint noise as of nails being driven into a board. It was intermittent; first I thought I heard a couple of thuds, then a long silence as of some artisan studying his work, and at last, when I had just dismissed the matter as my fancy, several swift muted blows. Still, it was so far away that I must have fancied it. I went to the window, which gave on the air-shaft, and tried to peer out, but the glass was thick with frost.

Somebody knocked at the door. I have got to confess that the heart rose queerly inside me as I said, "Come in." There was a sort of chirping, and the wrinkled face of Teddy was poked round the knob.

"'Ullo, sir!" he said, grinning. "Didjer ring, sir?"

Wrath was useless. I told him sharply to bring some coal and kindle a fire; he nodded several times, blinked his eyes rapidly, and disappeared in a scent of hair-pomade. Presently the rattle of the coal-bucket approached. Singing to himself in his cracked voice, Teddy busied himself with the fire. He had just lowered the damper, and a cheerful roar was throbbing up inside the grate, when I heard the hammering again. It was as though something were being built—a scaffolding, say, or—

I was pacing about the room when my eye fell on one of those odious neckties, of sunburst colours, which women take such delight in giving as Christmas gifts. I held it up, simulating open-mouthed admiration, and I could see the gleam in Teddy's look as he watched me. I said:

"Seen any more ghosts, Teddy?"

He dropped the coal-shovel with a crash and backed away. "I ain't never seen 'em!" he shrilled, doubling his little fists in terror. "Gawd's truth, I ain't!" Then he began to whimper.

"Well, well, it's all right; they'd never catch *you*, Teddy. Should you like this necktie, and maybe a shilling or two besides?"

"'M," he muttered, watching me furtively. "But I ain't!" he added, with glaring passion. "I does wot they tells me, don't I? Ain't no spook a-going ter get *me*, is there? When they sends me hon errands, I alwis comes back right 'ere. Alwis! And when they gives me money for things, I alwis gives 'em the right—"

"I know, Teddy. I know you didn't see anything back there today."

"Ow, I wish I *'adn't* seen it!" he cried, his mood changing. "A-lookin' right at me, it wos; a-lookin' right up—" His staring eyes looked into some crackbrain country beyond my shoulder. Then he picked up the scuttle.

"*Up?*" I repeated, carelessly. "Looking up at you? Did you go to the staircase then, Teddy?"

He turned and bolted from the room, not even stopping when I started after him to offer him the necktie. Ah, well! I went to the fireplace and raised the damper with my foot. The roaring fire was grateful; sitting down before it, I spread out my hands. A harlequin wind sported in the chimney...

The lock clicked on the closing door. Bencolin stood with his back to it. He wore a dead-black dressing-gown, which accentuated the angles of his thin and gigantic form; his head was hung forward, and even across the room I could catch the upward glitter of his eyes... Striding to the hearth, he took from the pocket of his dressing-gown an automatic pistol and a police whistle, which he laid on the mantel-shelf.

(The rattle of dice in the box.) I said, "Well?"

There were other articles—a thin leather-bound book and some sheets of manuscript. He arranged them in a line with the nicety of Christmas gifts, and turned back to me. The man was outwardly cool, but his nostrils were dilated, and in him smouldered a subdued, terrible joy.

"Well, Jeff!" Relaxing in a smile, he sat down lazily in a chair across the hearth. From the mantelpiece he took a bottle of brandy and a glass.

"What's up?"

"The calf," he answered, "is now being fed on choice viands to make him more alluring bait... Specifically, Lieutenant Graffin is wandering round public houses and night clubs, searching out the most crowded places, trying to drink himself into a state heroic enough to venture home. I may add that he is being carefully shadowed by Talbot's best men. We want no premature attacks."

"And precisely what is the plan tonight?"

"Why, Jack Ketch is to have his chance at Graffin. The trap is ready."

"Aren't you putting a little too much faith in a sheer theory that Jack Ketch will go after Graffin tonight?" I asked. "Suppose he doesn't take the bait?"

"I do not think it will matter in the slightest whether he goes after Graffin or not. We should catch him just the same. I am simply preparing for every eventuality... You will see before long. Can I count on you to obey orders without asking why?"

"Naturally."

"Even if they involve as deadly danger as you are ever likely to encounter?"

"Why not?—But I should at least like to know what this is all about. You make all these mysterious remarks... Where is Talbot, by the way?"

"He also is obeying orders." Bencolin's face clouded over. "Jeff, if I have misread the signs, if I have made the slightest error in all my calculations, then there are unutterable horrors in store for all of us. A theory, nothing more!—" He stared at his hands, opening and closing them spasmodically. "I am playing with lives, God help me! If I fail Talbot, he will be the one to suffer. He has put himself blindly in my hands."

I hardly heard his last words. Faint, slow, insistent, the ghostly hammering had begun again. I thought, too, that I could discern footfalls.

"There it is!" I cried. "There! Do you hear it?"

"Hear what?" he asked, pausing with glass uplifted.

"Listen!"

This was *not* a trick of fancy. Knock, knock; a pause; knock, knock, knock, the stealthy blows beat again. Surely any sane person could hear it! Surely Bencolin was not chuckling and cocking an eye at me in a sympathetic way. "My dear Jeff," he said, "you are getting overwrought. Perhaps you are not in shape to—"

"This is some damned trick of *yours*," I said, venomously. "You hear that noise as well as I do; you're not deaf. Well, if you're trying to play on the murderer's nerves, all right! But say so. Don't stand there—"

"Have it your own way," he answered, sighing. His voice became sharp: "Easy, old man! Take it easy. Are you with us or not?"

"All right, all right. Go ahead."

I lit a cigarette. He nodded, as though approving some theory in his mind, and drew out the armchair on the other side of the hearth.

"We may have some time to wait. Graffin hasn't come in yet; if there are any demonstrations in—the other quarter, I shall be notified. In the meantime, we must possess our souls in patience. But I think I can fill in the interval amusingly by telling you some pertinent facts." He was silent for a time, with the brandy bottle dangling from his hand. Then he looked at me with that squinted sideways glance, and asked, casually, "Jeff, where did El Moulk go on the night he left here in his car?"

I said: "Now, frankly, isn't that a fine question to ask *me*? Scotland Yard please copy. To Ruination Street. To hell, maybe. To—"

"Use your wits," he suggested, gently. "What do we know about it?"

"We know, then, that he *started* for Mademoiselle Laverne's house. On the way there he was attacked..."

He nodded again in that absent fashion, and held up his hand.

"I am glad you mentioned those things," he said. "Those are the two pieces of evidence we have. Those are the two pieces of evidence we were intended to have. And both of them are wrong."

I shrugged my shoulders helplessly.

Bencolin went on: "His stick and gloves were found in the car. Therefore we were to assume that he never reached his destination. A box of orchids was found beside the stick and gloves. Therefore we were to assume that his destination was the house of Mademoiselle Laverne."

"Well, he telephoned her to expect him."

"Say rather that Mademoiselle *received a phone message* telling her to expect him shortly after seven; then, the message said, they would go out and dine. The sender of the message explained his strange voice on the phone by saying that he had caught cold... You talked to El Moulk, Jeff. Did he have a cold?"

"No—"

"Ah, I thought not. Now this message was sent about six o'clock. *Early in the afternoon*, before any such appointment had been made—in fact, before he even knew whether he could locate her—he apparently ordered a corsage from the florist. This strange '*cold*' is also commented on by the man at the shop. Now, Jeff, if you are going out to dine, does it ever occur to you to *carry* a corsage to the lady? You have them send it to her, do you not? The other proceeding is rather ludicrous, particularly if you have ordered those flowers many hours earlier. Somebody calls at the shop for the corsage—a very tall man, we learn. Certainly not El Moulk. Was it somebody in his household? Joyet would not answer the description, even if he had been in London—which he was not. Graffin? From the description it is possible, but we have ascertained that he did not leave the club all day. And it was not a club servant. The thing looks queerer... Finally, what happened to this mysterious corsage after it was obtained at the florist's? The car was overhauled before it left the garage, and nothing like a corsage was in it then. You saw El Moulk come down the stairs and enter his automobile. Did he have the box with him then?"

"No. I am sure of that."

Bencolin made a deprecating gesture. "There is no use dwelling on this point at length. Obviously our mysterious 'man with the cold' put in both phone-calls. It was not El Moulk. El Moulk knew nothing about either the appointment or the orchids. In short, it was somebody who was neatly producing evidence that El Moulk intended going to Mademoiselle Laverne's. In case we should never find out about the *appointment*, our man with the cold considerately wanted to give us evidence that he was going to see a woman. Hence the orchids. Since they were not in the car before El Moulk started, and since he did not take them to the car himself, clearly they were put in afterwards—after El Moulk had left it—by the tall gentleman who obtained them at the florist's. They were left as a false lead after Jack Ketch had caught his prey."

The thing was so blatantly plain as he explained it... I flung my cigarette into the fire and lighted another. Bencolin chuckled.

"We have established, then," he mused, "that Jack Ketch wished to mislead us as to El Moulk's destination. By the stick and gloves, we are intended to believe that he was lured out of the car (by a stratagem, I suppose) and attacked then... Let us see what really happened. Call up in your mind a picture of those gloves as we examined them. The right hand one, you recall, bore some curious dust-marks?"

I nodded. Those smudges on the tips of the fingers and thumb, and the broad level smear across the centre of the palm, were distinct on an ominous white hand in my fancy...

"You have told us yourself," the detective resumed, "that when he entered the car he was wearing those gloves unstained. By the cleaning of the automobile, we know that he could not have got that terrifically thick dust coat—very black and heavy—on his way, even if we can fancy a posture of his hand by which it could have come about. Then, of course, he got it *after* he got out of the car somewhere. Of course, also, he was still wearing the gloves, since the dust-marks are of fingers inside them.

"And yet," cried Bencolin, "we are asked to believe that, somewhere on this ride, El Moulk was lured out of his car, attacked, and dragged off. What a nightmare of impossibility, Jeff! El Moulk, wearing his gloves, steps out. He is set upon and struck down—after which, in his abductor's power, he very carefully removes his gloves and places them neatly, one on top of the other, in the rear seat! The sheerest nonsense, old man, that the credulous gullet of man was ever intended to swallow.

"It is plain that El Moulk quitted his car of his own free will. He wore his gloves, and he carried his stick—you recall those thick mud-stains over the top of the ferrule? The chauffeur sat solidly at the wheel, unalarmed, unsuspicious. El Moulk was unsuspicious, though he travelled behind bullet-proof glass... He had reached his destination."

Red flames and yellow writhed among the black coals. Wild things were beginning to take shape there between the bars of my grate. Bencolin's voice, low and hypnotic, drifted as though from a distance:

"Remember, Jeff, that the stains on the glove were dust, not mud. It was a wet night. Any marks of mud, any marks he obtained *outside*, would have hardened. These stains came from inside a house: the house to which El Moulk was going, the house to which he did go...

"See, in your imagination, the top-hatted dandy leaving his car in the fog. See him crossing some street, entering a house, and then, in the darkness, fancy *on what* he rested his hand so as to stain the glove in this particular and significant pattern..."

Smudges as of grasping at the fingers and thumb, broad flat dust in the palm; I saw in the grate, as in a monstrous blazing mirror, a gloved hand reaching out to touch—

"A stair-rail," I said, quietly.

There was a long silence, and then the splash of brandy poured into a glass. Bencolin laughed suddenly.

"That," he said, "was what I was looking for when you saw me examining the stair-rail with a candle. This elaborate mummery merely means that El Moulk drove around the block, parked the car in the alley, and ascended the rear staircase to his own apartments!"

XV

The Street of Strangled Men

THERE ARE TIMES WHEN THE UNMISTAKABLE, THE OBVIOUS, crashes down on one's brain with a blow like a blackjack's. A curtain snaps up, lights go on, and what was so terrifying is revealed in one surge of disgust as a sheet, a broomstick, and a candle-lit pumpkin. One kicks the pumpkin in wrath, to see it fly apart… Now Bencolin had risen, and was leaning in that familiar position against the mantelpiece, regarding me amusedly.

"I found the glove-marks, of course, on the stair-rail. When you saw me," he continued, "I thought surely you would realize for what I was looking. And then, this afternoon, when I gave such clear indications to all of you as to just where Ruination Street was located, I fancied you would be certain to see the obvious conclusion."

"Then Ruination Street—"

"Is the alley behind this house. It has been glaringly apparent from the first. I will explain that curious name in just a moment." Smiling, he stared deep into his glass and swirled round its contents.

"But why, in God's name," I said, "*why* should a man call his chauffeur, get into his car, and drive around to the rear of his own house?"

"Exactly, Jeff. Why should he? That is the very point which sent you in the wrong direction. When a man leaves his house, you do not naturally suspect that he is coming straight around to it again by the back door. That was what El Moulk bargained on."

"What *El Moulk* bargained on?"

"Yes… Have you forgotten that curious scrap of conversation we learned from Joyet? Just before Joyet left for Paris, El Moulk spoke to him, and do you remember what he said? '*If my plans work out, I am going to trap this Jack Ketch—trap him at work. I have found a helper right here at the club.*'

"Jeff, El Moulk thought that night that he was laying a trap for Jack Ketch. And in reality he was playing into Jack Ketch's hands. What must have happened is very simple. The murderer, unsuspected by El Moulk, makes friends with him. He tells our Egyptian that he has noticed some curious happenings in El Moulk's rooms—possibly he even tells him that he has seen Jack Ketch at work. So he suggests this trap. Why not (he urges El Moulk) why not start out one evening in his automobile as though he were to be out for some length of time, and then come up softly by the back stairs again? Jack Ketch will be deceived, and show himself in El Moulk's rooms. Hidden, the Egyptian can get a look at him…"

The detective made a deprecating gesture.

"Not a very clever idea, is it? But El Moulk was frantic enough to fall in with any suggestion. He never planned to go and see Miss Laverne that night, because he intended to spend it watching for Jack Ketch."

I rose and began pacing about the room. Bit by bit, the whole plan was becoming clear…

"And do you see the murderer's damnable cleverness? By planting in everybody's mind the assumption that El Moulk had left this house, then this house was the very last place the police would look for him! He lured his victim out—and lured him right back again. Consequently, he would have the police searching all over London, anywhere in the whole city, except directly under their noses. I think, Jeff, it can rank as one of the most brilliant devices in the annals of crime."

His eyes were very bright, and his voice held a tense note of admiration.

"Do you see the picture, Jeff? As El Moulk comes up those stairs in the dark, the murderer is waiting for him, crouched on a landing. Possibly Jack Ketch had even arranged to watch *with* him, unsuspected by El Moulk even as yet. Expectant, triumphant, the fly comes unhesitatingly to the edges of the web, and the spider is smiling..."

"But where was El Moulk intending to stay while he watched?" I demanded. "We have heard that Jack Ketch seems to be able to go in there and leave his gifts without being seen. El Moulk couldn't just walk in the staircase door and sit down; *that* would be no trap for a person who walks as invisibly as Jack Ketch."

Bencolin pointed his glass at me.

"And there you come to the whole crux of the plan," he said. "It is the reason why the murderer was able to snare El Moulk with the Egyptian's full consent... Have you never heard the story that in this building there is a lost room where they held their revels in the old days, and where Lord Rayle kept—?"

"But that's nonsense! They've told me—"

He shook his head. "I very much fear, Jeff, that it is far from being nonsense. Surely it must have occurred to you that, since Jack Ketch is able to walk in there unseen, with all doors locked, he had some means of reaching El Moulk's rooms—some *secret* means of entrance?"

I put my hands to my head. "And those rooms were formerly used by Lord Rayle—!"

"You have hit it exactly," replied the detective. "Now is it clear? The murderer must have mentioned to El Moulk that he knew of the existence of some secret room, some place communicating with the Egyptian's apartments. So, suggests our ingenious Mr. Ketch, he will show this to El Moulk, and there they can watch for the coming of the killer.

"Oh, it was done with admirable completeness! The delighted fly walked straight into Jack Ketch's lair. Then a blow over the head, a sponge full of chloroform—" He shrugged, spreading out his hands.

"So, then, he has El Moulk and the woman—in this house—*now*—"

"Yes."

"And you know even where this secret room is, I take it?"

"Of course I know where it is.—Don't you?"

I thought, looking at him, that the man was merely indulging his theatricalism. Then, as I met the tired, impatient glitter of his eyes, I knew it was no pose. He was irritated by the slowness of all of us—weary and bitter with all brains which could not comprehend truth in an instant. He stared back at me now as though he could not believe his ears; then his tense hands relaxed and he raised a quizzical eyebrow.

"I see you are in earnest," he remarked. "And yet we have evidence which tells us exactly where it is, so that we are able to lay our hands on it without a single instant's groping...

"No matter! We have decided that El Moulk and the woman are hidden in it. And tonight—"

"Wait a minute!" I protested. "There's no tremendous need for this sneering. I *understand* that the entrance to this secret place communicates with El Moulk's rooms, of course... What I meant was that I didn't know where to look for the entrance when one was *in* El Moulk's rooms, and—"

"The entrance is not in El Moulk's rooms," he said, gently.

"But you said—!"

"Oh no, Jeff; I said nothing of the kind."

"I give up," I said, despairingly, and sat down by the fire. "Go on."

"And tonight, as I was saying, we are going to trap Jack Ketch either when he visits his lair or when he goes to take Graffin. But do you want to know why 'Ruination Street' was brought in by the murderer? Look here!"

He took the book from the mantelpiece and held it out. *"Tales of the Lost Land*, by J. L. Keane. Jack Ketch sent El Moulk this copy. He marked in blue pencil one of the translations, the same one which El Moulk was translating and whose manuscript we found on his desk. Let me call your attention to it. It begins in the usual way:

> The mighty King User.maat.ra had a nephew named Nezam Kha.em.uast, who was a scribe learned in all the ancient writings. He had a friend, Uba-Aner, who was a captain of war, and his councils were weighty among the men of blood—

"Our scribe, one may gather, was quite a pacifist. Now take El Moulk's translation, which is practically the same as the other, and start here."

His finger indicated a place. I drew the lamp over. While the wind rustled in the chimney, and the snow fell on London, the naïve chronicle ran in soothing periods:

> —returned from the land of Gutium rich in honours, and in many slaves, and the gold of valour, and with garlands of flowers about his neck. So that when Nezam looked upon his friend, he fell into a rage like the cheetah of the south. In Thebes there lived a woman, beautiful in her limbs, whom Nezam wished for himself, and so well for him; but her eye saw Uba-Aner, who bent double the great war-bow—

My eye ran on rapidly:

—and went and stood in the presence of the Great King, and of his nobles. And Nezam accused him, saying that he had performed treachery against the King, and against all the chieftains of the army. Wherefore was he tried by justice, and who should stand against the word of the nephew of User.maat.ra? And so Uba-Aner suffered death. But Ra heard the prayer of Uba-Aner. And Ra was stirred to anger. And it so occurred that on the night of the full moon, when the moon had eaten deep and was fat, Nezam walked in the street which is called Ruination—

I let out an exclamation, and looked up at Bencolin, who nodded.

—for that it is the Street of Traitors, and filled with the cryings of each *ka* which is an enemy of the King. And as Nezam walked there glided behind him, like the serpent, a leathern bowstring, which no man moved by his hands. And it leaped in the air and coiled about the neck of Nezam, and killed him. Wherefore was his race cursed forever—

Handing the sheets to Bencolin, I sat back. "You see?" he asked. "They were looking for it in old London; actually it was in old Thebes. Without this, we should never have understood Ruination Street even when we solved the problem. Or we should have known about Ruination Street and still not have known where to look for El Moulk."

"Then it's of no consequence to the case…"

"On the contrary! Had it not been for this idle story, we might never have had our case at all. El Moulk believed it. That was what put the fear into him. Suppose that you, for example, had been selected by Jack Ketch as a victim for these parcels by the post, these houndings and suggestions. Why, you would simply have gone to the police. You would have forced things out in the open. The persecution might have bothered you, but it would never have reduced you to that cringing terror which tortured El Moulk. Imagine him sitting there night after night by his green lamp. Imagine the horrible blackness that came on him the first time he ever saw that papyrus—when he saw his own story acted out with grisly exactitude, and his doom written for him four thousand years before his birth! Can't you see him screaming and crying, but believing inexorably that the bowstring would leap on *him*?"

"Which it did," I said, grimly.

Bencolin folded up the sheets and slipped them into the book. He murmured:

"I wonder! Tonight we may test the potency of Egypt's gods..." He picked up my watch, which was lying on the table beside the fire. "It's nearly twelve; Graffin should be in at any minute."

"You still haven't given me any clue," I suggested, "as to the location of this secret room where Jack Ketch has his hideaway."

Folding his arms, he studied me.

"You have not shown any appalling ingenuity so far, Jeff. Very well; I will give you a clue, and see what you can do with it. It is true, is it not, that Jack Ketch seems to have been in the habit of paying visits and leaving things on El Moulk's desk in his absence?"

"Yes, of course."

"It is also true that there is a certain *peculiarity* about all the objects left that way. They were all books, or pieces of rope, for instance, or that little wooden figure..."

"I see no peculiarity about them. Odd, yes, but—"

"Be quiet and listen. These things were left on the desk. Whereas the model of the gibbet, the glass duelling-pistols, the cremation jar, were sent by the post." He paused.

"Well?"

"That, Jeff, is the clue."

"Really?" I said disgustedly.

He made a flourishing gesture. "The key to the whole affair, Jeff! A nursery riddle which might have been propounded to you a few years ago. Why is a book like a piece of rope? Why is a model of a gallows like pair of toy pistols? Answer me, and you have Jack Ketch's secret. Answer me, and the doors of truth fly open."

The telephone on the wall rang stridently. It was the signal for which Bencolin had been waiting. I felt my heart pounding as he took down the receiver. He listened a moment, said, "Good!" and hung up. When he came back to the fire he was slapping his hands together in exultation.

"Now then, Jeff, your instructions.

"Graffin has just come in from his tour of the night clubs. He is very drunk, but he can still navigate. The bar is closed downstairs, and if he wants a drink he will have to come up to his room. I don't think he will linger downstairs. The man is nearly frightened out of his wits."

Taking up pistol and police whistle from the top of the mantel-piece, Bencolin handed them to me.

"Put these in your pockets. When you hear him coming along the hall outside here, go out and accost him. Make any excuse you like, but find some pretext to accompany him back to El Moulk's apartment. When you get there, sit down and talk to him. You'll have no difficulty; he is so terrified that he'll jump at the chance to have company, and he has no suspicions of *you*. See that he drinks himself into a stupor—keep pouring drinks into him until he's unconscious. Manoeuvre him into some conspicuous position in the big room. Is that clear?"

"Yes."

"If possible, try to find some pretext for opening all the curtains of the windows when you go in. If you can't do it without exciting his suspicions, don't try. Wait until he has gone under, and then open them. Stand over him as though you were bidding him good night, wave your hand, and go towards the door to the front, as though you were going to your own room. That lamp doesn't shed much light, and once you get outside its circle you can't be seen. Sit down in a chair by the door, conceal yourself as much as possible, and *wait*. Don't make any noise. No matter what you see, don't shoot unless it is absolutely necessary. I can't bargain on all circumstances, but if at any time you think you have Jack Ketch in a corner, blow that whistle. Got it?"

"Right."

He hesitated. "Now I don't have to warn you that Jack Ketch is as dangerous a little playmate as anybody in my experience—"

I held out my hand at arm's length. My chest felt constricted and my heart was thudding, but the fingers were perfectly steady. He nodded.

"Hush!"

From the passage outside drifted the noise of somebody swearing, and the noise of a blundering progress up the stairs. The person seemed to be tripping on treads. Once the voice broke into song, ending in a grunt as though the singer had suddenly balanced himself against the wall... Bencolin went over swiftly and turned down the lamp, so that only a pin-point of light illuminated the big room.

Now unsteady footsteps grew louder along the passage. Graffin was singing again, muttering to himself. With my hand on the knob, I looked back to see Bencolin standing by the lamp, his finger on his lips for silence. The voice of the singer grew hysterical; the footfalls hesitated, shuffled, and then, with a grim rising of the song, they stumbled forward again.

I opened the door.

XVI

At the Turning of the Knob...

THE PASSAGE WAS WELL LIGHTED, BUT, EVEN SO, GRAFFIN staggered back, clutching at the wall to save himself from falling. He wore a top-hat and a dandified overcoat from whose collar dangled a white muffler. His face was so white that the clotted blue veins stood out on his forehead; the redness of his snipe nose was intensified, as were also his oyster eyeballs. The eyes rolled. He gasped,

"Oh! It's—you! I—"

"Sorry to startle you, Lieutenant," I said. "I was going down to pay a call. I can't sleep, and there's nothing to read in my room; I thought perhaps I might borrow a book."

He stared for a second, and then his face lighted eagerly.

"Yes!" he cried, seizing at my shoulder. "Yes, by all means! Glad you did. Delighted! Delighted—extend hospitality. Books, thousands of books; take any of'm. Perhaps you'd like—little drink, eh?"

He put his arm about my shoulder and kept eagerly talking about thousands of books as he lurched down the passage. He laughed; he slapped my shoulder and called me a goo' fellow. As we reached the door an expression of sly cunning crept into his look. He whispered:

"Perhaps, Mr.—what's your name?—yes, perhaps you wouldn' mind going in ahead of me and lighting lamp?" Deprecatingly, "'M a bit indisposed; you know how it is… Tck!"

"Of course," I said. It was not pleasant to go across that great scented room in the dark. I nearly knocked over the lamp in my blundering progress, but presently the green globe shone out. Graffin came in hastily and locked the door. He blurted, "Th-thanks... Lock other. Burglars!" he explained.

As he went over to fumble with it I wondered whether it would be advisable to leave it locked. If Jack Ketch were to have his chance at Graffin— Still, I could unlock it later.

"Draw curtains," he explained now, winking at me wisely.

"Don't you think we might as well have a little air—"

"*No!*" he cried, grabbing at the curtains and regarding me like a child whose toy you have attempted to take away. "Draw curtains," he repeated, with dignified firmness.

As he was taking off hat and coat an idea seemed to strike him. "Where's Joyet?" he cried.

The thought had only just occurred to me. Where was the valet? I had neglected to ask Bencolin; very probably he was included in the detective's arrangements, and the stage was to be left to Graffin. "Funny," the man mumbled, peering about. He lifted his voice to bawl, "*Joyet!*"

There was no answer. He shouted again, in a voice which must have been audible on the floor below, without result. Graffin's red eyes blinked round curiously; once he started for the door leading to the bedrooms, but he thought better of it.

"Sit down, Mr.—er—sit down, do. You're not in a hurry, are you? No, no; you just sit down, and we'll have little drink. Books," he swept an arm about. "Take choice. Have drink."

He sat down in lordly fashion in the chair before the table, peering at me from beyond the lamp, and from under the table he produced a bottle of whisky only just opened. The cunning look came back.

"H' stupid of me! H' *bloody* stupid! Only one glass. Perhaps—er—there's glass in bathroom; you go out that door, turn to left, and carry straight on; can' miss it. D'ye mind—?"

I saw him clutching at the edges of the table, following me with his eyes as I left. Gingerly I stepped through the door, closing my hand on the butt of the pistol in my pocket. The door to the left in this small alcove... beyond lay darkness. The rooms were very cold, and the windows mere frosted blurs on darker gloom. I could distinguish dim shapes of furniture. Several times I ran into a chair. And gradually the dim rooms grew endless and whirling, as though I were lost in a maze; distorted blurs wove before my eyes. Tile! Tile beneath my feet now. Groping cautiously, I found the edge of a glass shelf; then my fingers brushed the edge of a tumbler, and it fell into the washbowl with a hellish clatter which made my heart jump.

A board creaked in the room beyond. Standing motionless, I listened. The sound was not repeated.

No, the glass had not broken, though the noise of its crash still tingled in my ears. I picked it up and started back... *What was that?* It seemed to me that the door of a high wardrobe, whose mirror shone faintly from the opaque white of the windows, was being pushed slowly open. I could see the dim reflection slide at an angle along the mirror. My watch was ticking audibly in the vest pocket under my dressing-gown. No, this was another illusion. It was my own shadow. If I moved the hand which held my pistol, a corresponding shadow slanted on the mirror. But panic at this black and bewildering emptiness had laid hold of me, and, had I seen anything like a man moving inside that wardrobe, I know that I should have fired without challenge. (Nonsense!—pull yourself together! If Jack Ketch really does put his hand on your shoulder from behind something, what will you do *then*?)

Back in the large room again, I breathed more easily. Its vault stretched up high and ghostly, and those eerie green curtains were drawn over mysterious recesses, but at least there was blessed light.

Graffin looked at me eagerly. He let out a cackle of laughter, and asked in a tone intended to be jocose:

"Didn't meet up with any burglar, eh, my friend?"

Revulsion at this leering creature rose in me; this whining blackmailer who had taken such delight in torturing El Moulk, and now crouched in fear for his own scrawny neck. The neck would, I thought, afford a good hold for the hands; it was so long that you could put one above the other. (*Whew!* What an idea! Where did that come from?) I put the glass on the table and replied, coldly:

"No burglars. I thought I saw Jack Ketch once, but I was mistaken."

His hand jerked on the whisky bottle. The rheumy eyes grew wide, slowly; then he seemed to reconsider, and said, with pathetic eagerness:

"Oh!... Pulling my leg, eh? Ha, ha! By Jove! that's rich! Pull my leg—course." He forced out a few cackles of laughter, and wagged a playful finger. "Don' joke like that, m' friend. Bad for me; bad heart. It *was* a joke, wasn't it—eh?"

"Yes, it was a joke," I said wearily.

He poured out two drinks, almost filling the tumblers. With back-thrown head he was gulping his down, so that the red neck was elongated and the Adam's apple surged up and down in jerks. The *hammering* started again... Back jerked his face into view. He said, "What—was that?"

"I didn't hear anything."

"Oh... fancyamine. Righto. Luck." Another tilt of the glass.

One more of those; just one more. Let him finish that glass, and he was done for. I made a tentative motion in my chair, which he apparently interpreted as a preliminary to leaving him.

"Oh no. Mus'n't go. You don't wan' go," he said, persuasively. "Look here, you like piano? Play piano for you!" In the delight at this idea, he got up and stumbled towards the bench, throwing eager glances over his shoulder. The spectacle had begun to sicken me a little. "Play a piano. What d'youlike? Play anything. What d'youlike?"

"Whatever you wish. Have a drink."

"Tha's it! Li'l' drink. Have li'l' drink." He stumbled back to the table, and then scurried towards the bench again. Sitting there with his shoulders hanging, he stayed motionless for a time... Then the chords crashed out.

A thrill ran through me. He had not lost that uncanny, that magnificent touch; it was as though, of all his shaking faculties, only the hands were alive. Only the hands were swift, sure, and inspired. He played Chopin with a kind of exquisite madness, and the throbbing sorrow of the damned. At his left the colours of the mummy-case shone by the light; above him the green curtains stretched far up to a dizzy height. The back of his bald head bobbed foolishly... For a long time he played, and then the fury and softness died away. He seemed to forget about it. He turned round, snuffling, and looked at the floor.

Knock, knock... knock, knock, knock...

He lifted his head, and I said, very loudly: "That was superb! Play some more. Play—" My voice was almost a shout.

Knock, knock-knock, knock...

Graffin got to his feet and staggered back to the table. He was quieter now; you sensed, somehow, that the bottom was reached; it was as though he crumbled before my eyes. He said in a whisper:

"I'm done. I'm done. I can' stand it—any longer. He's buildin' g'lows for me."

The last words were so low that I barely heard them, and his head sank down into his skinny hands. He mumbled: "You'll put me in prison. Y'r the police; pumme in prison..." Suddenly he sat upright and smote the table a blow with his fist. "But I'll tell! I'll tell, d'y' hear? Rath'r go prison than stick this longer. *He* won' get me. If I tell you, you won' let'm gemme, will y'?

"I knew the kid. Kid was in service with me; r'ported dead. *I*"—a couple of large and ludicrous tears appeared in his eyes—"I got court-martial. Cow'rdice, d'sertion, they said. Lie. Going shoot me. War ended; kicked me out service. Went Paris. R'c'gnized kid. The kid with El M'lk... No duel! No duel atall! El M'lk shot D'lavateur, hear? *He* shot D'lavateur! Got proof!"

With weak fists he was pounding on the table and glaring at me, choking as he tried to speak faster.

"Come closer!" He beckoned, and I went to the table. "Made El M'lk pay money keep quiet. Then learned—livin' here—the kid's..." His voice mumbled off. I did not dare speak for fear that tenuous thread would be snapped or his brain would freeze again to silence. I held my breath.

"That's who Jack Ketch is! Made 'im pay me fif' thouz'n' for proof... Ogod! I was crazy!—Tried work him 'n' El M'lk both, hear?" Graffin was trying desperately to speak with coherence, and his rheumy eyes were glassy with the effort.

A pause, during which he breathed heavily.

"El M'lk didn' know who was sendin'—things here. Didn' know Jack Ketch was..."

"*Who?*" I demanded, and seized him by the shoulder.

"Lemme be!" said Graffin, snuffling. He looked puzzled; the thin thread had snapped. He stretched out his hand for the rest of the whisky. "What 'z I tellin'? Oh! Yes. Jack Ketch—"

Hiccoughing, he suddenly fell across the table senseless. His head struck the top with a sodden thud, and one sprawled arm knocked over the bottle, so that the spilled whisky crawled in a puddle about his face. Now only his swinish breathing was audible...

Presently I drew back. Rousing him was impossible. For the first time I realized how cold it was in the room. I looked round at those vast green walls, at the cold relics and the four brass lanterns. A premonitory chill crawled in me at the unearthly silence. Well, now for it! Remembering my instructions, I went to the windows and drew the curtains wide. The snow still fell with silent insistence. In the glass I could see a reflection of the green lamp, and Graffin's head as he lay with his face buried in one arm… Was somebody watching, was somebody listening, that I was required to go through that rigamarole of a farewell?

Very distinctly I said, "Good night, Lieutenant." I slapped him on the shoulder, tipped my hand to my head, and walked out into the shadow. Over by the door into the passage to the outer hall I stopped, and softly drew a chair across the door. Seated there in densest shadow, I had my back against one locked door, and could command a view of the other two.

The vigil had begun. Too late I wished for a sweater or some warm coat; the silk dressing-gown was infernally cold. I settled into a comfortable position and resigned myself to wait…

No noise penetrated from St. James's Street except the occasional whir of a cab. The little pulse of my watch beat steadily. Sometimes Graffin would mumble and stir; I could see his head shine beyond the green lamp. Marble floor in squares of black and white. Dark green carpet. Black marble mantelpiece at my left; four blue vases, and the tinted "Judgment of the Soul." Lofty shelves. Gilded cabinets. Three windows—how the snow was piling up, little by little, on their ledges!—with the faintest reflection of the room in them. *Tick-tick, tick-tick*—that was my watch. *Tick-tick, tick-tick*. Darkness beyond the windows. Pilgrim. Was Pilgrim awake? Did he know what was going on in his marionette-theatre? Pilgrim, Colette Laverne. A flashlight showing her ripped body. Cut it!

Dallings, Mount Street, Sharon. Sharon, the Mediterranean, Sharon's arms, a slow warm bath of sleep. Sleep, Macbeth shall murder... Murder. El Moulk.

Round and round my thoughts ran, like a squirrel in a cage. Murder—El Moulk, El Moulk—murder, or like the slow swing of a pendulum which lulls one to... sleep no more; Macbeth hath murdered... *tick-tick, tick-tick*.

Dragging hours. I had lost all sense of time. This period of staring at the room had twisted it out of all proportion, as a word will grow meaningless by being repeated over and over. The brass lanterns swung backwards and forwards on their chains; the black granite "Hathor" on one gilded cabinet tilted sideways! all things began slowly to revolve, as in one of those rolling barrels at the amusement parks, and I sank fathoms into the luminous depths of the green lamp. In some conjuring trick, playing-cards spurted from a magician's hand. They were all face-cards, whirled out in a shower. Face cards: El Moulk, Graffin, Pilgrim, Sharon, Talbot, Sir John, Joyet, Dallings. "Choose a card, ladies and gentlemen. *Choose a murderer...*"

Falling off to sleep, I jerked myself upright. A pain shot through my cramped limbs. The room was snapped into focus again.

Somebody was walking on the stairs.

The tick of my watch had somehow got mixed up with the heavy pounding drum of my heart. What time was it? Had I been asleep?

Somebody was walking on the stairs.

My hands were numb with cold and I shuddered. I fumbled in my vest pocket, and strained foggy eyes at the luminous dial of the watch. Half-past two. Had I been asleep? Half-past two, in the weird hours of the morning when there is even a different *feel* in the air, when the silence is nearer death than sleep.

Sly, soft, but distinct, the footsteps mounted from the depths of the house. On every landing they paused, as though the walker were listening. Jack Ketch was coming… Good God! I had forgotten to unlock the door!* Let him have free access. Let him put out a hand to take Graffin; then one blast of the whistle… It was maddening how slowly the footfalls ascended, but it gave me time. I got up softly and crept on the deep carpet across to the door to the enclosed staircase. My very legs felt light, and there was in me a horrible pounding excitement. From under a crack in the door a gust of air pricked up gooseflesh on my ankles. Softly, so softly that I could hear the drumming silence, I eased round the key in the lock. The footfalls were coming nearer; I could even discern their *scratch* on the dusty treads of the stair. Facing the door, I drew sideways to the right into the shadow of the curtained shelves. Let him see his prey lying helpless across the table.

The footfalls stopped. My heightened fancy could even pick out breathing beyond that door. I gripped the handle of the weapon until my wrist ached. Graffin moaned dimly in his sleep, and his loose arm slid down off the edge of the table…

Soft and insistent, there was a knocking at the door.

Silence. Distorted, the green-lit room reeled over itself in the enormous roaring we call quiet. Then the knocking was repeated. It was persuasive; a spider-sweet lure of a knock which urged you softly to open. Very gently the hand called you.

The knob began to turn.

---

* At this point in the first edition, readers were offered a refund for returning their copy to the bookseller having resisted the desire to break a physical seal over the subsequent pages "to discover how this ghastly vigil terminates and end the fearful uncertainty and harrowing suspense of this tale."

XVII

"The Name is—"

I LEVELLED THE AUTOMATIC TO THE RIGHT HEIGHT, BRACED myself against the shelves, and put the lip of the whistle into my mouth. I felt very cool, with a ghastly courage and extreme clarity of thought.

A pause. (Come on, damn you! Come on! One sound—shot or whistle-blast one or the other—so come on! A deep, rolling undercurrent of drums: this is the finale, you know, Jack Ketch.)

Still there was no movement, and the knob had ceased to turn. I stared at it, literally for minutes. To this day I can see its white porcelain in my dreams. What was delaying him? Was he standing out there on the landing, listening? Had the mere brushing of my sleeve against the curtain of the bookshelves, the ticking of my watch, warned him? I cursed with that soundless tightening of the jaws which makes them ache. Excitement was oozing; courage was crumbling—if he didn't move soon—

Had he gone? No; I should have heard any step on that stair. In which case I should have to take the initiative. By opening that door I could come face to face with Jack Ketch. But be careful! Bencolin has laid a trap: suppose this is one of the police? No. The whole furtiveness of that behaviour meant only one man... I grasped the knob, turning it to make no sound, and suddenly I threw open the door.

He was not on the landing. Only a little light filtered out from the green lamp, but it was sufficient to show me that there was nobody. There mounted the trap to the roof. There descended the staircase.

Dusty, deserted, and cold. Was I going mad? Surely I would have heard any sound of his descent on those steps! The thing was impossible; he had not just vanished into the wall. Stay! Back to me began to float old stories—the tales of a lost room hidden somewhere in the club. Perhaps they were not maundering legends. Perhaps, somewhere in this crazy old pile, there really existed a lost room where Jack Ketch held his unholy gambols, and he had flown away through the wall to caper round the tall gibbet of Nezam El Moulk. Hollow walls? Oh, impossible! Meanwhile, I was exposing myself directly against the light…

I stopped. There was a draught here, but it seemed to me that I felt a colder current of air which seemed to come from *above*. My eyes wandered to the ladder stretching up into darkness, up twenty feet or more to the gigantic height of these rooms and the trap-door. I could not see the trap, but by that current of air I knew where Jack Ketch had gone. His hidden lair was above. If I could track him there!…

Had he seen me? Probably not, since he had not closed the trap. On the other hand, he might be lying in wait, and I had no light. But it was foolhardiness or nothing: besides, Graffin was safe so long as I knew my man had gone up. On a wild impulse I took the key softly out of the door and locked Graffin in, dropping the key into my pocket. Retreat was cut off now. I could not let my courage go, for I had to meet Jack Ketch in the dark.

It was black on the landing, except for a faint crack of green under the door. Groping my way over to the ladder, I hung the whistle by its cord round my neck and began to mount. Testing every footstep, never trusting my weight until I knew it would make no noise, I ascended into a colder current of air. The source of that mysterious hammering grew more clear. Now I thought that the gloom above was a little lighter; just a fringe of blue which might mark a partly opened trap, and a straight current was stirring the hair on my head.

The gun was cumbersome. Once I almost dropped it, and I clung to the ladder for a moment in nausea and cold sweat…

My head was through the trap, and one groping hand touched wood. I waited for the chaos of a pistol-butt on the head, but nowhere was there a sound or a movement, and the imaginary lights of the crash faded. The trap was entirely open, as I found by groping cautiously about, and I hauled myself over the edge.

I was in some sort of attic, but of its nature or extent I could form no idea. A cold wind stirred in it, and I thought I detected the rustling of paper; but that weaving, foaming darkness was impenetrable. My fingers rested on… I moved them back and forth… polished hardwood. This was a most extraordinary attic, "for refuse," as they said at the club. It was a smooth and solid floor, and undoubtedly would not creak. Mercifully, I was wearing rubber soles.

And then the appalling folly of my conduct struck me. This garret must be enormous; for one person, without a light, to attempt tracing Jack Ketch in it while Jack Ketch's prey lay in a drunken sleep below was sheer madness. Should I blow my whistle, and trust to Bencolin's having men about to sweep the place from end to end? Should I—

A light appeared ahead. I was still sitting at the edge of the trap, exposed to any beam; now I rolled over swiftly and backed away. *Now* things must be narrowing down: we were not to hear this murderer's sly step at our doors, and his knock by night, without one terrible glimpse of his face. O God! I had dropped the whistle! My hand in the pocket of the dressing-gown found only a pack of cigarettes… I dropped on my knees and groped, with the sensation of one caught against a wall. There! It clinked faintly against my foot. Meantime the freezing cold had grown. Of course there must be a window corresponding to the one below; it was open, and I was near it… There was the light again. If I judged its position correctly, it must be against the far wall directly opposite me—that is to say, the wall whose corresponding one on the floor below was occupied by the piano and the mummy-case.

At first it crept out in an oblique white line, which broadened into a fan against the dark background. The light was coming from *inside* that wall. Now something was silhouetted against it. A man? No, it was too immensely tall. It shone on bricks; it shone on the height of an immense chimney. Between wall and chimney, along the side of the chimney, a door was opening. Now, slanting out across that fan of light, I saw the shadow of a man. It was grotesque, and incredibly tall, so that it bent across the roof of the garret. Its wavering outline was contorted as though the man were laughing, but I heard no sound. Pointed nose, open mouth, shaking shoulders, all were exaggerated. And by some trick of the light, the man seemed to be wearing a tall hat. Surely that could not be—*Graffin*, whom I had left in a stupor downstairs? I must be mistaken. The gaunt shadow swung backward and forward in slow pantomime, as to a secret music.

Somebody laughed. The light went out.

On the back of my neck I could feel stinging snowflakes as I stood by the open window. Now was no time for a funk; now was the time to use every wit. In darkness I began to move forwards. At one point during my idle vigil downstairs I had fallen to estimating the dimensions of the room. Allowing two feet to a pace, I had decided that it must be a little over fifteen paces wide. Adding four more for the width of the landing, I could tell just when I should have reached the source of the light. The chimney stack must be a dummy, since the fireplace below was on the other side of the room. If there were any obstructions, I should simply have to risk a noise… Seven paces I counted, eight, nine, ten, eleven, twelve, thirteen, fourteen…

My outstretched hand touched the wall. Could I have misjudged the width by a distance of over ten feet? No, this must be some other wall; five paces difference was too much. And yet, groping to the left, I ran into the brick chimney. It ran out a great distance from the wall, possibly six feet, and was of proportionate length. There must be a difference of ten feet between the wall of the room beneath and *this* wall, with six more for the projection of the chimney. There was the explanation of the secret room! The casual eye would never have noticed it with lights on. Coming up from the trap, one would glance at the other wall, forgetting the landing below, and estimate that the distances tallied. Only by pacing it off in the dark could the deception of the eye be overcome. In other words, the secret room must run the entire depth of the side of the house, with a dummy wall all along, and a false chimney-projection as a sort of anteroom.

Holding to the side of the chimney, I circled it to find the right-hand end where the door must be concealed. A sound attracted my attention—the faint noise of an unguarded step, then the *scraping* of a foot, and another, dying away. Somebody was going down the ladder.

I whirled round. That opening of the secret door was now clear. Jack Ketch was not reconnoitring; he had been leaving his lair. Somewhere on that black expanse we had passed each other. I had missed him. I had bungled my chance. Was he going after Graffin? I had almost sprung forward for the trap—whose location was now hazy in my mind—when there came the unmistakable sound of footfalls going *down* the stairs past the top landing. Certainly Bencolin was not such a fool as to leave the whole house unguarded! There must be guards to stop him. In the meantime…

Bewildered, I had lost my head completely. I had failed; I didn't know now what to do, and each minute the steps were dying out. In another moment I should have shouted, when my hand slid around the side of the chimney and found—an opening. Jack Ketch had left his secret door ajar. That meant he must be coming back, and now I was on the threshold of his secret.

My forehead was bursting. A fetid and musty smell was in my nostrils from the aperture in the chimney-side; the air was warm, and I thought I could see a vague glow of reddish light. There were other odours, too—heated iron, and the nauseating sweetness of chloroform. The door was a whole section of brickwork, very thick. I wriggled through the open space.

The hand holding my pistol touched a cold substance which made me gasp with deliverance. It was a candlestick, on some sort of table by the door, and then I could feel the warm top of the taper. The cigarette-lighter was in my vest pocket. I kindled the wick...

The dim flame swept aloft, under huge and moving shadows. I was in a large vestibule, stretching up to a great height, but for a moment I refused to believe that I had not stepped through the portals of a nightmare. It was curtained in folds of black velvet, with arabesques of gold writhing under my light. The draperies were moth-eaten, mildewed, and decomposing, a wilderness of leprous finery. Under my feet gleamed that same evil pattern of black and gold. The smell of chloroform was more pronounced, and also the smell of heated iron...

The flame of my candle was reflected in a high mirror, whose gilt plaster frame had peeled off in strips, and I saw the reflection of my white face. Cracked gas-globes drooped from a chandelier nearly eighteen feet above my head. On my left, in the outer projection formed by the false chimney, I thought I could distinguish a couch of some sort, and near it a trap in the floor. On my right was a curtained door leading to unknown depths, but the light was too dim to distinguish any definite shapes.

Setting the candle down on the table where I had found it, I grasped the pistol and went towards this curtained door at my right.

Somebody moaned.

I stood still, quivering to the chill of that dim, unearthly sound; but I could not locate it. It might have come from beyond the door, it might have been in this room. Cautiously I drew aside the black-and-gold drapery over the door. A long musty passage ran at right angles to it, apparently the length of the house. And then I realized that shuffling footsteps were coming along this passage from the bowels of the den...

Jack Ketch was not alone, then. Jack Ketch had a confederate! I knew, I could swear, that the murderer himself was not in these hidden rooms now; this was somebody allied with him... The shuffling footsteps grew louder, approaching the curtained doorway. I heard a voice now, upraised in a dreadful whining singsong.

"Where are you?—Where—are you?"

Faint, chilling, it swept in a low wail along the evil walls. "Where—are—you?" creeping with the plaintive blindness of a soul groping in the endless corridors of hell. The steam of heated metal stung my nostrils not a foot away. I flattened myself against the curtains of the wall as the drapes over the door trembled to the movement of a hand. Now in the doorway, dimly lighted by the candle, peered a figure. In its hand it carried something whose tip glowed a ghastly whitish-red. Again the thin and strangled wail beat bewilderedly against silence: "Where are you? Where are..."

It had not quite time to screech out before I sprang. I whirled that tiny figure by the throat and crashed it up against the wall, driving the gun-point into its stomach. Its legs wriggled horribly; the glowing tip of the poker staggered in the air and fell.

"Keep quiet!" I snarled. "Keep quiet, Teddy!..."

A frenzied gurgling, and the sound of my own panting breath. The light of the candle fell over my shoulder on his contorted face, a wrinkled horror with lips drawn back from the gums, slobbering. A fish-like film was over his eyes, and streaks of sticky hair-oil ran down across my hand at his throat. I had him pinned against the wall like a child crucified. With twisted limbs against a black-and-gold background, he stared at me. I could smell the white-hot iron burning a hole in the carpet. *Teddy!* I was shaking all over in sweat, and by his glassy protruding eyes I knew I must be choking him to death. Dropping into the jargon of the nursery, I spoke words which, whispered in that mad place, must have seemed the climax of all madness.

"Teddy make a sound," I whispered, "and—" The gun-point rammed again into his stomach.

Slowly I lowered him, relaxing the grip at his throat. This crack-brained boy, then, was a confederate of Jack Ketch, and even now he was heating the irons for the monstrous sacrifice. Still holding him by the neck, I backed through the curtained doorway with pistol ready.

It was none too soon. Even as I did so, through the half-opened brick entrance to the lair drifted the sound of scraping wood and a low thud. Somebody had closed the trap-door to the garret. Jack Ketch was returning to his hideaway.

In the twilight, drawing the curtains half open, I crouched with my captive. I could not even see the flame of the candle. It stood behind a projection of the wall which hid from view the outer entrance. Caught in a draught, its waving gleam sent shadows scurrying over the unsteady draperies of black and gold. But that ghostly light illuminated the path which Jack Ketch must take. Now his foot-steps were approaching the outer door! I wanted to shoot, to yell, anything to end the maddening slowness of those beats. The carpet smoked and glowed in little edges of fire from the fallen poker...

He came closer to the door, and I felt that my chest was bursting. He came inside...

Into the candlelight loomed a tall figure with a shadowed face, one shoulder humped. Yes, his face was invisible, but I saw the fingers of one long white hand crooked like a claw at his breast. He seemed to be swaying, he seemed to be peering for the tiniest whisper of danger. The tensity of that roaring moment ran tight and snapped. A board creaked under my foot. He whirled...

"Put up your hands!"

A blast from my whistle shrilled out deafeningly, and in that snapping of the strain I realized that I had relaxed my vigilance on the captive under me. Teddy writhed and rolled from my grasp, letting out a strangled shriek. A pudgy hand seized the fallen poker. I saw the glowing tip spin aloft, over my shoulder as I dodged, and I *heard* its crash against my skull. My head seemed to leap out and far, whirling in nowhere; there was a chaos of splintering lights, and the room reeled in nightmare...

Somebody was still blowing the whistle! Even in that inferno I knew that I had flung Teddy across the room, that I had even hurled my gun aside, and that I was springing for the throat of Jack Ketch. He was there ahead of me, weaving; he dodged back, throwing back his hands, and the candlelight fell on his face— No, no; this was crazy, mad, delirium; it was *not*—!

One yell burst from him. There was a crying of many voices. There was a rush of feet, and figures bolted through the door. Figures carried Jack Ketch back against the wall, manacled and fighting. The great draperies were ripped from their rods. With the din of his shouts in my ears, I swayed in sickness; the pinwheel lights rushed at me, my legs buckled, and I was whirled out and far into crashing night...

The face of Jack Ketch was the face of Sir John Landervorne.

XVIII

Handcuffs

THE FACE OF SIR JOHN LANDERVORNE...
Its sallow and bony austerity, its shining grey hair, its clipped beard and moustache. The inscrutable grey eyes under their thin brows, lids pinched down. The high cheek-bones, shadowing those eyes. The high-bridged nose, and the thin lips compressed.

I do not know whether it was with me in the mists of unconsciousness, but I know that it was the first thing I saw afterwards. I was first conscious of a nausea, a blinding headache, and the blurry sound of voices. I was half sitting, half lying against the wall, and I raised my head. Then I knew that the room was lighted by many flaring gas-jets, and opposite me I saw Sir John's face.

Some struggling idea flickered into my brain—Jack Ketch. He was— Oh, nonsense! A dream, a crazy vision, hammered out on the splintering anvil in my head! He was sitting in a chair just across from me. I smiled at him, but he did not return the smile. His face was wooden, but it was strained in a look of wildness round the eyes. He was very pale, and he breathed heavily while he blinked at the light. He looked ill. He wore a grey suit and his hands were folded in his lap. Then he shifted his position, as though the light hurt his eyes, and I saw that there were handcuffs on his wrists.

The splitting headache made me want to close my eyes, but I had to solve this bewildering riddle. I could see only that little segment of the room where Sir John seemed to be alone. Then there became visible legs which appeared to belong to Talbot, and there were blurry words:

"—to warn you that anything you say may be used against you."

Sir John seemed to be roused. He drew a few deep breaths, and his heavy gasps were dying out. It was as though the mists of a nightmare were being driven from him. Grey and impassive, he twitched his head with impatience.

"Don't be a damned fool, Talbot," he said.

Afterwards he smiled in his wintry fashion. "Yes, by all means spare the rigamarole. You've got me, and you know it. A 'fair cop,' isn't it?"

"Then you don't deny—?"

"Why the devil should I deny it?" asked Sir John, curtly. "You've your witnesses, haven't you? I shall swing for this, of course. But you might as well understand"—he lifted cold eyes—"that it doesn't matter a snap of my fingers to me."

I struggled to a sitting position, trying to take in the details. The room hardened before me. All the gas-jets were lighted. Near me stood Talbot, looking rather haggard. Behind Sir John's chair was a police officer in plain clothes, holding the arm of Teddy—who was crouched back against the wall, his hands over his eyes. On the otto-man to the left of the entrance—that dim couch I had seen when I came in—sat a figure which drove the last mists from my eyes. It was Nezam El Moulk. He was very pale and tousled, with the stubble of a beard, and the jauntiness of his sickly face had gone. He held hard to the edges of the ottoman to keep himself from shaking, but his yellow eyes glared with hate.

Now through the curtained doorway to the interior stepped another person. It was Bencolin. The Frenchman was cool and impersonal; he regarded Sir John as he might have looked at some curious insect, and Sir John flushed bitterly. There was a silence…

"Would you—would you like to make a statement?" Talbot asked. There was a dead finality about all this formal courtesy which made me shiver.

Sir John rose. He stood gaunt and tall in the middle of the little room, his stooped shoulders blocking out the yellow-blue flare of the gas-jets. He looked almost frail then, except for the thin, contemptuous set of his face. He stared straight ahead, frowning.

"I will write you out a statement," he said, "if you will take me down to my rooms now. There must be no misunderstanding—"

He paused, and looked suddenly towards Bencolin. Cold and aloof as ever, but with the coming darkness in his eyes, he added, stiffly:

"I believe you win your wager."

"I believe I do," replied the detective, indifferently.

Sir John said in a harsh voice: "I shall have to send you my cheque instead. Friends!" He rattled his handcuffs. "Friends! God help us!" Bencolin bowed. What went on behind that Satanic mask I had no idea; it showed only the edge of a cruel politeness and an eyebrow lifted mockingly. I felt that he was with difficulty restraining a smile. Still Sir John did not move. He glanced down at the handcuffs on his wrists and examined them curiously, as though suddenly he could not understand...

"I think you may take these off, Talbot," he said. "I shall not repeat my earlier outburst..."

The inspector stepped in quickly and unlocked them. Then Sir John asked Bencolin, as though he could not stop torturing himself:

"You knew this—all the time, didn't you?"

"I suspected, yes. The man who called himself Keane was—"

"He was my son," said Sir John.

A pause. The struggle in Sir John was shown only in his too-quick breathing, but at any moment you felt he might give way. He clenched his fists. Now in that grotesque room he seemed to tower. He glanced over towards the ottoman, and for a second his body was contorted as I had seen the outline of that shadow shaken with hate. El Moulk let out a cry...

"You swine!" shouted Sir John. "He was my son!"

That terrible voice rang in the hollow room.

"Easy, sir!" said Talbot, and grasped his arm as he stiffened; "easy—"

For a moment Sir John stayed motionless. Then his grey face turned slowly. His voice was not loud, but it was thick and unnerving.

"Put those cuffs back on me, Talbot," he ordered, holding out his hands. "Put them back on, man!"—The outstretched hands trembled. "Good. Good. Thank you… Now…"

He was growing a little unstrung, and he turned blind eyes to the flare of the gas.

"You see," he said, hesitantly—"you see, I was—very fond of that boy. He was—everything I had, and I was proud—I—thought he died—like a gentleman…

"And," Sir John added, "I think—he did die—like a gentleman. But not the way I thought, you see? I didn't know—some swine had made him—hang himself—for something he didn't do. And when I learned it, I…"

Checking himself, he swallowed hard. Iron reserve hardened his jaw.

"Be good enough to take me downstairs, Talbot," he said.

Talbot motioned towards the entrance, from which another plain-clothes officer appeared and took Sir John's arm. Then the inspector nodded to the second one, and Teddy was impelled towards the door. It was all done in frozen pantomime, with no sounds except the faint click of the handcuffs and Teddy's muffled sobs.

"Go easy on him, officer," said Sir John. "My statement will exonerate him. He only did—what I told him." At the door he paused. He hesitated, as though he were weighted down by exhaustion, and his near-sighted eyes blinked at us; but he wore his gyves proudly, and he smiled.

"I have one last instruction for you," he said in a steady voice. "In the front room of this—suite, you will see a highboy in the left-hand corner. In the drawer of that highboy you will find definite proofs that Nezam El Moulk shot and killed Pierre De Lavateur on November sixteenth, ten years ago. I bought them from the man Graffin. There is a photograph, among other things. I ask you to use these proofs, Bencolin, and you will have no difficulty in sending him to the guillotine. In the same room you will find the Laverne woman bound and gagged in a closet. She may have smothered by this time; I sincerely trust this is so. You will also find the short sword with which I killed the chauffeur and the pistol I used to shoot Sergeant Bronson; they will be useful at the—at the trial. I think that is all." He drew himself up, nodding curtly. "Good—good evening, gentlemen. I shall—probably not—see you again."

… When he had gone there was a long space of silence, while Talbot walked aimlessly about the room, running his hands through dishevelled hair and muttering. That last speech left a bitter taste, a sick reaction of futility and doom. In that drugged hour of the morning the cold minutes ticked towards dawn. The inspector turned his drawn face.

"I expect I had better go and untie that woman," he muttered.

"I have already done so," said Bencolin. "She has been drugged, but she will recover shortly…"

Somebody spat out an ugly word. We turned towards El Moulk. While Sir John was there, the Egyptian had been cowering back against the wall. Now he was crouching on the ottoman, glaring. He put up a hand to straighten his hair; the numb arm moved with an effort, shaking, and his wrists were red-scored by the galls of a cord. About his neck was still a thin rope of what seemed to be woven steel wire, and it looked as though it had been soldered on. Its long coils rattled against the wall behind him, and the end was fastened to a beam in the roof… Suddenly he broke into a torrent of such abuse as I have seldom heard from any man. His shrill voice was raised frantically; he shook stiff fists and grovelled there in his chain like a dog on the leash.

"Be quiet!" cried Talbot, "if you please!—"

The yellow eyes whirled on him. "He thinks I will go to t'e guillotine, eh?" shrilled the Egyptian, beating his chest. "By God! he will learn better! I will spit in his face. I will—"

"Be quiet, please!"

"I will not be quiet! I will not be quiet! I will show him!" The steel galled El Moulk's neck, and he grabbled at it, still writhing about on the ottoman. "Are you goin' to set me loose? Are you goin' to make me sit here like a dog with this thing round my neck? Are you? Speak up, you stupid louse—*are you?*"

A mottled red surged in Talbot's face. He responded, quietly:

"It's been welded on, Mr. El Moulk. We shall need cutters to remove it. I've sent for them; if you will be patient, we shall have you free directly."

"My wrists!" moaned El Moulk. "Oh, my poor wrists! And my legs! I can' stand up yet. That dog! Oh, that—"

"Look out for that trap!" snapped Bencolin, as the Egyptian tried to stagger to his feet. Cowering, El Moulk sank down again.

The detective was indicating the trap in the floor I had previously noticed, a few feet in front of the ottoman. It was several feet square and constructed of two leaves. In each of the leaves was set a staple; through both of them a wooden stick ran to the floor on either side, holding it up and closed. The thing looked very flimsy.

"Step on *that*," the detective added, "and you'll go straight through to the room below. I think—*Tiens!* Jeff's awake!" He walked over, smiling, and bent to shake me by the shoulder. "That skull of yours, old man, is uncommonly thick. It was only a glancing blow, but I shouldn't care to take it on my own head. Here, have a drink.—All right now?"

"All right," I said, taking the proffered flask. "But my head—God! Help me up."

"I confess, Jeff," he said, as I got weakly to my feet, "that I never cast you for any such stellar rôle as you played tonight. You were to watch Graffin, and it seemed to me you were safely accounted for. I assure you I had several bad moments when I saw you walk through this door and light the candle…"

"You saw me?"

"Why, yes. Talbot and I were in the garret all the time, on the watch. It nearly disorganized our plans, this venture of yours. However!"

"Of course," I said, bitterly, "you knew where the secret room was."

Talbot mopped his forehead. "It was touch and go for a while," he said. "When I heard *two* people wandering about in this garret… phew! We never thought you'd get mixed up in this, and we couldn't grab our man until we knew which one we were grabbing in the dark." He looked about with some bewilderment. "Then this place is directly over the big room. Still I don't see—"

"Come here," requested Bencolin. Kneeling by the trap, he hooked his finger in the parallel staples and gently withdrew the wooden support. Then he lifted the leaves. "Now look down and tell me what you see."

Talbot and I approached the edge. Even El Moulk started out of his lethargy, mumbling, to peer below. Some twenty-five feet or so beneath us, and slightly to the left, I saw the table with the green lamp. Graffin's bald head still shone there, sprawled across it beside the overturned bottle of whisky.

"As I told you," Bencolin continued, lowering the leaves and hooking them into position, "I was intrigued from the start by this tale of somebody who was able to enter the apartment, with doors locked and servants on the watch, and leave souvenirs there. At first I thought, of course, of a secret passage in the walls somewhere. Then I heard that all the souvenirs had been left in just one place—on the centre table. Never at the door, or in the bedrooms, or anywhere else except *on this table*. The inference was obvious: Jack Ketch was able to reach no place *except* the table, which suggested that things were being dropped from above. And when I remembered what sort of gifts had been left there—"

Squatting by the trap, he looked up at me.

"You recall what I pointed out to you, Jeff?—the peculiarity of all the objects found on the table? They were all solid, *unbreakable* things. Books, a little wooden figure, a piece of rope. Whereas fragile and breakable things, like that gallows-model, or the glass pistols, or an earthen jar, had been sent by the post—clearly because they would have been smashed had they been delivered in this other way. It became clear that Jack Ketch was sending gifts from the ceiling without ever being seen at all."

"Then down there this afternoon," said Talbot, "when you raised all that fuss about rare old something-or-other brass, and got out the stepladder, and climbed up to look at the lanterns, you were really looking—?"

"At the ceiling, of course. The trap is artfully painted, and hidden so ingeniously that it would go unnoticed by any eye not looking for it; but reason told me it must be there. And, once having located the trap, it was not very difficult to trace this hideaway… Of course, I couldn't tell you then what I was searching for, because I already suspected Sir John, and to let him know I had guessed the presence of the secret room would have been ruinous. Even as it was, he had several of his worst moments down there, if you recall his behaviour."

Talbot dug his hands in his pockets and shook his head bewilderedly.

"You already suspected him?" he demanded. "Sir, he was the very last person—"

"Nonsense, Inspector," Bencolin interposed, brusquely. "His guilt was so glaringly apparent from the first that I wonder how you overlooked it. Man, he made a horrible blunder at almost every turn! Of course, I was puzzled for a time by certain features of it, because I hadn't yet met our half-witted Teddy; but, once Teddy entered the picture, the whole sequence of events became plain."

"Well, it isn't clear to *me* even yet," muttered Talbot. "Especially how anybody could have seen anything suspicious in his behaviour..."

Bencolin sat down in the chair which Sir John had occupied. The reaction was on him; he looked old and tired, and the harsh light brought out the pouches under his eyes. For a moment he sat there brooding and ruffling the grey patches at his temples with nervous fingers.

"Very well," he said abruptly. "Let me tell you, then, just what course the murderer followed. Let me tell it to you as though we did not know the identity of the murderer, and then you will see how inevitably it links up.

"Much of the story you already know, so that you can fill in as I go along. Jack Ketch was obviously somebody to whom the dead 'Keane' had been very dear. Such careful and murderous planning, such overwhelming devotion to his object, was not possible merely to some friend of 'Keane.' There was nothing lukewarm about *this* vengeance; a blood-relative was concerned, and a tigerish lust for retribution.

"Jack Ketch, after mourning Keane as dead for nearly ten years, learns the truth. He has been brooding in his devotion. All his thoughts have been centred on the dead man; all his love, all his hopes and plans in life, died with Keane. The ghastly shock of learning what really happened! The slow realization—the insane flare of hate—the quiet ferocity with which he prays to his God for vengeance! Then the loving care with which he sets out to scheme... Night after night, meditating on each subtle horror he will inflict on—"

"*Don't!*" shrilled Nezam El Moulk. "Don'—talk—like that!" The Egyptian was fingering the steel rope about his neck, and his lips were drawn back from his teeth in a contorted grimace.

The steel rope rattled. In all our minds loomed the grey set face of Sir John Landervorne, the quiver of his nostrils, the cold eye where lay an edge of madness. I could see the twitch of those long white hands...

"He has learned of this secret suite of rooms. In his brain flowers a plan perfect in its details, and he chuckles nightly over a brilliant and intricate plan. For months he has been torturing his victim; and now, at the anniversary of Keane's death, he is ready to act. We have determined already that he has made El Moulk's acquaintance. We know how he lured him out that night, lured him round to the back of this house—is that correct, my friend?"

"He—he tol' me," the Egyptian muttered, "we would watch for Jack Ketch from *here*. I did not know about t'e trap. He tol' me. He said we would watch from t'e roof. We came in here, and then—"

"At what time was this?"

"Just after seven; fifteen, twenty minutes. He was so friendly! I had tol' my chauffeur to wait for me in the alley... no, *he* tol' my chauffeur to do that! I didn't. I wanted to send Smail away, but he said no. He took me up here, and all of a sudden he smiled at me, and— What happened to Smail? Why didn' *he* come and—"

"Because he had to die to fulfil Jack Ketch's plan. When you were disposed of, the murderer crept downstairs again. Smail was waiting in the foggy alley. A few quick blows with the short sword…"

Bencolin turned to us.

"And do you see now that he needed a confederate? The nice balance of his plan demanded that he have an alibi. Some one, not himself, had to take that car away. It could not be left there in the alley to tell exactly where El Moulk had gone. It must be taken away… And precisely there is where Jack Ketch's plan miscarried! He wanted his confederate to drive the car out on some lonely road and leave it there, far from the club…

"Gentlemen, I knew there had been a confederate from the first time I looked at that car. If Jack Ketch were mad, he was at least *consistently* mad. He did not slice gilt tassels and glass buttons off a chauffeur's uniform; he did not steal bright nickelled pistols, and cheap gold watches, and hack at fingers after imitation diamond rings. That sort of conduct was not a part of his madness. He did not return automobiles to the club. Above all, *he was not such a tiny person that, when he sat driving the car beside the dead chauffeur, he could not be seen at all by people on the other side!*"

Bencolin smote the arm of the chair.

"But, gentlemen," he said, gently, "who, of all the people we met, was the only one who went wild at the sight of bright shiny pieces of metal? Who was the sort of thief who would steal a gleaming brass watch—and pass up a platinum cigarette-case because it was dull and unattractive: not valuable like the brass watch or the trumpery gilt tassel? Who alone was small enough to drive that car and be hidden by the vast bulk of the chauffeur?—When we met Teddy in the passageway this afternoon, I knew without question who the confederate was."

Talbot nodded. "Oh, it's clear!" he said, bitterly, "it's clear!—But then when he was in the rooms this afternoon, and he got such a fright that he ran out screaming—"

"He was returning the loot," said Bencolin, "because Jack Ketch made him do so. Stealing those things was no part of our murderer's plan; he was scrupulous and conscientious, Jack Ketch was. So Teddy was bringing back the pistol, the tassels, the watch... Of course, I knew it as soon as I saw them—"

"You knew it when you saw them?" cried Talbot. "In God's name, how?"

"The dust, man; the coal dust!" replied Bencolin testily. "Didn't you notice that black dust on the red bandana handkerchief? Of course, Teddy had them wrapped in his handkerchief at the bottom of the coal-scuttle. By the way, it was Teddy who had been smoking that cigarette; you know his weakness for smokes, I think..."

"But the book, the *Murder Considered as One of the Fine Arts*! Surely he wasn't reading..."

"Oh no! Sir John did that, I fancy. He was afraid we would realize it was Teddy who had been at work there, and, finding the book on the desk, he simply opened it while Jeff's back was turned—the rest of us were out of the room, you remember. Then he called Jeff's attention to it. As I told you, nobody had been reading it at all; the pages were uncut."

"Then Teddy went in there to return the things—and got no fright at all?"

Bencolin chuckled. He drew a cigar from the pocket of his dressing-gown and contemplated it whimsically.

"Oh yes, Inspector, he got a fright! A colossal fright, I am inclined to think. He came in, he laid the fire, and from the scuttle took the things he was to bring back. He lighted one of El Moulk's cigarettes and opened the drawer...

"And do you remember what he saw? In the drawer, right before him, was a huge picture of Smail! Suddenly there leered up at him the features of the dead man who was already beginning to haunt him. The courage he had possessed the night before, when he had been willing to drive the car for the possessions of the dead man, had already gone. His conscience was working. That picture must have leaped before his eyes like an accusing ghost. He takes back the things he has stolen—and up springs that leering jack-in-the-box, that horror from the grave!

"He shrieked and ran. Sir John, meeting him in the hallway, realized what had happened. Did you notice that all the time he was trying, apparently, to make Teddy tell what he had seen, he was in reality digging his fingers into the boy's shoulders—warning him to be silent? He knew Teddy was too frightened to speak."

And as Bencolin settled back to light his cigar, there drifted back to me the words which Teddy had spoken in my room that night: "A-lookin' right *up* at me, it wos; a-lookin' right *up* at me!—"

XIX

The Trap Falls at Last

"WELL, THERE IS NO USE DWELLING ON IT," SAID BENCOLIN, shrugging. "You can see that this crack-brained boy disrupted the whole plan. He was told to take the car out, far away somewhere in the wilds, and leave it there. Didn't he tell us once that the great ambition of his life was to own an automobile? Joyously, crazy to drive, even willing to drive with the dead man on the seat, so long as he can run a limousine—out he goes, on a crazy joy ride all over London! There is your explanation."

"But why the devil did he bring it back?" asked Talbot.

"I think I can answer that," I put in, still remembering my conversation. "I talked with him tonight. One idea was stuck in his head; something like, 'No matter where they sends me, I always comes right back here. Always!' He was frantic on the point."

"Yes," replied Bencolin. "He probably was; I fancy he had received some sharp comments from Jack Ketch on that piece of business. Why, picture it! Fog or no fog, at once frightened and delighted, the half-wit roars round on his journey—you recall how he paid no attention to any traffic signals? Fortunately for him, it was so foggy that people looking at the car would imagine the big chauffeur was driving it. It was only when you looked at it closely, as Jeff did, that you noticed anything different. Fortunately, also, the fog enabled him to leap out of the car when he arrived at his destination, and to escape unseen. By the way, Jeff, I called your attention to that excessively cramped space in the front seat. It was bad for the chauffeur, but it went very well with Teddy's short legs. Anyhow, that was the flaw in

Jack Ketch's plans—he never bargained on the lunatic conduct of his accomplice. It must have given our killer some very bad moments when we were pursuing the car down Pall Mall. Oh, Sir John was as startled as we were..."

"Sir John! Sir John!" snapped Talbot. "All right—grant everything you've said so far. Nevertheless, there's nothing which might have indicated *him* as Jack Ketch. Suppose he did squeeze Teddy's shoulders; that might mean nothing. You've no proof that he was the one who opened that book while Mr. Marle's back was turned; not a shred of proof! How could you possibly have connected him with the crime?"

"At first," said Bencolin, reflectively, "I think it was the fact that the murderer knew you."

"Knew me?"

"Yes. You got a telephone message at Vine Street, 'Nezam El Moulk has been hanged,' and the rest of it. This call was put through during the time we all were at the theatre. The curious point was that the caller asked to speak to *Inspector Talbot*. Not just the Vine Street police-station, but very definitely Inspector Talbot; you told us that yourself.

"That startled me considerably. How many people in London, do you think, know offhand the name of the detective-inspector in charge of their district? Do you know it in New York, Jeff? Do I myself know it in Paris? In particular, we had decided that the murderer was somebody at the Brimstone Club, and it was somebody who knew his metropolitan police very, very well. Well, who at the Brimstone Club definitely *did* know the name of the Inspector at Vine Street? Sir John Landervorne—because after the murder of the chauffeur he himself suggested ringing up Talbot to summon him here!

"Still, it was only an idle speculation. Then I suddenly remembered that it was while Sir John was in there, phoning to summon

Talbot, that the little wooden man must have been hung on the toy gallows in the lounge. Now, whoever hung that toy on the rope was obviously the murderer, because the toy had last been seen in El Moulk's possession—"

"I showed it to him!" El Moulk cried suddenly from the corner. "The wooden man! When I met him and came up here with him, I showed it to him, and he took it from me—!"

"Ah yes. Now just cast your minds back. We had left the little gallows in a cabinet by the fireplace when we quitted the lounge at six o'clock. Somebody took it from the cabinet, put it on the centre table, and hung the toy from its rope. *Who knew the gallows was in that cabinet?* Just three people! Just three people knew where it was—you, Jeff, Sir John Landervorne, and myself.—And who alone had access to the lounge unobserved, after the murder of the chauffeur? Sir John Landervorne, who was telephoning to Vine Street for Talbot at his own suggestion, because—"

"—because," supplemented Talbot, "the telephone box is right opposite the door to the lounge."

"Precisely. So I asked myself: Could Sir John have put in that other telephone call also? That sinister call telling that El Moulk had been captured? And I knew that he could have done so, since, while we were at the theatre, none of us had seats together. He could have slipped out and called from a public box, unobserved. Well, then! Was it also possible that he could have been the one to spirit El Moulk out of his automobile? When I learned that El Moulk had merely driven around the block, and that the chauffeur had been murdered *not more than twenty minutes after leaving this club—*"

There came to me a recollection of sitting in the lounge, waiting for Bencolin and Sir John to go out to dinner. El Moulk had left a little after seven. It was half an hour before Sir John appeared...

"I see you agree with me," Bencolin said, yawning. "Of course he had lured El Moulk up from the alley, killed the chauffeur, and despatched Teddy with the car—we know that now—before coming out with us. Really, he had no alibi at all! Whenever important things were happening, he was always absent. Just as he was absent this afternoon, when he called for Miss Laverne. No wonder he could convince her he was an official at Scotland Yard—convince even her suspicious nature! He must simply have shown his old official papers, and she felt quite flattered at being escorted by an assistant commissioner. Ever think of that? Or have you thought of that expression of startled incredulity on the dead face of Bronson? Bronson knew him, naturally; and to see his former assistant commissioner confront him with a pistol..." Bencolin shrugged.

"But what about the telephone call she received this afternoon—from Mr. El Moulk?"

Bencolin looked over inquiringly at the Egyptian.

"*He* made me call," said the latter; "Yes—I know what you mean! He made me call. I tol' her there would be a detective call for her; I tol' her I was *safe*. I tol' her I had only pretended to disappear, and I was hiding, and not to be afraid of Scotland Yard, because they were helping me!"

"Did you tell her to inform everybody that she was going to the Yard?" asked Talbot.

"Yes! Yes! I tol' her to say that, because then the murderer would be put off t'e track, you see? Then, I say, she can come here and together with Scotland Yard we can catch the murderer—"

"But where the devil did you call from?"

Bencolin interposed: "I can show you when we explore this very interesting place. There is a very antiquated telephone here, which is tapped in on the one in El Moulk's rooms below. Undoubtedly they used it when Rayle staged his revel in these apartments, and, so long as the phone below is in working order, so is this one. It was perfectly safe for him to use this one—since, if the suspicious Mademoiselle Laverne traced the call, it would have been found to come from the Brimstone Club, and her last suspicion would have been alleviated."

There was a pause, while Bencolin stared at the floor.

"The details we have yet to learn," he said, finally. "I can only guess at them now. Graffin and young John Landervorne were undoubtedly in the same corps of the service during the war. Young Landervorne's plane, I remember, crashed near the end of the fighting, and he was reported dead. Graffin was kicked out of the service about the same time. Anyhow, Graffin must have known him. Both of them turned up in Paris—young Landervorne in a hospital, it seems—and both became acquainted with El Moulk. The fact of the young man's being a dabbler in Egyptology (as witness that book he wrote) would give cause for friendship..."

Bencolin stopped suddenly, from what cause I could not fathom. All of us were forgetting that El Moulk himself was listening, crouched against the wall. Talbot seemed to understand that something was wrong, and he inquired, hurriedly:

"How do you suppose Sir John learned about this place?"

"Teddy, in all probability; Teddy in his wanderings may have stumbled on the entrance. I can't tell, naturally."

"There is just one last question," said Talbot. "The shadow which Mr. Dallings saw—the night he was wandering in the fog—"

"That," said Bencolin, "should have been explained to you when you saw the little toy gibbet. Don't you remember the monstrous shadow of it which the firelight threw on the wall of the lounge? Dallings saw the same thing, on a window-blind, with somebody's hand walking the little toy man up the steps. And, Inspector," he bent forward, "it was another signpost which pointed straight to Sir John Landervorne. Dallings saw that shadow *here*, as you should have realized. And he saw it on a ground-floor window—the window of somebody whose rooms give on that alley. Do I need to tell you that the ground-floor apartment at the back is occupied by Sir John?"

"Good Lord! If we had been able to see that at the beginning—!"

"You would have seen through it all?" Bencolin sat back quizzically. "Yes. But that was the climax of all reasoning: Sir John sitting up late, brooding over the toy he had constructed, laughing in delight at what he had constructed. Even, I imagine, as he fashioned those calling-cards...

"That was the fact which brought it home to me most clearly that Sir John must be the murderer. Finally, the crowning indication of all was the fact that, of all the people at this club, his rooms alone were in proximity to these. His rooms gave on that staircase. He alone could reach the secret chambers without being seen. It was *his* private staircase, too, and with it he could prowl about whenever he liked."

"There is just one other point," I put in. "Somebody, at some time after one o'clock in the morning, knocked on Mademoiselle Laverne's door and left a card there..."

"I fancy it was Teddy," the detective replied. "The card was bloodstained, if I remember correctly, and was probably stained while he was sitting beside the chauffeur. Very likely he had instructions from Sir John to leave the card at the door somewhat earlier, after he had left the dead chauffeur somewhere. In the excitement of his ride, Teddy probably forgot all about it. Then, after he had taken the car back to the Brimstone at midnight, he remembered his mission. And he executed it. It was fortunate for him that he met nobody on his walk to Mount Street—he's a bit conspicuous, you know. The interval between the time he took the car back and the time he left the card at her door he undoubtedly used for getting rid of the bloodstains on him—changing his clothes, I imagine. He couldn't walk through London as he was."

"A child!" muttered Talbot, "a child doing all that—!"

"He's no child, I assure you," Bencolin snapped. "Don't be deceived by his stature; he is twenty-five years old, or more. Certainly he can't be more than four and a half feet tall, but he was tall enough to squeeze himself in and drive that automobile. During the war I knew an ambulance driver who could barely see over the windshield, but he handled heavy cars on roads full of shell-holes without a single mishap.* It was my recollection of this fact which started me thinking of the possibility."

He brushed a hand over his eyes.

"I have led you along a tangled trail, gentlemen, and I think I have shown you how each step followed the last. And when we learn the truth, we find that the truth works out just as most things do in this life. The only sufferers by all these wild happenings are a poor devil of a detective sergeant, shot through the heart, and a chauffeur who lies in potter's field. It seems now that—what do the motion pictures say?—'with hearts cleansed and souls uplifted, Mr. El Moulk and his charming lady may walk hand in hand into the sunset, twin hearts that—'"

He turned his head slowly. On his face was a thoughtful and deadly smile.

"At least, you may walk in that fashion until I have the pleasure of sending one of you to prison for perjury and the other to the guillotine for murder."

He rose slowly, and the scrape of his chair on the floor was the only noise in that abrupt and chilling silence. His jaw was shadowed and lined harshly; in the dead-black dressing-gown he seemed to soar

* Mentioned in Lieut. C. S. Melisse's *Mémoires de la Grande Guerre*.

against the curtains of black-and-gold, and the flare of the gas threw high upon them the shadow of a horned head. Now the hooked eyebrows were drawn low over glittering eyes...

El Moulk was crouching on the ottoman; he sat transfixed, but slowly a glare of triumph mounted in his eyes.

"You think so?" he said softly. "You think so, eh?"

"Sir John Landervorne fastened that noose round your neck," Bencolin went on, as though he had not heard. "I think he was going to make you walk on that flimsy trap after he had torn out your bowels. He would make you walk on it, and down you would drop—down, do you see?—twenty feet down, and the steel rope would snap your neck to a nicety. And he would leave you hanging there for us to find, with all his evidence cleared from here... The death reserved for you, my friend, is not quite so picturesque, but I assure you it will serve my purpose as well. The Red Widow deals with necks, my friend, quite as effectively as any steel rope. In all my career no murderer has ever escaped me—do you hear?" His voice was still poisonously gentle. "That is why I was so anxious to save you. That is why I interested myself in this investigation, and spared no pains to see that you were delivered from the hands of Jack Ketch. I wanted to take you back to Paris with me: to go out at dawn and have your neck shaved by that exquisite little barber we know of..."

El Moulk was trembling, but it was with an insane triumph. The coils of his rope rattled against the wall. His yellow eyes were distended: he writhed on the ottoman, horribly, as though he had more than one pair of arms and legs...

"I am goin' to tell you something," snarled the Egyptian. "Listen, you—you—" His words choked him. He stabbed his finger at the detective. "By God! you're not goin' take me back! Do you know why? Do you know *why*? They kep' me drugged up here. Yes! They kep' me tied. Yes! But do you know what I did? While the kid was here, I got partly free. Didn' you hear me *knocking*? Didn' you hear me swing this rope against the edge of the door…"

So much for the knocking; but now none of us paid any attention to it. We were watching him as he panted, and his words ground on:

"Before that man, he came up and drug me again, do you know what I do? I have bring the kid in here. I have offer him a gold-piece I have if he will take those paper—that photograph of me Graffin have taken—he sneak out, damn—he sneak out and take of me when I kill De Lavateur—" His English was growing incoherent; he steadied himself. "I have offered him the gold-piece if he will burn it all in the fire where he is heating the irons to torture me! And he did—*he did!*"

A screech of eldritch laughter convulsed him. The stubble of his beard, the wild disordered hair, his blackened shirt front…

"And now there is no proof! I shot De Lavateur, and there is no proof! Jack Ketch they have captured—I am free! You can' prove it! I am free! And the curse is broken, too."…

Suddenly he seemed to realize something. The light of fanaticism deepened as in the crash of a blinding revelation. "The curse," he muttered, "the curse is not—" He flung up his arms. His voice, shrill in victory, tore through the silence:

"The gods are dead! I have killed them! Dead is Ra! Oh—dead is Anubis! Dead is Sakhmet the avenger! Dead are the gods of my people, and hunt me no more! Dead are the gods of Egypt!"

He leaped to his feet. Glaring, spitting, crying at Bencolin; he whirled as in a crazy dance-step. Dancing in mad laughter, he took a step forward, full upon the trap in the floor.

It was all over in an instant. One shriek alone he uttered. The wooden stick snapped, and I had a momentary glimpse of his skinny upraised arms and his fallen jaw. With a booming crash the trap dropped; rustling, the steel line ran out and jerked taut with a snap that shook the beam, and twenty feet he fell into the room below. We did not even need to hear the *crack* as the steel knot broke his neck...

In an unearthly silence, while the echo of his cry still rang, Talbot and I walked to the edge. He was swinging limply, his head on his shoulder, just above the green lamp. Below him, Graffin lay across the table in swinish slumber, with his bald head shining dully. Shuddering, we turned our eyes away only when a low, gay, melodious sound fell on our ears in the ghastly hush.

Bencolin was humming a little tune, and smiling.

THE END

THE ENDS
OF JUSTICE

I

IT HAS OFTEN BEEN REMARKED THAT IN M. HENRI BENCOLIN'S most baffling case he did not interfere until it was too late. The convicted murderer of Roger Darworth was sentenced to be executed at Blackfriars on May fourth. On May third, on one of those drowsy evenings when the English countryside is in full bloom, Bencolin was taking tea with his old friend Sir John Landervorne. They sat among the purple lilacs, shaded by a rustic arbour, and a bright singing stream ran past them. Up over the terrace were the grey gables of Sir John's house, stark against the last fire of the sun; a sleepy twilight hovered over them.

The gaunt baronet stood by the tea table, lighting his pipe. Bencolin sat watching the rippling water. He wore careless grey tweeds, and needed a shave, for his black beard was scraggly and his hair rather wild. Beyond him, dark against the lilacs, sat Bishop Wolfe, with his narrow face and slow-blinking eyes, blond hair parted carefully in the middle. It was a devout face, an earnest face, but the eyes were a bit palely blue, and rimmed with red. His clerical garb was neat, and his nails polished.

"It was opportune," Sir John was remarking, "that you should come here at this time, Bencolin. I wanted you to meet Bishop Wolfe. You said that you had been away some time, I think?"

Bencolin lifted eyes that were very tired.

"Six months," he said, and smiled. "In the south of France."

"You succeeded?"

"I got my man," the Frenchman said. "Come, come, this is in the nature of a vacation, my friend. You don't want me to talk shop, surely?"

"Well, I know you. You would be interested, wouldn't you, in hearing of a churchman turned detective?"

"From what I have heard," Bishop Wolfe put in, raising his colourless eyebrows, "I personally should be much more interested in a detective turned churchman."

"Are you referring to my religious ideas?" asked Bencolin. "Well, well, one sinner more or less doesn't matter, does he?" He smiled at the stream. "Am I to gather that Bishop Wolfe did detective work?"

While the bishop made a protesting motion, Sir John went on enthusiastically: "Well, rather! He solved the most perplexing case *I* ever racked my wits over!... Did you ever hear of Roger Darworth?"

"The spiritualist?"

"Call him that if you like." The baronet shrugged. "He always impressed me as a stagy fake, you know. And I suppose you know Tom Fellowes?"

Bencolin slapped the table.

"Know him? I'm proud to know him! I always admire these crazy young hellions; they do all the things I should like to do..." Bencolin scratched his head, and looked apologetically at the bishop.

"Your instance is bad for your case, M. Bencolin," said Bishop Wolfe with sudden harshness. "Would you like to commit murder? Fellowes did."

Startled, Bencolin leaned back and stared at him with his wrinkly black eyes.

"My friend," he replied quietly, "I do not doubt your word, of course, but when you tell me that Tom Fellowes committed murder, I find it hard to believe. No, no, I tell you! Ah, monsieur, I who know the wickedness of the many know also the goodness of the few. Were it not for Tom Fellowes' money, thousands of children in London would die every year. It is he who feeds them. Were it not for Tom Fellowes' money, hundreds of maimed soldiers in France would die. It is Tom Fellowes who supports them. Does not your church take cognizance of that?"

"I am not sentimental like you, M. Bencolin," said the bishop, stroking his colourless hair. "I judge a man by his fruits. Fellowes killed Roger Darworth; I am surprised that you have not heard of the case."

"It *is* strange, old top," put in Sir John. "It was a sensation. Fellowes is to be executed tomorrow. I'm sorry about it, naturally, for he seemed to me a splendid fellow. But the evidence was conclusive."

"Then," said Bencolin, "will you be so good as to tell me about it? Fellowes to be executed… It's unbelievable!" He passed his hand over his forehead. "I count myself a good judge of men, but if Fellowes is a murderer, I shall acknowledge myself an utter idiot."

"The English law courts—" said the bishop.

Bencolin made an impatient gesture.

"Damn the English law courts!… I'm sorry," he apologized, catching himself up and looking at Sir John with a wry smile, "but I don't understand just yet. Will you tell me about it?"

"I will give you the facts," responded the churchman with precision. "You shall then make whatever judgment you like on your ability to size up men, M. Bencolin. Sit down, please, Sir John… No, thanks; I don't smoke."

He waited until Bencolin had lighted a cigar and whirled a wreath of smoke around his head. Then, in the fading twilight, Bishop Wolfe, with his hands folded in his lap, began his story.

II

I had known Roger Darworth a long time. He was a devout man, for all he meddled with spiritism, and his belief in communication with the dead was sincere. He sought to establish it with the zeal of a scientist. I have seen him give demonstrations in which the most extraordinary things occurred; Darworth bound and roped in a chair at one end of a darkened room while bells were rung, tables moved, spirit hands materialized. Of course, my religion did not permit me to sympathize with him; but I respect any man's beliefs, except atheism.

The personality of the man was vibrant. His eyes had an uncanny penetrating look, and would change from blue almost to black; he had a great skull, with plumes of reddish hair, and a loose-jointed, powerful figure. He used to walk the streets of Bayswater at night, under the moon, head sunk forward and hands clasped behind his coattails, mumbling to himself. Well, of course, he had a violent temper, and used to play practical jokes on children (loved to scare them a little), but it was just his own particular humour. He gave a great deal to the church. Then, too, for some reason he always had a doctor about his house—a Dr. Joseph McShane, of whom you'll hear later.

I suppose you know of his relationship to Tom Fellowes. He was a cousin, and had inherited a great deal of money from his grandfather. Half of this money (it amounted to about a million pounds) was to go to Tom Fellowes on Darworth's death. Now, it has been proved that for all Fellowes' charity work, he was almost out of money; he had been begging loans from Darworth. It was just a part of Roger's whimsical humour that he would half promise a loan, and then laugh at Fellowes when Fellowes came for the cheque; the young scapegrace needed a lesson. Then there was the girl. You very rarely hear of an actual case in which two cousins, utterly unlike, are after the same lady, but it happened in this instance. For Roger's sake I am glad that this Cynthia Melford preferred Fellowes; she is an utterly frivolous chit, one of the type called "saucy" (ugly appellation!), with bobbed hair and what is known as "make-up." I am sorry that Roger took it hard when she became engaged to Fellowes. She was unworthy of him, of his colossal mind. She actually grew hysterical once when Roger, purely as a joke, sent her a dried arm from a dissecting room in a flower box.

Roger, as you probably know, lived in a big house in Bayswater, furnished in accordance with his sombre, studious type of mind. It was a model of neatness; Roger neither smoked nor was untidy, and to his orderly trend of life the slightest thing out of place was a horror. I often wish, in these careless, untidy days, there were more like him. He often had a group in to a séance, however, which he held in his vast library, shadowed with gloomy hangings and books, and with a red lamp burning on the centre table. Some of the most renowned scientists in the world have sat there, shivering (for the house was healthfully cold), and marvelled at the effects he produced. I can see him yet, sitting behind the glow of the red lamp, with his long white face and weird, changing dark eyes under the straggle of reddish hair. Then the solemn circle... the dark... the sudden clash of a tambourine, or ghastly spectral hands moving in the air, while, mind you, Roger sat bound and handcuffed in his chair.

One night last January (it was blustery, and driving with snow) Roger invited me around to his house. I remember the dully lighted hall when I was admitted, and Mock Yen, who was Roger's house-keeper and whom he always kept in Oriental costume. Mock Yen was an absurdity—he had a glass eye, which lolled grotesquely and made his face a thing at which Roger laughed constantly. Well, the door to Roger's library was closed, but as I approached I heard voices. I heard Dr. McShane's voice say:

"You realize, then, your own grave danger?"

And Roger answered:

"Oh, Fellowes has made his threats to kill me, right enough. I don't doubt I shall be dead within a week. But he'll hang for it!"

Then I knocked on the door, and they both seemed embarrassed. They stood by an old-fashioned grate with a gas fire, which sputtered blue flame over the hangings and the rows of books. McShane, a little fat man with eyeglasses and a bald head, stammered:

"Come in, come in, sir. I didn't expect you so early."

"Look here, Bishop," Roger burst out, kneading his big white hands over the fire and peering at me from around his shoulder. "I don't see any reason why you shouldn't know. That damned cad Fellowes has been after me again. I can't express to you," he cried suddenly, and I was actually frightened at the expression on his face, "the way I hate that bounder! He means to kill me. Why shouldn't he? He's got money coming to him. Five hundred thousand quid if I die. Why, it's enough to tempt your cloth, Bishop—but you needn't worry. I've put ten thousand pounds church money in my will."

I must confess that there are times when Roger's jokes were a bit hard to bear, though he meant nothing by them. He laughed and said:

"Listen, I'll tell you how it is. He wants to get married. If he'd kept his fortune and not thrown it about trying to help snivelling soldiers, he'd be a rich man today. He, who keeps up a fine brave pretence of money, with his Vauxhall roadster (and not a sixpence for petrol!) and his grand fur coat!... Well, he's coming here tonight. He was desperate. Said he'd got to have money, and I told him there might be a chance if he came around. But I'm afraid of him."

"Whiskey and soda?" said the doctor, reaching for the siphon.

"No... Now listen. I am going up to my study to finish up some work. You two remain down here. When you hear him come up on the porch, go upstairs quickly, and don't let him see you, above all! I'm supposed to be alone in the house. You know where my study is: at the back, at the end of a long hall. Well, the hall is brightly lit. At the other end, directly opposite my study, is another room. I've laid a fire there, and it's comfortable. You two go in there, and watch my study door after he has gone in. Guard me! If you hear the slightest sign of violence, come in. I tell you I'm afraid of him!"

"But hadn't you better see the police, if it's as serious as all that?" I asked. The man was actually in a chattering state of fear.

"And have them messing it up and creating a scandal?" he demanded. "No, no, I've done the next best thing. I've invited Sir John Landervorne here; he's enough in touch with the police to be effective, and enough out of touch to keep his mouth shut. He'll be here any minute. See that he follows the instructions; make him go upstairs and watch the door with you. Do you understand?"

"I don't like this, Mr. Darworth," said McShane, shaking his head. "See here, it's outlandish! This is a civilized world. You aren't a mile from Trafal—"

"Do as I tell you!" Roger ordered. "You understand, don't you; wait for Sir John, don't let Fellowes see you, and above all get to me in case anything should happen. I promised to see him alone."

His big loose figure went surging to the door in its black clothes that hung all baggily around him; the great mop of hair was flung back, streaming out as he went through the curtains. It was the last time I ever saw him alive.

III

Bishop Wolfe paused, and looked round at his companions, smoothing his hair. It had grown darker; the arbour hung in vague perfumed shadow, but with a sort of moving light about the water. In the silence Sir John stood up, a black silhouette against the pale sky. The action was unconscious; it seemed like an emotional upheaval.

"I am weary," said the bishop, and cleared his throat. "If M. Bencolin is interested, perhaps you will continue the story, Sir John. You have a minute attention to detail."

The silhouette nodded without speaking. Sir John had leaned against a post covered with trailing vines, supporting his chin in his hand, and was staring straight before him, still outlined on the pale sky.

"Yes, I am very much interested," Bencolin observed, talking in a voice that was low and extraordinarily tense. "I am very much interested in that conversation you overheard outside the library door, Monsieur l'Évêque. Go on, go on!"

Abruptly Sir John began to speak.

IV

I remember distinctly the time I arrived at the house, because the snow was beginning to thin out, and I could see my wrist watch. It was ten minutes after nine. The glass-eyed butler admitted me. When I went to the library, Darworth had just gone out, and Bishop Wolfe and the doctor were talking beside the fire. I was almost chilled by that house; not physically, but with a form of brooding repulsion that made me almost afraid to touch the hangings, as though I might get leprosy...

And the doctor impressed me unpleasantly, not like the genial bald-headed man Bishop Wolfe has described. He seemed always on the alert—sly, if you can understand, with pale blue eyes behind his glasses and one strand of hair sticking over his big forehead. He kept going over and looking out the windows, and for some reason asking, "Is it still snowing?"

I learned of the grotesque situation, after which the doctor turned to me.

"It's nearly nine-thirty," he said. "That's the time young Fellowes is due to arrive. You'd better go to the room opposite the study. I'll stay here. Now, don't argue! I can see what sort of mood he's in."

We left him waving his arms by the fire. I confess the thing was so absurd that it seemed we had all gone out of our wits. Somehow we *expected* a tragedy. You would have thought that we might just have stayed with Darworth, but we didn't. Just as the bishop and I got out into the hall, we heard footsteps on the porch. Like a couple of children, we hurried back, blundering through a dark hall, around a turn or so, falling over furniture, until we emerged in the hall Darworth had mentioned. It ran along the back of the house, fairly well lighted—just a narrow corridor with a door at each end. One door was closed. The other, opening into the room where we were to remain, was ajar. We went inside: a gloomy place, with heavy Victorian furniture and ghastly flowered wallpaper. A gas jet was burning over the fireplace. We stood behind the door, looking out through the crack and down at that blank door opposite: we could see it plainly, because another gas jet beside it threw a dull yellow light directly on the panels. The door was ugly, sinister: its brown boards and white knob stood out with terrible distinctness... Then, outside, we heard the front door slam, and voices in the hall. One voice was high and agitated; the other, which apparently belonged to Mock Yen, was low and baffling. I felt foolish, like a child looking through a board fence, but Bishop Wolfe was gripping my arm.

Suddenly the light was blocked. A man had come into the hall, swung with his back to us, and he was going down toward the brown door. He was tall; he wore a bowler hat and a great fur coat, and a trail of shadow slanted out after him. Gad, I can see him yet, striding down that faded carpet under the yellow light, pausing at the door, where the gas jet made a shining bowl of his hat and slid down over the sleek fur coat. As he lifted his hand to knock on the door, I could see a diamond gleaming on one finger. It was Fellowes, all right; the fur coat he always wore, and the diamond ring. A voice from behind the door said, "Come in."

As he went in, and the door closed after him, I heard Bishop Wolfe gasp. It was horrible: as though one saw a dead man, whose face was invisible, come in out of the snow like an avenger. Then silence.

We waited. God knows how long we waited, in a strained posture, with our eyes on the door, which fixed one's gaze like a bright lamp. There was utter silence in the hall, except for the singing of the gas jet and the occasional sound of voices from Darworth's study. Then it came out, with the sound of ripping cloth, like a ghost voice. It cried:

"Don't! Don't!" Darworth's voice!

Down the hall we went pell-mell. Nobody had come out. I turned the knob and threw the door open, at the same instant that I heard running footsteps behind me, and the doctor's voice crying from the hall:

"What is it?"

That cold study was before us, like a stage tableau. The dirty paper, the rows of books, a spirit cabinet, a mass of musical instruments all lying in a heap. The one window was wide open, and a wind whirled through it, tossing the curtains. An oil lamp with a green shade burned on the table. In a chair in the middle of the room sat

Darworth, his head back, so that we saw only the long neck and a part of his face. His hands and legs were handcuffed to the chair, in which he was still writhing spasmodically, and in his chest was stuck a long knife.

While we stood there motionless we could hear the jingle of the handcuffs as he twisted his hands. But I swear nobody was in the room; there wasn't any place to hide. While Dr. McShane ran toward him, the bishop turned to me.

"He's gone out by the window!" Wolfe said. "Hurry—look!"

I ran over to the window. When I put my head out, it was bright moonlight; the storm had cleared some time since, and the snow lay unbroken all over the tiny yard, which was fenced with a high wall. That was it! The snow had absolutely no footprint, or any sort of mark. I looked up, I looked along the wall. It was a perfectly smooth expanse of close-set brick for twenty yards around, at the sides and up; there were no windows—a fly could not have clung on that wall. Yet nobody had walked over the snow! I stood there gaping in the moonlight at the impossible nature of it. We had watched the only door, and it was impossible to leave the room by the only window. Neither had been locked, yet the murderer could not have left the room. He could not have left, but he was not there.

When I came back into the room Darworth had stopped writhing. He had been trying to speak, but that ceased also. He sat back, with his red hair hanging down toward the floor, the manacles shining on his wrists and legs, and his mouth wide open. That was all.

"Where is Fellowes?" I heard Bishop Wolfe say. "He *couldn't* have left here so quickly."

"Dead," the doctor was muttering and chuckling. "Dead! Got him just in the heart... Put that window down, will you, Sir John Landervorne? It's cold in here."

The bishop, who looked white and shaken, leaned against the table.

"Better get the police…" he faltered.

"Well, well," the doctor was saying to himself in a surprised tone. "It's not ten o'clock—it's not ten o'clock."

V

None of the three had noticed that the arbour was quite dark. Bencolin tossed his cigar in a glowing arc into the stream. They could feel him leaning forward as he spoke tensely; they could almost feel that he was seizing the sides of his chair.

"Go on, go on!" he ordered. "They piled up the evidence, I suppose? Tell me about it."

"The steps," went on Sir John, "were easy. Mock Yen testified to having seen Fellowes come in the front door just before we saw him in the hall. He said that Fellowes seemed agitated. Well, we searched the room. There was no secret way for him to have left. Dr. McShane did not see him when he came in the front door, but he heard his voice; unmistakably that of Fellowes. The crude details of the affair were as bad as those of an American thriller: Fellowes had stabbed Darworth with a carving knife. The knife was identified by Fellowes' manservant at the trial as coming from a dinner set in Fellowes' apartment. He had evidently handcuffed Darworth and stabbed him with premeditated care. But the devil of it lay in how Fellowes had left the room!"

"Did he confess?"

"No! Again a strange thing. He was arrested the next day, and swore that he had been nowhere near Darworth's house all evening. The night of the murder, he said, he had been in his rooms in

Half-Moon Street until eight-thirty. At that time, according to his testimony, he received a phone call from Miss Cynthia Melford, the lady to whom he is engaged, asking him to come to her apartment, which is some distance away—that he would find the door open, and to go in and make himself at home until she returned. She would not be absent long, the alleged message ran, and she had something important to tell him. Fellowes says he went there, though he admits that neither hallboy nor doorman saw him go in. He says he stayed there until eleven-fifteen, when Miss Melford returned.

"Well, she was questioned before she knew what was wrong, and told the investigator she had sent no message, being surprised to see Fellowes when she returned from the theatre. Then, when she heard of the crime, she recalled her statement and said that she certainly had sent the message... but the puzzling thing was why, in the face of so much evidence, Fellowes insisted that his story was true."

"What about his appointment with Darworth?"

"Fellowes said he had none. You can see that the evidence against him was overwhelming."

"Well," temporized Bencolin, "how did he get out of the room?"

"If he stuck to his story of innocence," said Bishop Wolfe coldly, "he could hardly be expected to explain *that.*"

Sir John hurried on: "But the most conclusive proof against him was unearthed by Bishop Wolfe. It was Bishop Wolfe who produced a witness who had seen Fellowes leaving Darworth's house."

"*What?*" cried Bencolin.

"Quite so. You remember my telling you of the little walled yard that encloses the window of Darworth's study? There is a gate in that. A Mr. John Simpson, who is a banker's clerk, was passing by outside—on the street that runs past the wall. Through the merest chance Bishop Wolfe unearthed him. As Mr. Simpson was crossing the street the night of the murder, he saw a man come out of that gate. There is an arc lamp near, and by its light he could see a man in a fur coat and bowler hat slip out and go running down beside the wall. So somehow Fellowes *did* get out the window."

Bencolin gave a sudden exclamation, like a shout of triumph. They heard him strike the table and cry:

"Of course! Of course! I might have known it!... What time was this?"

"Mr. Simpson didn't remember. One doesn't, ordinarily, but it was around the time of the murder."

"At least," said the bishop complacently, "it proved him guilty, however he left the room."

"You fools! You fools!" Bencolin snarled, with more excitement than Sir John had ever seen him show. "Don't you see? Don't you see that it proves him innocent?"

There was a queer crushing silence, after which Sir John began to grope around blindly and mutter:

"Strike a light! I've got to *see* you, Bencolin! What are you talking about?"

"Listen: one question about this thing," the detective said rapidly. "Do you remember anything about Darworth's will? He made one, didn't he?"

"It was an odd kind of will," said the baronet. "Darworth's would be. He left his house and a life annuity to Dr. McShane; a thousand pounds to the butler; and some other charities—the church too, I believe... For God's sake, you don't really doubt that Fellowes killed him, do you?"

Darkness lent a tinge of unreality to the conversation. It was like a ghost conclave, except that the little Frenchman's voice was much too vibrant. He snapped:

"You have your car here, haven't you, Sir John?"

"The Daimler."

"How long would it take you to drive to London?"

"Starting when?"

"Now!"

"By fast driving, I could do it in six or seven hours."

"Then get the car out! Get it out, I tell you! We're going to London tonight. You have influence; telegraph Blackfriars to stay that execution as long as they can—get in touch with the board of aldermen. Use my name! Quick, for the love of God! If I can see McShane before tomorrow morning, we may save Fellowes!"

"You're insane!" the bishop said. "I refuse to be party—"

They stood up, opposite each other, clergyman and detective, each vaguely visible, but the hatred that sprang between them lit each face like fire.

"Bishop Wolfe," Bencolin said quietly, "Pilate was more merciful than *you*."

Then he went out into the blue-shadowed lawn, striding up the terrace with Sir John after him.

VI

For three hours Dr. McShane had been sitting in the library listening to the clock strike. It was Roger Darworth's library, and he was master of it. In the great gloomy place, with lines of books and horsehair furniture, he sat at a table, playing with a child's toy Humpty Dumpty circus. The bright-coloured dolls of clowns, the wooden animals, the bandmen, the ladders and barrels, were all arranged before him under the light of a gas lamp. He had bought them this afternoon, on an impulse, and he was childishly chuckling now. The lamplight shone on his glistening face, with the eyeglasses stuck on a round nose, the startled eyes, the wisp of hair straggling down over his bald head. Dr. McShane did not understand why he should grow afraid every night. He never wanted to go upstairs, nor did he want to go into the back of the house, for he might have to pass the brown door of Roger Darworth's study. There, the clock was striking again. Four. The windows were wide open, so that occasional noises from the street were startlingly distinct in the night stillness: the clop-clop of hoofs swinging past, the rattle of a cart, the brawling voice of a huckster. Once the doctor thought he heard a motorcar stop.

If McShane was very nervous, it may have been due to the fact that he was steadily drinking himself into a stupor. Brandy at intervals had unstrung him; one of the toy clowns plopped off a ladder, and the clack as it landed on the table made the doctor jump... He kept imagining that people were moving around in the house, or fancied the click of the door latch, though he knew that Mock Yen must be in bed. Vaguely McShane wondered whether his glass eye stayed open while he slept. It might be disconcerting to find him asleep sometime, with one stary eye looking up at you while he breathed deeply in slumber.

He had pots of money now. There was no need to practice. He could get drunk all he wanted, thought McShane, and reached for the decanter. Dark in here; almost the way it had been when Roger Darworth gave his séances. It would be terrible to look up from the table sometime, and find Roger Darworth staring at him over the red lamp, the way he used to do...

McShane looked up then, suddenly and unaccountably. He sat with a toy elephant in his hands, motionless, with his eyes getting wider. There was a man standing by the library door.

He was only duskily visible; he wore a fur coat, and a bowler hat, and had one hand on the portieres of the door. A diamond ring glittered on the middle finger.

McShane did not move, or cry out. He felt the rumblings of the brandy in his stomach, his sight swam a little, and he felt nauseated. The toy elephant fell with a thump on the table.

"Darworth!" said McShane. "Darworth."

The stranger came forward. As he moved more into the light, McShane saw that it was not Darworth's face. It was a lean, tired face, with steady black eyes, black moustache and beard, and a hooked nose.

"I am not Darworth," the newcomer said, "but you recognize the costume, Dr. McShane. The police will be here to take you soon."

Behind the portieres of the door were two other figures, peering in the gloom. Over the shoulder of the man in the fur coat they saw McShane totter up behind the grotesque pageant of the toy circus. They heard him say:

"I didn't kill Darworth…"

"I know you didn't," said the man in the fur coat.

Abruptly the doctor pointed.

"Why are you wearing those things?" he cried. "It's… summer!"

"Because I found them in Darworth's study, doctor." The watchers saw the man in the fur coat lean on the table, over toward McShane, who was backing away. "You know about it. I found them in the chest where he had hidden them. Listen!"

"I won't! I didn't kill anybody!"

"Listen! What was the disease with which Darworth was dying? What was the disease that would have killed him within a month if he hadn't been stabbed?"

"There wasn't any… Oh, my God, get away."

"Yes, there was, doctor. You warned him against it. You warned him the night Bishop Wolfe came here. You knew Darworth's spiritualism was a fake, only another of his ghastly jokes. You knew he was a ventriloquist and a handcuff king. You knew that he had summoned reliable witnesses here to see a fake murder. You knew that when he left this room the night he died, and told you to wait, that he went to his room and put on these imitations of Fellowes' clothing; that he went out his own window, and came around to the front door to impersonate Fellowes. You knew he went down the hall, where Bishop Wolfe and Sir John Landervorne were watching, used his ventriloquism to throw his own voice into an empty room and say, 'Come in.' You knew he entered the room, stabbed himself with a stolen knife, and just as he was able to get out of handcuffs, so he was able to get into them after the knife was in his chest. You knew he bribed Mock Yen to swear Fellowes had really come in. You knew the whole thing was a plot to convict Fellowes of murder, since Darworth was dying of disease!" His voice went into a shout: *"You knew that, didn't you?"*

The strain of the battle could not last much longer. It was as though every nerve force of the two men was locked over the table with the circus, weakening with the faint grey light of morning. McShane's eyes closed; he choked, as though with sickness, and he sat down drowsily.

"All right, all right," he said.

Bencolin turned away from the table. He went trailing over to the window in his absurd fur coat, and put his forehead against the cool glass.

"Sir John!" he called in a dull voice. "Bishop Wolfe! Get me some water, will you? I'm sicker than he is."

VII

Sir John Landervorne came running into the room. The old baronet looked haggard after a night of driving.

"Where's the telephone? McShane!" he demanded. "Where's the telephone? If we can get the prison… Quick, where is it?"

McShane looked up with a lopsided grin, and cackled:

"I won't tell you!"

"Are you insane? Look here, wake up! A man is to be executed this morning—don't you understand that?"

"I won't tell you!"

Bencolin was still standing motionless, with his head against the glass. Sir John looked around helplessly, at the drunken smile in the chair and the grinning clowns on the table.

"Here it is!" clamoured Bishop Wolfe with eagerness, putting his head in at the door. "I found it in the hall. You can call them, can't you?"

When Sir John had gone hurrying out, Bishop Wolfe went over to Bencolin. McShane was pouring out another drink. The cleric, lit by the grey dawn and the dull gaslight, blinked his red-rimmed eyes, stroked his light hair, and said apologetically:

"I—I really don't see how you knew all this, sir."

Bencolin put up the window, breathing the warm wind that blew in. He turned his old tired mocking eyes.

"Why, you didn't recognize that the man who was seen leaving by the gate was not Fellowes at all, but Darworth in his costume," he said. "The witness said it was still snowing, didn't he? And at the time of the murder it wasn't snowing, so it was before the murder—it was the time when Darworth left his house, to return in the character of Fellowes. Please go away…"

"I know, I know you're tired," prompted the bishop in a flurry, "but Darworth must have known there would be no snowstorm to efface the footprints of a man leaving by the window after he killed himself."

"That," said Bencolin grimly, "was what he forgot. He thought, with the window open, it would seem that Fellowes had left that way, and that the snow would take away footprints. But it stopped snowing before the suicide."

"Why, we must have seen that he couldn't get out that way!"

"*You* didn't, Bishop Wolfe," said the Frenchman, looking at him with steadiness. "Oh, my friend, isn't it so obvious? Isn't it so ridiculously plain a plot? All the mummery, when Darworth could easily have saved himself from Fellowes if he thought the latter meant to kill him? Planting an audience who were not allowed to see him? A murderer handcuffing Darworth without the latter's making a sound, when there were men within twenty yards. How could Fellowes have done it? Why would Fellowes have invented a story so impossible as to be absurd, unless it were true? Darworth was resolved that if he was to die anyway, Fellowes should never live to enjoy the money that was coming to him. He could hardly enjoy the money, Bishop Wolfe, if he was hanging at a rope's end. God! It's so cheap and stagy..."

"But how did you know about his being a handcuff king?" persisted Wolfe.

Bencolin smiled faintly, and said with drowsiness:

"I'm a policeman, monsieur. My business is handcuffs. And I have seen Darworth give one of his séances..."

The sun was coming up, over the blank rows of houses, filling the areaways. A milk wagon clattered past. One sleepy housemaid threw up a window with a bang. And the warm light had something in it that held the heart, as though all the world had stopped its breathing... McShane rattled his glass and mumbled a few words. Then Sir John Landervorne appeared in the doorway. His face was perfectly blank.

"We're too late," he said. "He was hanged ten minutes ago. They haven't cut him down yet."

"I don't see that I'm to blame!" returned Bishop Wolfe nervously. "I merely did my duty to justice in trying to run down—"

"Shut up!" Sir John ordered in a toneless voice. He went aimlessly over to the table and began picking at the scattered toys, and tried to balance a wooden lion on a toy chair. Suddenly he drew a long breath, adding: "Well, he's dead."

A drowsy, deadening hush of summer, ruffled by light winds, was on the street and in the room. Bencolin took off the coat.

"I'm sorry I could not have got here sooner," he observed.

Then Sir John began speaking in jerky bursts:

"They said he—he died very well. He was not crying when he left Miss Melford. He walked out to the scaffold without—you know—stumbling or fainting. They had his coffin there. He smoked a cigarette on the platform and Miss Melford was crying, but she was waving to him. He smiled…"

"Where the hell is the rest of that brandy?" mumbled Dr. McShane, thrashing around him.

"Apparently the phone call that sent him to her house that night came from Darworth," went on Sir John, "and his mimickry! The conversation you overheard, Bishop, was about Darworth's health… Miss Melford will be around here soon. They've told her. We… shall have to face that girl, Bishop."

The bishop raised his earnest eyes, one arm up as though he were in the pulpit, the other hand on the lapel of his black coat.

"It is God's will," he said piously. "The ways of the Lord are dark, and His servants can only follow humbly. This thing, which seems so tragic, is but another manifestation of divine intervention for good. We must pray for Fellowes' soul."

Bencolin did not laugh. He did not feel like laughing. But he made a sound that was something like passionate fury, and his hand dropped from the window, and he turned.

"Oh, Bishop," he said, "when will you learn? When will you learn?"

BRITISH LIBRARY CRIME CLASSICS

ALSO AVAILABLE

Many of our titles are also available in eBook, large print and audio editions